Viktoria

L.J. Fox

L.J. Fox

Australian (British) English

First edition: 2018
Second edition & rewrite: 2026

Artwork by: Wendy Frere

No Artificial Intelligence (AI) has been used in any form with the art or contents of this book.

Publisher: L.J. Fox, Australia

For more information on books by L.J. Fox or to sign up for news, please visit https://ljfox.com.

We wish to acknowledge the Traditional Custodians of the land upon which we live and work, and pay respect to Elders past and present.

The feat of surviving is directly related
to the capacity of the survivor.

- Claire Cameron

Prologue

She peered out from her vantage point behind the large, gnarled tree, bent over from decades of coastal winds. Waiting, breathing lightly and barely blinking, she watched the fishing boat glide into shore. Having heard the purring motor for the past twenty minutes, the sound breaking the silence of her world. It started as a faint and distant humming, gradually intensifying until occupying her entire mind space. Finally! She had been waiting weeks for the keeper to arrive.

The boat slid to a silent halt as it breached the sand, motor extinguished, and four humans stepped out of the boat, landing in the knee-deep shallows. She could hear their squeals and voices, cheerful and excited as they picked up their belongings from the sand where the keeper had tossed them. Lifting her face and inhaling, she hoped to capture the faintest scent of them, but the breeze was not in her favour. She focused her attention back to the keeper still aboard the boat, wondering what was happening, and realised with a start that he was not intending to disembark. He was studiously throwing items from the boat onto the sand in his hurry to leave. She could see his familiar hat and the colour of his clothing as his body actively strove to purge the boat of foreign objects. She felt momentary panic and forced her breathing to regulate.

Looking back at the newcomers as they retrieved their items, shaking off the loose sand where they had been carelessly tossed, she saw the keeper signal with his hands to the males on the sand to push his boat back from the shore. A male stood staring at the keeper with his hands on his hips and she heard the gruff voice of the male, indignant at this hostile ejection from the boat. Shrugging his shoulders, the other male waded into the water, shortly followed by the angry male, and pushed the front of the boat. It easily floated back from the sandy bed.

Two males and two females, all young and vibrant, carefree and happy. She watched them silently from behind her hide-away tree. Her excitement at first hearing the boat arrive had now collapsed, spiralling down into a dull pain in her chest. She sighed in resignation and misery, as her eyes became watery and a tear escaped. The keeper had done it again. She shook her head not wanting this to be true.

A low grumble erupted from deep within her, vibrating as it worked its way up and out of her mouth, breaking the silence although not enough for the humans to hear. She wanted to scream her fury at the world and pummel the tree into oblivion, but it was imperative they remain unaware of her presence. Her sharp nails dug into the bark of the tree, hard enough to bring pain. Tears slid down her cheek. She wished her keeper would not do this to her. She disliked eating humans.

The earlier keepers had brought her newborn calves, baby goats and chickens, arriving in the small boat regularly with her meals. At times, they arrived and caught fish, cooking the fish for her, aware she disliked eating raw fish. She thought back to the delicious smell of the cooking fish as she waited back behind the trees for her meal to be ready. Her mouth salivated at the memory, and she could almost taste the food.

This most recent keeper provided animals most of the time, though his visits were becoming less frequent. Every now and then, humans arrived and the keeper deliberately left them as he just had.

She had not seen the keeper for several weeks now and was ravenous. Eagerly, she scanned the ocean horizon daily, desperate for any sign of the boat. The earlier keepers possessed a silent boat without the purring motor, and even though she knew the recent keeper arrived in a motorised boat, she still scanned the ocean, hopeful for any boat.

The hunger this time was the most severe she had ever experienced. The growling in her stomach had ceased some time ago and there were moments the thought of food made her nauseous. Her body had never felt so thin and skeletal with ribs jutting out and the outline of her bones painfully visible. She was not as physically powerful as she once was, tired out easily and was aware it was from lack of food.

There was now a total absence of animals on the island for her to hunt. She continued to search every day in case one happened to wash up as had occurred on the rare occasion. Even the birds seemed aware of her presence and avoided the island. Her ears were finely tuned for the slightest chirp but all she heard was the rustling of trees and the waves.

A few seasonal berries grew, and the old, abandoned vegetable garden occasionally provided a mutant, wild vegetable but the pickings were slim at this time of year. For the first time in over one hundred years, she contemplated her own death and fervently wished for it at times.

She watched the humans as they lifted their items onto their backs and made their way into the trees of the island. Time for her to make her way back to her shelter for a rest. She would watch them later when she had more energy. The humans would eventually find her. They always did. Four humans should keep her alive for some time to come.

She made her way back to the shelter, depressed and beaten, and her mind thought back to happier times.

Part One - The Island

L.J. Fox

Chapter 1
The Backpackers

"**I** FOUND AN ISLAND!"

"Huh? You what?" Matt asked, sitting up confused.

The three friends had been stretched out on the white sand of the beach staring up at the clear, blue sky and relaxing. The weather was hot, and a slight wind stirred the sand. All three sat up suddenly, shaking sleepiness from their consciousness and sand from their hair, and trying to understand what Jamie was talking about.

"I found an island ... our island," Jamie repeated, sitting down heavily on the sand facing the three friends. "I asked everyone with a boat within a kilometre of here and found one."

He paused to scan the faces of his friends, seeking comprehension of what he had just said and an inkling of excitement. All eyes were on him and he saw the first spark of understanding in their sleepy eyes.

"You found an island or a boat?" asked Kim.

"I found this old guy called Juan with a fishing boat and he knows an uninhabited island that sounds just perfect," said Jamie, wrapping his arm around Kim and pulling her closer to him. "He can take us early in the morning. His boat's a bit small but big enough for us and the motor looks ok."

"Awesome!" said Matt, his face breaking into a grin, the first of the group to respond favourably to this information. He reached across and the two men clapped hands together in a congratulatory salute.

For Jamie and Matt, this was a dream come true. After years of discussions about finding an uninhabited island to camp on, they were excited at the thought of being the first humans to pitch a tent, catch and cook fish and spend a few days in a serene, untouched location. It was a boyish dream, but one that had festered and grown roots over the years.

The two girls nodded agreeably at Jamie, not invested in the dream of an uninhabited island but still interested in the opportunity for great photographs for their social media accounts.

"This guy ... Juan ... his English isn't great, but I'm sure I got it right. He said the fishing is great out that way and no one ever goes to the island," said Jamie. "I thought we could camp there a couple of nights and get him to pick us up at noon on Wednesday. What do you think?"

His eyes moved between the other three, feeling a little deflated that the girls were not as excited as he or Matt were.

"Perfect," Matt responded.

The girls nodded and smiled agreeably, lying back on the sand. They were accustomed to Jamie and Matt's hare-brained ideas, having heard these ideas for years but more so in the past three weeks as they travelled around South America.

Both were confident in leaving the details of their adventures up to the two guys who always came through and delivered. They trusted their judgement and so far, the South American adventure had been a fun and interesting trip without major mishap. The two guys had been planning this back-packing trip since university days back in Australia and now seemed like the perfect time to do it.

" ... the archipelago of Juan Fernández ..."

Kim heard Jamie's voice and just caught the end of the sentence. She sat up suddenly, interested in what he was saying.

"What was that?" she asked.

"That's where we're going, the archipelago of Juan Fernandez. It's a series of uninhabited islands off the coast of Chile. There's beautiful wildlife like birds and turtles. That's where our island is."

Jamie grinned, pleased to finally spark interest in Kim after his work securing this boat trip to an island. He had studied the area in detail before the trip so was aware of the location and history of the surrounding islands. He looked at Kim and could see her eyes sparkling with interest.

She recalled seeing a documentary on television once about the archipelago and remembered how beautiful it was. Suddenly, this island trip seemed more interesting than it had previously. She had long dreamed of swimming with dolphins, viewing giant turtles in the water and bathing under a waterfall. Perhaps, this was her chance and she imagined the fabulous photos they could potentially take. An island without people, and a wild, untainted landscape did have a romantic appeal.

They discussed necessities for the trip and agreed they had everything in their backpacks that were needed, other than a small amount of food purchased from the local village before they left.

The last three weeks of the trip had been an exciting, off-the-track adventure. Jamie and Matt were keen to stay away from the standard tourist route and wanted to forge their own way around the coast, meeting villagers and viewing the fishing villages in more isolated locations. They reasoned that staying away from the mainstream areas meant they were more likely to see the real South America, and not the commercial version.

The girls had been warned well in advance that this trip would be an adventure on a shoe-string budget and expect to 'rough it'. Luxury items such as hair dryers, make-up and unnecessary toiletries were banned. Kim found it incredible that each of them had been able to fit their entire survival items into four backpacks plus bed rolls. Each couple slept in a small tent each night and ate dried or tinned food or what fish they managed to catch and cook.

Kim had cut off her shoulder length blonde hair and now sported a short, boyish hairdo which tended to spike on top. She thought she looked like Annie Lennox's baby sister and was mildly surprised to find the haircut made her feel liberated and care-free, almost gloriously butch. She never would have imagined feeling this way about cutting off her hair. During the last three weeks, she was thankful she had this short hair. Showers or baths were rare and she jokingly called their group 'the ferals'. They did encounter a few waterholes and streams but were wary wondering what else may be lurking and concerned over the quality of the water . She knew they probably smelled bad half the time, and were damn hungry quite often, but that was part of a back-packing trip. She would return home to Australia tanned, slim, muscled and with a greater knowledge and appreciation of the world around them.

Jamie and Matt often caught fish and cooked them over a campfire, becoming quite efficient with the catching, cleaning and cooking. Kim swore she would never eat a fish again once they returned to Australia, except for the battered variety.

Just this past week, she had become ill, possibly from swallowing water at one of the waterholes and spent five days with stomach cramps, vomiting and diarrhoea. She decided there was nothing worse than camping in forests and needing to run off behind a tree to puke or worse. Thankfully, it was over and she looked forward to a great dinner that night in the local village.

Once a week, they booked a cheap hotel for the night and made the most of the luxury of not camping. Kim would never again take the basics for granted such as the joy of showering in clean, warm water, a soft bed with a pillow, moisturising cream, a variety of food and wine, and even soft toilet paper. Total privacy was the most exquisite experience ever after camping with friends in the jungle.

Tonight, they were booked into a hotel in the local village of *Perudo* and leaving for the island early in the morning. Kim was dreaming of a slow, warm bath, washing her hair, a well-cooked meal and a romantic night with her husband. Before the trip, they decided to only make love on hotel nights, feeling it too awkward to make love in a little tent right next to Matt and Jenna.

Thinking of the romantic plans she had for the evening, Kim looked up at Jamie's lean, brown body with the hot sun behind him which showed not an ounce of extra weight and looking muscular and fit. His brown hair was longer than he normally wore it, tousled and sun bleached slightly on the tips, giving him a younger, surfer look. She grinned at the beard stubble, longing to run her hands across his chin to feel the prickles.

Later that evening at dinner in the restaurant with Matt and Jenna, all were drooling at the thought of a steak with local vegetables. Kim almost felt delirious at the delicious smells wafting out of the restaurant kitchen. A fresh loaf of bread was a good start to the meal, along with the smooth flavour of the local wine. The only Australians in the restaurant, they enjoyed the food, laughed and joked, and bantered jovially with their hosts.

At that moment, they felt the luckiest people on earth. Life was perfect with four best friends enjoying the time of their life, confident in the fact that one day they would tell their grandchildren about this trip.

The wake-up call was scheduled very early so they all retired to their rooms straight after dinner, feeling content and well sated, even slightly tipsy from the wine. Kim soaked in a warm, soapy bath until the skin on her fingers and toes became wrinkly. Wrapped in a white bath robe, she found sweet smelling candles, contributing to the romantic darkness of the room. Afterward, both fell asleep in each other's arms, content with the day and eager for the next.

Chapter 2
The Argument

"Who was that white man you were talking to today, Papa?" asked Marcos, turning to face his father.

The old man intentionally turned away from him, busying himself with coiling the ropes for the boat.

"Oh, just some stranger who wants to go fishing," he answered, quietly.

"Fishing? Is he on his own then?" Marcos asked, knowing there was more to it than his father was revealing.

The old man hesitated.

"Ahhh … no. There are three others."

"Four of them … and they want to go fishing? Why are you taking them?" Marcos persisted, his voice rising with his concern.

His father did not answer. After several minutes, Marcos grabbed his father's shoulder and turned him around sharply to look in his face. The old man looked his son straight in the eye with defiance. Marcos could see the coldness in his eyes, the determination and the arrogance and the terrible truth dawned on him.

"They are offering lots of money, son," the father answered gruffly, his eyes narrowing.

"NO! You cannot take them. Tell them NO!" Marcos said, his voice firm.

His father turned away again to fiddle with the ropes.

"It is good money. I will take them."

"You cannot do this. This is not right. I will not let you." Marcos stood firm and puffed out his chest. His voice had risen with his alarm at the situation.

Another minute ticked by before his father turned back quickly to look at him, eyes flashing angrily and face firmly set.

"Our family has looked after her for many years. This is what we do. You don't know anything."

He flicked his hand in the air, dismissing his son and turned away again.

"NO! This is not what we do. This is not what Grandpa did or his father did. THIS IS NOT WHAT WE DO. THIS IS NOT THE RIGHT THING! You are not doing this anymore. I won't allow it," Marcos fired. His face red and sweat breaking out on his forehead.

Juan's eyes flared and his fists clenched.

"What are you going to do, boy? You don't look after her yet. I do." The old man's face was flushed and set. His lip jutted out in his defiance.

"NO! You don't look after her anymore. This has to stop right now."

Marcos was now yelling at his father, oblivious to the scattering of other people near the fishing boats.

"What are you going to do, then?" the father asked.

Juan looked up at his son, who stood a head taller than he was. The old man knew his son and what he was capable of. He knew that Marcos was young and strong, and could easily overpower the old man, but he also knew his son was too placid and didn't have the steely nerve to stand up to his father. He felt smug and knew he was calling his bluff.

Marcos stared at him for several minutes. He felt his confidence and bravado leave him, and he looked away. He knew physical violence was not the way to solve the problem.

"I will do what I have to do. I should have done this a long time ago. Enough is enough." His voice was low and steady though he did not feel calm. He sighed a deep and slow sigh, then turned and walked away.

Juan sniffed in disgust and looked at the back of his retreating son, before turning his attention back to the boat. Marcos had expressed his thoughts before, but nothing ever happened. He shook his head, not understanding how his own son could have such different views from him. They were like chalk and cheese, complete opposites of each other. He would ignore this outburst knowing Marcos was all puff and no action. Marcos would go away and ponder on the discussion and surely, he would realise that this was a good deal. After tomorrow, Juan would have a lot of money and would not have to make another trip to the island for months.

Chapter 3
The Boat Ride

"**O**h, it's kind of small, isn't it?" Jenna queried, turning to Matt, her eyebrows raised.

Kim's first glimpse of the boat was one of disappointment and trepidation as well. She was not sure what she was expecting, but perhaps something larger, newer and more sturdy in appearance. This boat looked old with pale blue paint peeling from the hull and about half the size she was expecting.

"How long will it take to reach the island?" Jenna asked, turning to Jamie because Matt looked just as worried as she felt.

Jamie put his arm around Jenna to reassure her. He gave her a squeeze and plastered a big, confident smile on his face. "Just over two hours and the boat will be fine. Don't worry. I heard the motor run yesterday and it sounded perfect."

Kim remained silent but looked at the unconvinced face of Jenna and hoped Jamie was right. Matt seemed satisfied with the boat once the initial shock wore off and she felt confident Matt would have voiced concern if he was truly worried. Sometimes, they all trusted Jamie too much, she thought. He was always right. How frustrating it was to be with someone who was always right. How do you win an argument with someone who could do no wrong?

With the luxury of facilities at the hotel, they had washed and dried their clothes overnight and were all feeling refreshed, clean, fed and ready for an adventure. Kim and Jenna wore shorts of tough linen that fell just above their knees with socks and hiking boots. All four wore T-shirts as the weather was warm and humid.

A man stepped out of the boat and onto the sand. It was difficult to judge his age, but Kim estimated him to be sixty to seventy years old. His face was weathered and lined, leathery brown from many hours at sea. He wore a white shirt and white straw hat like many of the village men, although the straw hat had seen better days and looked frayed and shabby, no longer white. Silver hair could be glimpsed poking out around the side of the straw hat. He was not much taller than she was and almost appeared a little frail. She smiled as she thought he resembled his little boat in so many ways, once fine but now aged.

He nodded at Jamie and picked up one of the backpacks to load on the boat. Kim noted he was not the friendly type, offering no greeting or acknowledgement to any of the other three in their group and avoiding eye contact. She thought he was most likely one of the older village men who didn't have a high opinion of foreigners though they needed the income the tourists brought in. This village was not on the main route for tourists so there were not many English-speaking people here and money was tight. He was probably getting more money today than he had seen all year. Kim continued to watch him, contemplating his situation.

Suddenly, an angry male voice carried across the sand and Kim swung around to see a man in a black T-shirt marching towards them. This man was younger than Juan and she guessed it could be his son. He looked around forty years old with black hair greying around the sides, more heavily built than Juan and dressed in more modern attire. He was angry and fired off Spanish words in fast succession to Juan. The older man answered in angry responses, his words slow and firm.

None of the four friends knew any Spanish other than the very basics, but deduced the younger man was not happy with Juan taking the four of them out in the boat. He was gesturing at them and waving his hand at the ocean horizon while addressing Juan. Kim heard Juan say the word 'Marcos' so assumed that was the younger man's name. He gestured toward them with his thumb and seemed to be asking the older man a question. Juan turned toward the four friends and looked at them for a minute or so.

The four friends stood transfixed as this discussion took place. Were they about to lose their opportunity to visit the uninhabited island? Then he answered the younger man in a quieter voice. The younger man made an angry sound and stormed away across the sand. The four friends watched the back of the black T-shirt as it retreated across the sand toward the village. When the black T-shirt had almost disappeared into the village, the friends snapped out of their reverie. Jamie looked back at Juan.

"Everything OK?" he asked.

"Si," the old man answered nodding, then quickly looked away and resumed loading the bags on the boat. He gestured for them to help push the boat back off the sand and to board the vessel.

As she sat, Kim was grateful the seats had vinyl on them, and although worn and ripped in a few places, they were not sitting on hard wood boards. A two-hour trip was a long time to be sitting on a hard surface.

Once seated, the boat could easily fit the four friends with two on each side and Juan at the motor. There was no shelter and Kim was glad all four of them were wearing hats, although necessary to hold their hats on most of the way to prevent them blowing off. Again, she hoped Jamie had made the right choice with Juan and they would reach their destination safely. She glanced around and realised that there were no life jackets on this boat either.

The boat moved out to the open ocean and picked up speed, the motor not missing a beat. The trip felt that it went on forever and would never end. It was too loud to hear anyone talk and after an hour, Kim's backside became numb. Unable to stand up or move around, all she could do was wriggle and change seating positions to lean one way and then the other. Luckily, they passed a few small islands so there were sights to see including loud and colourful bird life. A number of islands were only a few metres square with trees, and a few were just rocks jutting out of the ocean. At one stage, she saw a number of dolphins jumping in and out of the water and on another island, among the rocks were a few fur seals, lounging luxuriously.

After two and a half hours, the old man slowed the speed of the boat. The friends sat up, suddenly aware of the change in speed, and looked around. Ahead to their right, an island came into view on the horizon and Juan pointed to the larger island with white sandy beach stretching the full length of the island, a canopy of tropical looking trees and large volcanic hill formations. It did look peaceful and beautiful, their island. Kim hoped the jungle was not too thick and there would be running water not too far inland. Secretly, she was relieved to know the island existed at all, then scolded herself for doubting Jamie and his instincts.

Along toward the right on the beach, she could see strange objects and as they drew closer, she saw wrecks of small, fishing boats. Most were just a skeleton of a boat, or splinters of wood and she pointed it out to the other three.

As they drew into the shore, the old man turned off the motor and they glided in, coming to a halt on the sand. Jamie and Matt stepped out of the boat into the shallow water and the girls, eager to stretch their legs, stood and turned to collect their bags. Juan was ahead of them and standing at the front of the boat, threw the bags unceremoniously one by one on to the sand. This seemed a strange thing to do when he could have just passed the bags to the passengers or stepped out of the boat and carried them ashore. Kim reasoned he was not accustomed to tourists and was unaware of the correct social etiquette.

The girls stepped down into the knee-deep water and the four friends headed for the dry sand. Jamie turned to Juan, still on the boat and preparing to leave, apparently not disembarking himself.

"You pick us up 12 noon Wednesday?" Jamie nodded his head waiting for an affirmative nod from the old man. Nothing was forthcoming so Jamie repeated.

"You pick us up Wednesday?"

Juan stopped and looked at Jamie. It was one of the few times Juan had ever maintained eye contact with him. His dark eyes were impenetrable and Jamie wondered what he was thinking.

"Viktoria be happy to see you," he said quietly in his thick Spanish accent.

Jamie tried again.

"You pick us up Wednesday lunch time?"

The old man nodded his head affirmatively and signalled for the men to push the boat away from the shore. They did and in very swift movements, the old man swung the boat around, gunned the motor and was heading off at great speed.

The four friends stood watching the boat speed away until it was just a small dot on the horizon. They looked at each other and shrugged their shoulders. None of them were particularly worried about Juan's lack of social skills or mistrust of foreigners. They just hoped he understood enough English to remember to pick them up as arranged.

"Jamie, if he doesn't pick us up, we volunteer you to swim back for help," said Matt, grinning at Jamie.

"Hey ... wasn't Robinson Crusoe based on one of these islands?" asked Kim.

"WILSON!" Matt yelled out and they all laughed.

After a few minutes of banter, they turned around to face the island. The sun was shining and glistening on the water, the sand was a lovely, pale colour similar to the beaches in Australia and the forest ahead of them appeared green and tranquil. They picked up their bags, slung them onto their backs and made their way toward the jungle.

Chapter 4
The Old Village

"I 'm starving," said Matt, looking eagerly at the others for agreement. "How about we find some shade and have lunch?"

They had packed sandwiches made up by the kitchen staff at the hotel before they left that morning, knowing they would need a quick lunch rather than try to catch fish or some other game in an unknown environment.

"You're always thinking of your stomach," teased Jamie.

Matt swiped at him with his hand and Jamie ducked his head, laughing.

They unpacked small, fold-up chairs, found a shaded area just inside the first line of palm trees and before long, had devoured a few sandwiches and half the water from their bottles. Although not unbearably hot, it was humid having rained off and on for a few days which left the air sticky and wet. Kim enjoyed her egg and lettuce sandwich, aware they may not catch any game for meals while on the island, so she wanted to make sure she had protein where possible. So far, they had always been fortunate enough to catch fish but that was not always guaranteed. Each of them carried dried biscuits, tinned food and beef jerky in case they became hungry. If they were lucky there would be tropical type of fruit on the island.

Jamie cleared his throat and addressed the group.

"I hereby dub our island, Melbourne II."

"Melbourne II?" queried Jenna. "It doesn't look anything like Melbourne."

"It doesn't have to look like Melbourne. It's our home for the next few days so it is our Melbourne. Melbourne II."

They finished their lunch and were sitting on little chairs relaxing and watching the turquoise waves gently lap at the sand from the shade of the trees when Kim suddenly held her hand out for everyone to pay attention.

"Listen."

Everyone froze, caught by surprise and judging whether to be alarmed or not. They listened for a few minutes, turning to look around them and each other.

"I don't hear anything," said Jenna, looking at Kim in puzzlement.

"Exactly. There are no sounds. Where are the birds?" asked Kim.

Everyone looked around and up at the trees. It was true. There was the sound of the waves lapping at the shore but that was all. There was no wind so no rustling of the trees or shrubs. The island was silent, eerily silent. There was not the slightest hint of any wildlife.

Matt stood up and turned around slowly, looking up at the trees.

"That's weird," he said and dismissed the idea.

For the past three weeks they had heard continuous bird life everywhere they went. Birds chatted and chirped, and at times, screeched at them. The only reprieve was when they were silent at night-time.

"Let's keep moving," said Jamie.

They packed up the remains of their lunch and little chairs and started to trek inland. Somehow, the playful mood had vanished, replaced by a strange feeling of something not quite right. Each of them discreetly looked up and around as they walked for signs of life. Kim thought it would only take the sight of one bird, or the sound of one insect for them to relax and the eerie mood to lift.

The jungle, which consisted of tall, palm trees and medium-sized shrubs and ferns, only seemed to last for about twenty metres when suddenly, they hit an open expanse. The shock stopped everyone in their tracks. Again, there was silence as everyone tried to understand what they were looking at. The expectation was that the jungle would cover most of the island, not completely end so close to the shore.

Ahead of them was cleared land with very few trees. It almost appeared as though the island grew jungle around the outside and cleared grass land on the inside, but the land had been cleared by man and was not natural grassland. There were dirt paths in many directions. One worked its way down through the middle of the land almost in front of them, and a few crisscross paths could be seen across toward the other side of the island. A larger path went directly right to left from where they were standing. They were standing on the perimeter path. Kim was aware that animals create paths to well-worn areas such as a waterhole but in this case, no animals had so far been seen and these paths looked too ... planned.

Huge rock formations appeared as small mountains covering the centre of the island. Tall rock faces jutted out in different directions with hues from dark granite grey to deep rust. The volcanic rock formations towered over the cleared grassland below.

"What's that?" Matt pointed to their left and down the cleared land a few hundred metres.

Everyone turned to look and walked closer trying to determine what the object was. They could see an old tree, leaning over as if the wind had been pushing at it for years, the dark gnarled bark hanging off in places, and under it, a jumble of old wood.

"It's a wreck of a house or a hut," said Jenna.

Everyone could see it now that Jenna had identified it. There was no telling how old the wreck of the hut was with the complete structure collapsed and rotted materials left. The wood would have originated from trees on the island but was a jumbled pile of old material now. Looking further around the immediate area, the remains of wooden fencing could be seen although mostly collapsed and rotted with vines holding parts of the fence together. There were also areas where feral plants had overgrown and Kim moved closer for an inspection, deciding the plants did not look like native flora local to the area. It had once been a vegetable garden and turned feral and wild when abandoned. Someone had farmed here or had kept animals. Why else build a fence?

"Ok, so the island must have once been inhabited," said Jamie. "They obviously couldn't make a go at it and left."

The others nodded in agreement. Although completely logical and evident, something about the ruins of a civilisation where people used to live and farm and were now gone was super creepy. Adding further to the eerie feeling that had clouded them earlier, the four friends felt disappointed in this find, as if someone had defaced their paradise. This no longer felt like their uninhabited island, their Melbourne II.

Matt tried to break the gloomy silence.

"There's going to be lots to explore on Melbourne II. But I think we should aim to find where we plan to camp soon so we can establish ourselves and do some fishing. It'll be dark before we know it"

The others agreed. Matt pointed further down the clearing, two hundred metres away, close to bushes and a cliff face.

"Look - I think I can see water over there. Let's check it out and see if it's fresh water and if there's fish."

"Could be a perfect spot to camp," said Jamie. "Protected from wind, flat, water and hopefully, fish."

They headed down the path which was just bare earth and the dirt had a slight reddish colour like clay.

"There must be animals around. Look at the path. There's no weeds or grass on it," said Matt.

Jamie bent down to peer at a few visible marks in the dirt. Although not convincingly footprints, the series of marks indicated some sort of trail and led down to the water.

"Maybe someone is still living on the island," Jenna suggested. "The old man said Viktoria would be happy to see us."

"I guess that's possible though I did say we wanted to be on an island where there were no people. I'm sure he understood," said Jamie looking at each of his friends. "Maybe he didn't understand."

Chapter 5
The First Night

They camped on the sandy ground next to the sparkling waterhole, on a picturesque site with flat ground and a cliff face towering above them. Shrubs, bushes and trees offered a backdrop to the water and provided shade. The water was clear and fresh and ran into the waterhole from the rocks. It was easy to see why people had once chosen this location to build a little village.

Even better, the water had plenty of fish and before long, Jamie and Matt had caught a bag full of fish for dinner. Meanwhile, the girls expertly erected the two tents and prepared the camp site, collecting dry kindling to start the campfire. There was plenty of dry wood to use once the fire was blazing.

The guys stayed at camp gutting the fish while the girls wandered over to the collapsed huts looking for wood for the fire. Gutting fish was one thing both girls refused to do. Kim felt nauseous watching it performed and would never be able to eat the fish later if she watched the cleaning of it.

The girls collected armfuls of old wood, careful to collect from the ground rather than risk taking any from the rotted pile which was as tall as the girls were. There had been several families living here at some stage and Kim counted at least twenty-two piles where there had once been a hut of some kind. She wondered where the inhabitants were, where they had gone. The old wrecks of boats on the shore where they had landed now added up.

As the sky darkened, they cooked their fish over a blazing fire and laughed and chatted. The initial disappointment at finding out the island had once been inhabited was fading now and they were feeling excited about exploring the next day. They were satisfied that no one else was on the island, and although there had been inhabitants at some stage in the past, there had been no one there for a very long time.

"Maybe we'll find a waterfall," said Kim hopefully. "There's running water and a rock face. We might find one around the other side of the cliff."

"I suppose you'll want a selfie in the waterfall?" Matt teased her.

Kim was always stopping for selfies in the strangest of places. She had her iPhone with her on the trip and when they were in a location with free Wi-Fi, she posted the photos to social media for friends and family to keep up with their travels. It had become a joke with them. She laughed too.

"Of course, and on that note ..."

She reached into her backpack and took out her phone, turned it on and waited for the screen to load. She was only turning the phone on for photos to save the battery life. There was no signal on the island.

"Right. Everyone - gather around."

She held the phone up in front of her for the selfie and signalled for the others to position themselves within the photo frame. Satisfied when she saw the four faces in shot, she snapped the photo. They moved apart back to their positions around the fire.

Jenna pulled a scrunched-up face and snorted.

"Ewwww. Can you smell that?"

She looked at the others, face still scrunched. They all breathed in and sniffed a few times trying to detect a smell. They shook their heads.

"Nope," said Jamie.

"What does it smell like?" asked Kim.

"I don't know."

Jenna squinted and sniffed again, trying to identify the smell.

"It sort of smells musky and sweaty, like someone who hasn't had a shower in a very long time."

She sniffed again and wrinkled her face.

Jamie slapped Matt's shoulder. "Matt, for Christ's sake, I told you to take a shower occasionally."

Everyone broke into fits of laughter.

"Haha. Very funny," Matt said, acknowledging the joke.

Jenna continued to smell the musky smell now and again throughout the evening. They could tell as soon as they saw her face scrunch. She was such a pretty and petite girl, with classical facial features so the scrunched up face made them giggle.

"Do you know what I feel like right now?" asked Kim, looking around.

Everyone looked at her expectantly.

"Err ... honey, we did that last night?" joked Jamie.

She pushed his shoulder in retribution. "Smartass. I feel like a good glass of red wine."

"Well. I'm sure we all do, but I can't see any bottle shops around here," said Matt.

Kim smiled secretly and rummaged around in her backpack.

"Well, it just so happens that I brought a bottle with me for this very occasion."

She produced a bottle triumphantly and held it up in the firelight. Jamie took the bottle from her peering at the label in the dim flickering light of the fire.

"Shiraz from Chile. How great is that?"

The friends were quick to retrieve their camping mugs from the backpacks and held them out for Jamie to pour the wine. They sipped the Shiraz savouring the smooth, rich flavour, toasting everything they could think of.

"To waterfalls."

"To Melbourne II."

"To friends."

"To a good time."

"To more fish."

"To exploring."

"To turtles."

"Turtles?" questioned the others.

"Yes, turtles," said Kim. "I want to swim with turtles. You know, Kevin Costner danced with wolves. Well ... I want to swim with turtles."

Jenna stood up. "Going to pee," she announced and headed into the trees behind where she was sitting. The trees were ten metres from the camp and the forest appeared to thicken behind the initial row of trees. The night was dark and the only light flickered from the campfire so she planned to venture just behind the initial trees to relieve herself.

She was only gone for a few minutes when she reappeared walking very fast, and sat down close to Matt, almost landing on him. The other three looked at her in surprise.

"Are you ok?" asked Kim.

Jenna was breathing rapidly and appeared agitated. Her pretty face was frowning and Kim thought she could see her shiver.

"I ... I'm not sure. I could smell that smell again ... really strong, and ... I heard a noise." Her voice was soft and unsteady.

"Did you get spooked?" asked Jamie.

She looked up at him and he could see genuine fear in her eyes.

"Yes. I ... I didn't feel like I was alone."

The other three looked toward the trees where Jenna had been. They scanned for any sign of life or movement. The trees at the front were tropical looking trees, similar to palm trees and the light from the fire flickered on the pale trunks. Beyond the trees it was just black and dark.

There was no sound or movement that anyone could detect, but it was unusual for Jenna to spook. They had been venturing into the trees and bushes at night for weeks in all possible situations and Jenna had never spooked before.

Matt put his arm around her shoulders to draw her close and rubbed her arm reassuringly.

"But the important thing to ask is .... did you pee?" he asked.

Everyone laughed and the mood lifted. They stayed up another hour chatting and finished the bottle of wine, but each could not help glancing over at the trees from time to time and listening for any sound. Jenna had moved around to the other side of the fire, not wanting to have her back against the forest.

Jenna refused to go back to the trees to relieve herself before bed, so Kim accompanied her and together, they found a handy bush closer to the waterhole.

Chapter 6
The Night Visitor

She ventured out of her shelter when the sun was retreating and darkness started to fall. She felt safer in the dark as it was harder for the humans to see her. Her eyes were accustomed to the dark as she spent time hunting at night, searching for any small animals active at night.

The smell of the burning timber and smoke excited her as it had been so long since she last smelled a fire. The odour of fish cooking caused her stomach to rumble, reminding her how hungry she was. She walked slowly and carefully between the trees, treading one foot at a time on the ground, careful not to step on anything that may make a sound. She regulated her breathing to be as silent as possible, not wanting the humans to be aware of her yet.

She knew she was salivating with the smell of the fish cooking on the campfire, but couldn't help it. Saliva ran down from the corner of her mouth and dripped from her chin down her chest. It was almost more than she could bear. She caught a whimper in her throat before it erupted and reminded herself that she had been hungry many times in the past and could manage it now. Not long to wait.

Standing quietly, she watched the humans for hours, peeking out from her hiding spot. They ate, they talked and they laughed, moving around and touching each other. She found their interactions fascinating. She had been alone for so long that it was almost difficult to remember being in the company of others, or how to interact with others. Flashes of memories came to her of others that she had known. Her eyes watered with the memories.

She could see these humans were two couples and gave a silent sob, catching it in her throat. She would never be part of a couple. Watching the four humans interact with each other and enjoy themselves made the loneliness seem overwhelming. She wanted to reach out, to touch them, to interact and communicate but had no idea how, or the courage. She wanted to let them know she needed cooked fish. Would they cook some fish for her? If only they could cook some fish for her, then there would be no need for her to hunt them. Maybe they could stay and cook fish for her regularly.

Watching the two couples for those hours was exciting for her and yet, incredibly sad and lonely. She was unable to drag herself away from the sight, smells and sounds of them. She was caught by surprise when one of the females walked into the trees right near her. It happened so suddenly she barely had time to move out of the way, having been lost in memories and not paying attention. Quickly, she slid behind a large tree and held her breath hoping the female had not seen her. She heard the female urinate, the smell sweet and strong, then inhale deeply and head back to camp. She let her breath out slowly and relaxed her muscles.

She continued to watch the humans and eventually, they disappeared into their little shelters and before long, she could tell they were asleep. She could hear the deep breathing, and light snoring from one of the males.

Slowly, she made her way out of the trees, creeping silently and almost tip-toed past the little shelters to where the fire was. Her focus was on the cooked fish. She knew they had eaten most of the fish but could still smell it and knew some remained. She just had to find it.

She rummaged around, upending items and tossing them aside, until she found a strange bag which contained cooked bits of the fish including bones. Every time she touched the strange bag, it made a rustling noise. Puzzled and wary, she poked at the bag with her finger, her sharp fingernail piercing the bag. Eventually, bones fell out onto the ground and she promptly picked them up and ate them, crunching the bones. She had never tasted anything so delicious. She devoured the bones quickly, licking her lips and desperate for more. She poked at the strange bag repeatedly, hoping more bones would fall out.

Hearing a human voice she froze, holding her breath. The voice had come from one of the little shelters and sounded sleepy. She couldn't work out if the voice was awake and addressing her or murmuring in sleep. After a few minutes of silence, she assumed the human had gone back to sleep so looked around at the backpacks and strange objects lying around, wondering what they were for. A large soft object caught her eye. It was brightly coloured and the colour drew her to it, even in the dark. When she held it to her face, she liked the feel of it and the smell of it, soft and soothing, and something she had never felt before. She wandered back to her own shelter dragging the colourful object behind her.

Chapter 7
The Face

The day dawned bright, sunny, and warm again. Jamie and Kim were the first out of their tent, blinking against the brightness of the morning. Jamie stretched having been squashed up in the short tent all night and needed to limber up his long limbs. Kim headed for the line of trees to relieve herself. She avoided the location where Jenna had felt spooked, though in the light of the day, it seemed innocent.

Kim wandered over to the fire to poke at the embers and see what could be resurrected. A few cinders remained deep down in the mountain of ash. She poked and blew hard on them and they flared enough that she was able to add leaves and ignite a small fire for breakfast. She marvelled at what a fabulous day it was and how fortunate they were to be in such a lovely spot.

Jamie found the bread and eggs and started the first batch of fried eggs on toast. He always said he could cook anything with a frypan, a fire and an egg lifter. He cooked an egg and a piece of bread together in one pan, perfectly timing the cooking so they were both ready at the same time. Then, he slid the toast and eggs on to the first plate and started on the second batch. The smell of cooking soon brought Jenna and Matt out of their tent.

"Do I smell breakfast? I sure am hungry," joked Matt.

Kim was hunting through Jamie's backpack and then her own, looking puzzled.

"I can't find our picnic blanket," she said.

"We were sitting on it last night," added Jamie, looking around.

He walked over to their tent and entered it, moving the bedding around to look for the brightly coloured blanket.

"Did you guys accidentally take our picnic blanket to your tent last night?" she asked Jenna.

"I don't think so. Let me check."

Jenna walked over to her tent, hunted around inside and came back shaking her head.

"That's strange," said Kim frowning and trying to remember if she had moved it before they went to bed the night before. Although not a terribly expensive blanket, each item in their meagre list of travelling possessions was important, and its loss felt.

She then noticed the shredded plastic bag that had contained the remains of the fish dinner from the night before. The remnants of the shredded bag lay scattered on the ground not far from the fire.

"Looks like there are animals on the island after all." Kim looked up at the others, holding the main part of the shredded bag up for them to see.

"They've gone after the kitchen scraps too. Maybe that was what was in the trees with you last night Jenna. Some sort of scavenging animal," she said to Jenna.

"Like what?" asked Jenna, a little freaked out at the thought of an animal near her in the dark trees last night.

"Like a fox or possum or something?"

"Maybe," Kim shrugged. "I thought I heard someone out here last night. I asked who it was but fell asleep again. Must have scared the poor animal half to death."

Their fears from the night before had seemed a bit silly, but what size animal could take a blanket away? Surely not a possum. Did they even have possums here?

After breakfast, they secured the campsite, ensuring there were no food scraps around and zipped up their tents. They left their backpacks at the campsite inside the tents and packed a small bag each containing a few essential items such as a water bottle, first aid kit and small amount of food for lunch.

"Let's explore," said Kim, excited at the thought of finding a waterfall or a turtle.

"Ok," said Jamie. "Let's start at the water and see where it goes upstream?"

They headed around the left edge of the water toward the cliff face. The massive rock formation loomed above them, magnificent in its many hues and angles. Matt was the first to discover the cave. A number of large boulders lay on the ground having tumbled down from the rocks above at some stage. One boulder was huge and as Matt stepped around it, he calculated it was the size of a Volkswagen.

Behind the boulder, he found an opening in the rock face. Excited, he signalled to the others and they followed. The opening was easily large enough for them to enter without needing to duck their heads down. The inside was dark but within a few minutes, their eyes adjusted to the dim light and they were able to see they were inside a large cavern. The walls and roof were rock and the ground felt soft under their feet where the water had recently flooded the cave.

Kim looked around almost expecting to see primitive drawings on the walls. It resembled the type of caves she had seen in books where ancient art was discovered. As they looked around, they could make out bits and pieces of bones and wood scattered around on the ground.

"Looks like this may have been a lair for some sort of animal. Not sure what bones they are but they look like young animals," ventured Jamie.

The others agreed. They left the cave and continued the investigation around the rock face beside the water. The going was tough in places where they needed to climb over loose rocks and rubble.

The island was not very large so it didn't take long to climb around to the other side of the cliff face. They were curious to see where the water originated from as it was fresh water and they didn't have to wait long. In a low-lying area on the other side of the rock formation, they found a natural spring where the water bubbled up to the surface. The pond was the size of a large swimming pool and the water looked dark and clear. The pond was surrounded by plants and ferns. The scene was one of beauty and serenity.

Although no waterfalls could be seen, there was a section at the back of the pond where the water streamed down a few rocks and fanned out to another smaller pond below. Close enough to a waterfall, thought Kim as she removed her boots and socks, and climbed down to the smaller pond below and sat on a rock with the water fanning over her shoulders. The water was cool and refreshing and the other friends joked and chuckled at the sight of Kim creating her own waterfall.

Careful not to get the phone wet, she held the phone out and took a few selfies then climbed out of the pond to have a look at the shots.

Flicking through the photos she had just taken, she suddenly frowned and stopped, staring down at the small phone screen. Using her fingers to spread the photo out larger, and angling her head for better light, she suddenly gasped.

"Oh! Look. Look at this. What the hell is that?"

Jamie took the phone from her and with the other two looking over his shoulder they studied the photo in front of them. It was the four of them from last night with the campfire behind them. The photo was dark but each face could be clearly seen, reflected from the campfire, as well as the face in the background beside a tree.

"What the hell ...?" said Matt.

Jamie spread the photo so the background face was zoomed in as far as the iPhone would allow. It was a face, pale against the dark surrounds, and at the height of another person, but the body was in the shadows of night and could not be seen. Zoomed in, the resolution of the photo was not good enough to gather much detail. The face was a little fuzzy but it was definitely a face.

All four friends looked at each other in shock. Kim could feel her heart beating fast and adrenalin rush through her body. They were not alone after all. This person had come into their camp last night and taken food scraps and her picnic blanket. She looked across at Jenna and thought Jenna looked close to tears.

"Matt, sit her down," she instructed, firmly.

Matt guided Jenna and the four of them sat down on the surrounding rocks. All were speechless, lost in their own thoughts and fears. Jamie was the first to speak.

"Ok. So, we're not alone. Someone else is here on the island and was in our camp last night."

Jenna's eyes teared up and Matt tightened his hand in hers.

"If this person wanted to hurt us, they would have already done it last night."

Kim blinked, thinking how vulnerable they had been, snug in their tents while an unknown person was stalking them. As he talked, Jamie felt more rational and confident in what he was saying. He was convincing himself as well as the other three.

"There must be someone here and they were curious about us but too nervous to come and meet us."

"Eating fish bones? Someone must be very hungry," said Kim, nervously.

Jamie grimaced. "Yes true. We'll just have to be careful and stick together. No one go anywhere on your own. Let's assume this person is hungry and will probably watch us and try to get food again," said Jamie.

"Should we leave food out for him?" asked Jenna.

"That could be a good idea. Let's all think on it."

Everyone nodded, but the holiday atmosphere was now gone. Fear and trepidation had crept in and now their thoughts were on protecting themselves and survival with an unknown person lurking.

"We can't even phone Juan to come and get us. We don't have a phone number and he doesn't speak English," said Jenna, her voice shaky.

"He may not own a phone. He's from a poor village," said Matt.

"Could we phone someone else to come and get us?" asked Jenna.

"There's no signal," said Kim, solemnly.

There was no choice but to wait until the rendezvous with Juan the next day. It was only another twenty-four hours.

Chapter 8
The Smell

"Ewww. Smells like something's dead," said Jenna, always the first to capture any scent.

There had been little change in the landscape for what seemed like ages. They headed away from the rock face and water to explore the island across the other side from where they had landed. Before they reached the far shore, they came across what appeared to be a well-worn path running parallel with the beach. On either side of the path were thick trees and bushes. This island had a diverse range of scenery and terrains. They were beginning to think they must have circumnavigated the entire island as they felt they had been walking for hours when they became aware of a stench. As they walked, the foul smell became stronger until it was nauseating.

Despite the revolting smell, they continued walking, wondering what the odour could be, considering they had not seen any animals on the island, only some weird ghostly person hiding in the trees. The smell forced the four friends to breathe through their mouths. Kim reached in her bag and produced a bandana, tying it around her face as a mask. Matt and Jamie searched on either side of the track for a dead animal, or whatever was creating that smell. It didn't exactly smell like a newly dead animal. They continued to walk warily, looking for anything out of the ordinary.

Eventually, to their right ahead they could see a structure, a type of building, faint aqua green through the trees. It seemed so strange for this to be sitting here and a faded, peeling aqua green of all colours. Kim wondered if they were hallucinating.

This structure was different from the others they had encountered. It was still old but newer than the hut remnants they had seen, and still standing, though parts of the roof were falling in. The outside of the building had been from island timber and once painted an aqua green colour. The green was still visible though the paint had faded and chipped and much of the wood was rotten. The windows didn't contain glass and stared at them like eyeless sockets. The roof had been wood with a thatch and was mostly still in place with one section having collapsed. The entrance had also collapsed, and a tunnel led into the hut.

"Well ... what on earth?" said Matt to himself.

The four of them stood staring at this apparition of a hut in front of them, not believing their eyes.

"Surely no one could live there now. It's in bad shape," said Kim. "The smell is coming from the house."

Jamie nodded.

"Yes. An animal must have gone in there to die."

They all nodded in agreement because nothing else made sense. The thought crossed Kim's mind that the last of the villagers may have died in this hut in more recent times, and she hoped that was not the case.

They continued staring at the hut as no one knew what to do. Common sense told them to turn around and walk away but none of them could do it. They needed to know what the smell was. Needed to know and yet, no one stepped forward to be the first.

A slight noise – a shuffling sound – reached their ears. All of them heard it and slowly turned to look at each other.

What was that?

Kim felt the hair on the back of her neck stand up. The sound had come from within the hut. Was something still alive in there? No one said a word, but each knew what the other was thinking. They must go and see what made the noise. It could be an animal or person in need of help. They couldn't walk away. They also needed to know what that smell was but no one moved. Fear of the unknown gripped each person and they remained rooted to the spot, listening for more sounds but there was nothing. Minutes ticked by.

Jamie was the one who eventually spoke. "Come on. We need to check it out."

The other three looked at Jamie not knowing what to say. He spoke with a courage that Kim did not feel and chided herself for being such a chicken. Logically, it was probably a dying animal that had kicked an old piece of furniture in its death throes. What else could it possibly be?

"I hope the smell's not worse in there," Kim said.

Jamie swung into action. He looked at each of the other three, took a deep breath, and stepped forward.

"Come on then."

The other three followed though keeping behind Jamie. Kim went second, followed by Matt with Jenna at the rear. They hesitated at the collapsed entrance, Jamie examining it and checking it was ok to walk through. A small entrance remained, one that had been used consistently for some time judging by the wear on the ground.

"There's a cobweb, so we know there are spiders on the island," he joked to lighten the mood.

"Guys, I think I'll stay here," said Jenna, quietly.

Kim could see Jenna was petrified and Kim almost suggested she would stay with her, but Jamie and Matt started moving and she automatically followed.

The smell was horrendous. Kim adjusted the bandana, to stifle it as much as possible. It appeared dark and dusty inside the tunnel from the collapsed roof, and the three friends hesitated and readjusted their eyes to the dim light.

Kim felt the hair on the back of her neck rise again as she looked at this tunnel entrance and felt prickles go up and down her body.

Could she hear something?

Could she sense something?

There was no discernible noise, yet she felt a presence beyond the entrance, inside the hut. Was this a natural intuition? Was there a low-level sound? She didn't know. She glanced at the faces of the two men wondering if they felt what she felt. Everyone was standing staring at the entrance. They all knew there was something in the hut beyond the doorway and they could sense the presence just as she could.

Jamie looked at Kim and she could see fear in his eyes. This was not a look she had ever seen on his face before, her confident, courageous and logical man who always got them out of trouble. This face chilled her to the bone and made her realise that her fears were real and everyone else was feeling the same.

The three friends looked at each other and Kim wanted to scream at them that they should just leave right now but she couldn't find her voice. Jamie stepped forward and they followed him. Ducking their heads, they entered the tunnel entrance and turned directly to the right.

Chapter 9
The Gates of Hell

They walked into the gates of hell.

The room was dark, stinking and larger than it appeared from the outside. As Kim scanned the floor for her footing, she saw piles of bones, rib cages, long bones, masses of small bones, animal skulls, hides and she thought she glimpsed a human skull. The stench was overpowering and the room felt alive and humming as swarming insects crawled over the debris.

Something was towering above in the middle of the room only metres away. Something dark and looming, and above their horizontal line of sight. The three became aware of the presence at the same time. Slowly, they raised their eyes from the boneyard floor up to view what their minds fought against.

Eyes looked back at them. Eyes focused on them.

Kim would later wonder what she felt at that moment, standing in that dim, putrid room staring up into the face of a demon. All she could articulate was she felt a strange shift in her whole being, like her world had fallen off its axis, the world had stopped ... civilisation had died ... humankind had ceased ... life meant nothing ... and the world struggled for breath in its death throes. She was in hell looking into the eyes of a demon.

A cold pulsing sensation ran down her body, she could feel her heart beating as if it would burst out of her chest, every hair on her body stood on end. She was not sure if she had urinated or defecated but something had let go and her organs had turned to water. She felt a strange primeval fear and a sudden knowledge of times gone by and a terror ingrained in her DNA. This was not the first time they had met, human and demon. Kim felt this, deep in her bones, the primal enemy.

The demon was studying them with interest, human-like eyes stared at them unblinking. There was no fear on the demon's face, no hatred, no anger, no emotion. The look was one of longing, of anticipation, of waiting to see what they would do next. Later, Kim would try to remember the details but at the time it all happened so fast.

The demon perched on a large beam of wood running horizontally across the room about waist height. Kim's eyes were drawn to the bright blue and red checked colour picnic rug hanging over the perch. The demon sat on its haunches, squatting, with its feet gripping the wood. Toenails that looked like claws, large, sharp and with black at the tips.

The demon looked very human-like and yet, it didn't. It looked animal-like and yet, it didn't.

The demon's body held powerful muscles and the torso looked very toned and strong, skin taut, tough and brown with a sprinkling of dark hairs. Strong shoulders, arms and biceps and yet, the body was thin and ribs were visible. The demon was female though the breasts were not large and the features were not feminine. Kim knew it was a female but could not tell why she knew. The hands were human-like but larger and the fingernails stronger. The face was primitive, coarse and almost Neanderthal-like. A large nose, deep set dark eyes and an intelligent look with long, dark brown to black hair tangled down past its shoulders with a smattering of natural dreadlocks.

Some sort of appendage was visible beyond her shoulders, pointed and yet, Kim couldn't make it out. The dark, intelligent eyes held her in its steady gaze not just at her, but into her soul. Kim resigned herself in those few seconds that this was the end of her life.

Matt was the first to react, throwing his head back and letting out a guttural scream that roared in her ears. The scream pierced the silence in the room and automatically, Kim opened her mouth to scream but only an empty hiss erupted. It was enough to release the three from their paralysis and spur them into self-protective action. With a flurry of urgent activity, everyone fell over themselves in the rush to leave the hut. Matt led the way with Kim and Jamie scrambling behind. Kim felt she had no control over her legs as total panic took over. The scramble was chaotic and frantic as fear turned into sheer terror. In times of sheer terror, people are capable of such extreme speed, strength or courage. Matt rocketed out of the hut and Jenna, waiting outside, took off following him. Kim and Jamie raced behind Jenna in absolute terror. Kim was not aware of her legs or what pace they were at. She was vaguely aware of falling over a few times but leapt back into a full-on run within a split second.

Kim was certain the demon would capture them at any moment, and sheer terror kept her moving. She had no idea how they arrived at the cleared area as she had been unaware of the direction they were running, just blindly followed Matt and Jenna.

In panic and without thinking, they had all turned inland and ran toward the centre of the island, back toward their camp site, intent on adding as much distance between themselves and the demon as possible.

Five hundred metres further, Matt yelled to stop. They all stopped, heaving from exhaustion and exertion. Kim's chest hurt and she bent over gasping for air and could hear the others panting and trying to catch their breath. After a few minutes, she felt able to breathe a little deeper and the pain was subsiding. She straightened up and looked behind, and with shock she realised Jamie was not with them.

Chapter 10
The Rescue

"**W**HERE'S JAMIE?" she screamed at the others. "OH MY GOD! WHERE'S JAMIE?"

With running blindly in panic, no one had looked behind, only ahead, too afraid of falling if they tried to look behind. No one knew whether Jamie had been behind them or not. Kim started to panic and Matt tried to calm her down, grabbing her shoulders.

"We'll go back and see where he is. Maybe he went to the beach."

Was it possible he had turned to the left when they had turned to the right? His old football injury prevented him from running as fast as they could. In the blind panic, everyone had only thought of running for their lives. There had been no thought of the fact that Jamie couldn't run fast.

The walk back was slow and step-by-step, holding on to each other by the arm, squeezing each other for reassurance. They were heaving from the exertion of running and Kim knew she was making high-pitched distressed noises, but she had no control over it. She was on the edge of becoming hysterical. They continually monitored to the left and right, afraid the demon would suddenly materialise from the jungle and jump them. Near where they had turned to run inland, they saw movement and a black shadow raced into the bushes. It happened too fast for any of them to see any detail, but they all knew what it was. The bushes rustled.

All three stood frozen watching the bushes to see if the demon would reappear. For what seemed like an eternity, they stood still and silent, scanning the bushes ready to flee. Kim was the first one to look away from the bushes. Another further one hundred metres, she saw a shape on the ground and screamed.

'JAMIE. OH MY GOD, JAMIE!"

They ran to the supine figure of Jamie on the ground. Blood was everywhere, covering his upper body and a huge pool was gathering beneath him, the blood darkening the dirt. His eyes looked upward at the sky but were unseeing and they knew he was dead. A gaping slash ran vertically across his jugular and it looked like he had bled out.

Kim fell to her knees screaming and threw herself across his body. She shook him and hugged him, calling his name repeatedly. Jenna also fell to her knees sobbing uncontrollably. Matt put a hand to his forehead and stood above them mumbling.

"OH MAN, OH MAN, OH MAN."

Time seemed to stop. Kim sat back and placed Jamie's head on her knee, rocking back and forth and sobbing. His eyes were open and she looked into those eyes but knew he couldn't see her. He wasn't there. She could not comprehend that this man that she loved was lying on the ground with no life left in him. This man who always had so much life in him, so much life to live. It just couldn't be real. None of it could be real. Where did he go? Where had his life force gone? Where was his soul? Were they dreaming? Was this a nightmare and they would wake up soon? She couldn't bring herself to close his eyelids because that would be accepting that he was dead. She whispered to him between sobs, looking into his eyes, looking for him.

"Jamie. Please, please," she rocked and begged him to wake up.

"Can we do mouth-to-mouth or something?" Jenna yelled at Matt.

Matt was pacing back and forth, running his hands through his hair continually and mumbling. He stopped and looked down at Jenna, then at Kim holding Jamie's head.

"It's too late. It's too late," Matt broke into a gentle sob and fell to his knees next to them. He put his face in his hands and openly sobbed.

Kim caught her breath and looked at Matt.

"He can't be dead. Matt, he can't be dead."

Matt continued his gentle sobbing. Jenna reached out and took Jamie's hand in hers and affectionately rubbed his hand across her cheek. She settled her sobs and looked across at Matt.

"What do we do now?"

Matt took his hands away from his face and looked at her through red eyes. Their eyes held as they tried to grasp their predicament and what it meant. Kim heard the voice but couldn't even think of anything except the fact that Jamie was gone. Part of her wanted to curl up and lay down beside him. It was too hard to picture going on without him. Nothing else seemed to matter.

Matt stood up. He knew that Jenna was relying on him and that he needed to calm down and take the lead. He glanced around the bushes but there was no sign of any movement. He gently placed a hand on each of Kim's shoulders.

"Kim," he said, gently.

There was no response and Matt could feel her body shaking with her sobs.

"Kim," he said, more firmly.

"We can't stay here. That ... that ... thing might come back. We have to think of what we're going to do."

Matt and Jenna looked at each other and waited for Kim to respond. Through tears Kim looked up at Matt and nodded.

"We can't leave him here."

"No," Matt said, firmly. "We will not leave him here."

There was no way off the island until the next day when they were to be picked up. Matt felt a strange feeling when he thought of Juan. Did Juan have any idea that this demon was on the island? Surely not. Surely, Juan would not have suggested this location and brought them here if he had known. He frowned, feeling uncomfortable all the same.

With the apparent ease which the demon had killed Jamie, Matt worried if any of them would survive another day on the island. Would the demon come back and kill all of them, pick them off one-by-one? It seemed a good possibility. Waiting until tomorrow was not an option. He didn't want to announce these thoughts to Kim and Jenna at that moment, but he was sure Jenna was already thinking the same.

"I think we should go and inspect those boat wrecks we saw to see if we can use any of them. Maybe we can leave the island."

This seemed like the most logical thing to do to Matt. Position themselves on the beach with the ocean behind them, and where they could see anything coming. Hopefully, they would find something in the wrecks that they could use to leave the island as long as it could float and hold the four of them.

Kim stood and took one of Jamie's arms and Matt, the other. His body was a leaden weight and they both found it difficult to lift the limp body. Awkwardly, they dragged Jamie with them down the path, through the narrow jungle and on to the beach. Although still gently crying, Kim's sobs had subsided with the effort of lifting and dragging Jamie along. She looked across at the bright turquoise water where they had landed. It no longer looked beautiful to her.

They were aware that at any moment, the demon could jump out of the bushes and attack them, but there was no choice but to push on. Kim decided there is a point with fear where it cannot grow any worse and when you reach that pinnacle, you automatically have the courage of a doomed person. It was such a relief to move out of the trees and on to the sandy beach. It was more difficult to drag Jamie across the sand as their feet bogged down into the soft sand. They moved down close to the water line and placed Jamie down, tenderly.

The three sat down next to Jamie to gain their breath back. Their eyes were fixed on the tree line in front of them searching for the slightest movement. Matt was not sure exactly what they would do if the demon did spring out of the bushes and run at them, but run into the water was the most likely.

After they had rested for a while, and there was no sign of anything from the jungle, Matt decided to wander down to inspect the boat wrecks. Jenna and Kim stayed with Jamie's body and kept a look-out.

Kim glanced at her watch and could see they were running out of daylight hours. They had a few more hours of daylight at best. Then what? What would happen when night fell? Everything felt so hopeless. She closed her eyes and wept for Jamie. Heart wrenching sobs that tugged at Jenna until the two of them were openly sobbing. With their arms around each other, the two women comforted each other in grief.

Kim knew that Jamie was intended to end up as one of the skeletal remains in that room with the demon, as they all were. Seeing the three of them approaching looking for Jamie must have scared it off. She pictured the demon dragging Jamie back to that room of horrors and trembled violently. 'Chilled to the bone' took on a new meaning.

Matt returned thirty minutes later with the bad news that there was nothing salvageable they could use from what he could see. Everything was completely rotten and not buoyant enough to float.

Jenna started sobbing again and Matt wrapped his arms around her, feeling defeated and useless. Jamie would have known what to do. Jamie always knew what to do.

"What will we do?" Jenna asked.

They all felt hopeless and it was only a matter of time before the demon came for them. Sitting ducks. They would all end up adorning the room of carcasses. Kim looked back at the water behind her. How far was the nearest island they had passed on the boat coming in? Too far she knew, especially with the body of Jamie to take.

Matt looked around seeking a solution. He knew the girls were relying on him to work out what to do. He had to step up. It was his turn. Their lives depended on it. He looked again at the wooden boat wrecks.

He suggested they camp on the sand near the water edge. He would build a large fire using the old rotten wood and they would take turns staying awake. Kim shuddered as she realised this was to watch if the demon came out of the jungle at them. Matt had brought back a long-pointed piece of wood as a weapon. Who knew how effective it would be against a strong demon, but it was all they had. Their backpacks were back at the camp site and no one was going back for them. They would go without food for tonight.

Matt started collecting pieces of old wood from the boats for their fire and Jenna helped him while Kim stayed with Jamie. She looked back at the ocean again. What about the tide? Would it go out or come in? This could make it awkward to camp beside the water. She watched it for a while and decided it was going out just a little at a time.

They started a pile of wood that grew and grew. They were going to need a vast amount of wood for a fire to burn all night. Kim hoped the demon would be afraid of fire but remembered it had investigated their camp site the night before when the campfire was going so it had not been afraid. Even if she was not afraid of it, it would give them light and may help them see her approach.

About thirty minutes had passed when she heard Matt shouting. Fearing the worse, she jumped to her feet in an instant, heart racing. Matt was jumping up and down waving his arms and yelling, but he was facing the ocean. She turned and looked across the water and could see a large speed boat heading straight toward them. She thought she was hallucinating for a moment, but the apparition grew larger and the sound of the motor grew louder.

It was an official looking boat, so much larger than the fishing boat they had arrived in, and she could see three occupants.

Matt and Jenna ran down to where Kim was, shouting and waving their arms. They watched the black-coloured speed boat slow down and glide into shore. Two of the occupants were police officers. She could see the brown colour of their uniforms and recognised the other man as the angry man from early yesterday morning. He jumped out of the boat and walked over to them along with one of the police officers. Looking down at Jamie, he pulled a grim expression and turned to the police officer. They spoke for a few minutes in Spanish and then he gestured with his thumb toward the boat.

"Come."

The angry man and the police officer lifted Jamie up and into the boat and climbed aboard. Kim sat on the floor of the boat still cradling Jamie's head on her lap. She wouldn't sit on one of the seats and leave Jamie on the floor alone. Matt and Jenna sat together on the back seat and Matt wrapped his arms around her. Jenna rested her head on his shoulder. She was mentally exhausted.

The man introduced himself as Marcos but didn't ask any questions. The police officers seem to only speak Spanish. The three of them didn't feel like talking so it suited them not to explain or try to bridge the language barrier.

As the boat was gliding backward, pushed back from the sand and the police officer was preparing to start the motor, a loud sound penetrated their awareness. It was a long piercing and haunting roar. It went on for several minutes, beginning as an angry sound and then fading to a forlorn moan. The sound shattered the quiet atmosphere and sent shivers down the spine of those present.

The demon knew they were escaping.

The motor roared to life and the boat took off back to the village.

Part Two - The History

L.J. Fox

Chapter 11
The Goodbye

Standing high on the rocky outcrop and surveying the barren plain below, the hunter sighed and as she did every season, wondered what had happened. Only weeks ago, this had been green, grassy land with plenty of animals for hunting, water in the waterholes and abundant birdlife. Suddenly, the animals were gone, the water gone, the birdlife vanished and the earth was bare and dry as far as she could see. Where had it all gone? Where was the water? How would they live?

A few other adults sat up on the rocks and she gazed around at the flock, wondering if they had the same thoughts. The world was brown and dirty as far into the horizon as they could see with small dust whirlies spinning on the bare earth. Unwittingly, the talon on her foot scratched at the rock and she looked down to see the pale marks made against the dark grey of the rock. She wasn't sure where to look or how to react to this lack of food and life.

Every year they witnessed this event and continued the struggle to find food over the months until the rain returned and the waterholes filled with water. The food had become very scarce for much of that period and they often suffered hunger. Sometimes, they only found small game such as rodents or reptiles, and she shuddered at the thought of the reptiles. She hated them, those slinky, slithering shadows but her life was a struggle, and she was bred to take food wherever it was available.

She sensed a difference this season to other years. The winds were hotter, the land more barren and the rain less frequent. The drought had lasted a long time and she wondered if the land would ever recover. Over the decades, she had witnessed the trees die off and the bushes thin out across the great expanse of landscape. Humans were building more of their shelters, and the remaining jungle was ebbing away from the development. The hunters were being pushed further back into unfamiliar territory and a land that no longer met their needs. It was a frightening time for the hunters, having existed here for hundreds of centuries and been so strong in numbers at one time. They had been in existence when massive reptilian creatures roamed the earth and barely survived the Ice Age. Now, they faced a threatened existence with low numbers and a disappearing homeland. Even the hated hyenas had disappeared, and she could not remember that happening other years. The vultures still sat among the bones picking what they could and waiting. She wished she was fast enough to catch one of these for food and licked her lips, wondering what one would taste like. What were these birds waiting for? Were they waiting for the carcasses of the hunters themselves?

Although there were no spoken words among the hunters, there was an understanding. Their species could not survive hunger each year and more importantly, they could not survive without water. Their bodies could maintain over long periods of time without food, although the resulting loss of weight affected their strength and the mothers nursing infants were unable to produce milk, but none of their bodies could survive without water.

The lives of the hunters in this paradise was over and it was time to find a new Utopia. They all knew it, this unspoken logic, and were aware it was just a matter of timing. She wondered where the new paradise would be and how far away. This home was all she had known. Would they all go, or just the adults? She looked down the hill at the youngsters playing in the dry rock area, flapping their wings in preparation for future flight. Their mothers sat with backs against the rock face watching their wards. What world would there be for these youngsters?

The sound of low, grunting noises reached her and she turned to the alpha male standing higher up the rock, looking down over the barren landscape and letting them know his displeasure and concern. Many of these youngsters on the rocks below were his offspring and the threat of starvation and dehydration was a major concern for him. As alpha male, he was in charge and responsible for ensuring food and water. Other males standing around also made guttural noises, agreeing with his thoughts and sentiments.

She felt movement to her left and turned to see a strong female land near her, only metres away. The strong female was carrying more weight than she was, having carried more weight on her before the food ran out. Stretching her wings out, the strong female deliberately touched her with her right wing. This was considered a rude gesture, and she immediately realised the strong female was not happy with her being in such close proximity to the alpha male. This female was still young and suffered from a jealousy she needed to overcome. Due to the low numbers of hunters remaining, there was no such thing as monogamous relationships. She ignored the strong female's attempt to rattle her, which would also be considered rude, aware there were more important things in life than a mate. She heard the strong female snort and knew she was not happy. This also went ignored.

It was still early in the morning and cool enough to consider searching for potential food or water sources. Would they be hunting today? Which direction may house animals that had not already fled the area? Perhaps there were a few rodents living in holes underground.

The alpha male spread his wings out horizontally and began flapping them, increasing the speed as he lifted off the ground. Gaining momentum, he slowly rose and descended where the females and youngsters milled about below. Seeing this, the other males followed suit. This was goodbye and they all knew it. The adult males saying goodbye to their mates, their youngsters and the old and sick members of the hunters.

She could hear loud exhaling and wailing and knew the females were crying. She uttered a few wails in sympathy and her own goodbye to her family. Down below, she had a mother too old to make this journey. The youngsters were now looking at the alpha male and wondering what was happening. Clinging to their mothers in fear, the youngsters whimpered and a pregnant female sat down in shock.

She wailed again, the urge to protect this group so instinctive to her; a need to take them to a new place, a safe place, where there was abundant food and water. Perhaps one day, she would also become a mother to a youngster. She craved this so badly, almost obsessively, but in lean times it was not the right time for her to breed. That event would not happen until they found a new Utopia.

The alpha male trailed by the other males flew back up to the top of the rock to stand with the rest of the adults. He landed on a large rock in front of them and looked around at each of them, checking if everyone was ready. With a roar, he leapt off the rock and flew above them with the adults falling behind. She could hear the wailing below and continued hearing it long after it was no longer possible to hear the ones left behind.

Chapter 12
The Village

Carlos arrived back at the island very concerned and agitated. He was thankful his village existed on this remote island and not in the mainland village where he traded fish on a monthly basis for meat or fruit. Luckily, the distance between the two was many hours by rowing boat so his village was very isolated.

On his latest trip, there had been a huge ship in the harbour with large white sails and masts almost up to the clouds. He rowed into the harbour, in awe of this tall ship which was a beauty to behold with its wooden decks. It was the most impressive ship he had seen in the harbour in all his years of visiting. Occasionally, ships arrived to refuel with food, water, fruit, meat and resources but Carlos had never seen one as grand as this one.

He couldn't help but row closer to the ship to inspect it at close quarters. The closer he drew, the more he could detect a horrendous stench that made him feel sick to the stomach. On board, he could see dark faces peering down at him, people with chains on their ankles and he could hear the clinking of the chains as the people tried to walk. The faces looked stricken, dirty and desperate, and he felt sick looking at them.

On earlier trips, he heard there were ships that contained slaves as the crew, forced into labour. He heard this talk on the dock and at the trading tables and the news rattled him. The masters of the ship were dressed in their finery and trading on the docks for meat, spices and fruit. They were on a journey to remote countries to sell these slaves but needed to stock up on food and resources on the way. He also heard most countries had banned the slavery practice but unfortunately, it still happened. His people on the island had never believed in treating anyone as a slave.

He didn't want any part of it. No man should be treated this way and he refused to trade with these men in their finery. He quickly rowed to shore, sold his fish and traded for a small kid goat which he managed to secure in the small fishing boat by binding its legs together. The little white goat bleated constantly, and he couldn't get out of the harbour fast enough, rowing as hard as he could. He would never forget the dark faces watching him as he left, the sound of the chains on their ankles, or the putrid smell coming from the ship. He was sure that mainland civilisation was doomed.

Reflecting on life on his trip back to the island with the little goat serenading, he was thankful for his peaceful village, the simple life and wonderful island inhabitants. If this latest scenario was where the mainland was heading, he had been doubly blessed. His people had lived on islands for generations and mostly fished for a living. They had lived this life for hundreds of years and were native Mapuche Indians, local to the area.

His ancestors moved from island to island via canoe, taking their belongings with them to start over, settling on their island around one hundred years ago. A group of over sixty villagers resided on the island, in a happy, small community, building huts and farming the land. Although village life was challenging, everything ran smoothly, peacefully and the villagers had never been hungry and were close to self-sufficiency.

Over the years, they had brought in goats, calves plus chickens and now had a great little farm of animals which supplied them with meat, eggs, milk and hide. They grew vegetables and fruit from planting orchards and vegetable patches. With natural fruits on the island and a variety of fish to catch, they never went hungry.

Occasionally, one of the younger members wished to return to the mainland for work or marriage or arrived back at the island with a new wife or husband. All the everyday life and events surrounding the inhabitants of the island had been near perfect ... until the day a flock of demons flew in.

Chapter 13
The Demons

Carlos and several men from the village spent the morning in the fields ploughing, when a series of shadows were cast on the ground they were working on. It had rained overnight but the day was fine and sunny with no rain or storms expected. Carlos didn't even look up as he pictured a flock of birds flying low. He didn't really give it much thought until the men became aware of strange sounds, a series of hisses, grunts, moans and squeals. What on earth could make such noises? The first man to look up screamed out in fear and stumbled backwards making the sign of the cross on his chest. Quickly, the other men raised their eyes to the skies.

Carlos could not believe what he was seeing. Large human-type creatures with large wings were flying across the sky above him. Surely, he was imagining it. The fear of the men around him guaranteed he was not imagining it. There must have been at least fifty of the creatures in formation, similar to a flock of birds, with many gliding as they descended.

This flock were planning to land on the island and the men realised at the same time. Suddenly, there was a panic to reach their families with tools thrown to the ground and men sprinting across the ploughed field, calling out to their loved ones in alarm.

Most of the women had been preparing food in the huts and raced outside at the sound of yelling. A woman in the vegetable garden started screaming and pointing up at the sky. At her scream, other women started screaming, children were crying and people were running in all directions. Panic and chaos ensued. No one was sure where to run.

The flock circled above the island gliding lower, looking for a place to land and scanning the island for threats. They didn't feel the humans were any threat as they continued their descent. Carlos reached his wife who had been near the garden and pulled her arm to follow him into the hut. He took charge and spoke with authority, inviting those around the immediate area to come inside the hut. A dozen people followed him inside along with a number of children. The screaming women had stopped, silenced by the men who had reached them, and the villagers were now hiding in the huts and peering out the windows in fear.

The flock landed on the tallest of the rocky outcrops, almost a rock mountain on the interior of the island. The outcrop towered above the valley where the huts and fields lay. As the creatures landed, they grabbed at the rocks with the talons on their feet. Slowly one-by-one they stretched their wings and then folded them in.

There was much noise from atop the rock with the creatures twittering and squealing, snorting and grunting. Carlos looked up at the figures of these creatures, clinging to the top of the rocky outcrop and he felt the world had ended. Surely, the devil had summoned all the demons to come to this island and end the lives of the villagers. He crossed himself and prayed.

His people held a mixed religion of Catholicism and the native Mapuche traditions and superstitions. There were no explanations for this other than the demons had come for them. In his hut, several of the people were crying and some were praying on their knees. For now, they had no choice but to wait and see what would happen. He wondered how the rest of the villagers were faring and was certain it was the same as the people in his hut. He was the leader, the chief of this village, yet he had no idea what to do.

Very few of the villagers managed to sleep that first night, whether on beds, with a blanket on the floor or in a corner of a hut. Carlos chose to remain awake and keep watch out the window for anything that may happen. He was sure there were many people in the other huts keeping sentry as well.

Just before the sun went down, most of the flock moved down the rocky face of the outcrop and sought refuge on a shelf with a rock face at the back. He noted many of them curled up like a human, and others remained upright. Only a small number stayed up on top of the rocky outcrop guarding. Maybe doing exactly what he was doing right now, guarding his people. It was a long night.

Chapter 14
The Confrontation

Carlos watched the creatures awaken early the next morning as he had not slept and kept vigilant all night. The night had passed quietly and slowly and the only noise he heard was a village baby cry and the roosters crow towards daylight.

On the rocky ledge, he could see the sleeping creatures stir and rise. They stretched their wings out and flew to the top of the rocky outcrop. Again, there were strange noises and flapping of wings and a few creatures suddenly leaped over the edge of the cliff face, gliding and then flapping their wings to fly across the fields. They swooped low over the huts where the villagers were hiding. Carlos wondered if the time had come for their lives to end. He could hear screaming from other huts and wondered what he should do. Should he stay cowering in this hut? Should he confront the creatures and ask them to leave? Should he try to fight? His wife, sensing his indecision, wrapped her arms around him and rested her head on his shoulder. He gently touched her face and then with determination, he walked out of the hut.

He marched out into the open field and stood watching the creatures circling the field. He hoped his courage would not fail him. A large male creature flew above him peering down at him then circled lower and lower. Carlos watched as the creature determined there was no danger and landed ten metres away and stood facing him. This was the closest Carlos had been to one of these creatures, so he studied it intently. This was a male and very strong, with a lean, muscular body and large talons on his feet. He was very human-like in many ways and yet much bigger, stronger, coarser and with some unusual features. He could see bumps on each side of its head and realised that they were a form of horns like the creatures from hell.

The male creature appeared to be studying him as well. Carlos thought that the creature did not appear afraid, and he figured he was scared enough for both of them. Carlos summed up his courage and took a step toward the creature. He raised his right hand and threw it up toward the sky.

"GO AWAY!"

The creature blinked and moved his head slightly to one side but did not appear to be afraid or intimidated. Again, Carlos stepped forward and raised his voice.

"GO AWAY!"

The creature did not move. Carlos was aware of a few of the other creatures slowly circling above and wondered if they were waiting to see what would happen, or waiting to fly in to protect one of their own.

Carlos was about to repeat his little show when the creature let out a deep sigh and made a clicking sound with its mouth. Carlos had no idea what this meant. Was it trying to communicate with him?

The male creature started flapping its wings and then rose and flew across the field with the other creatures following. Carlos stood there puzzled trying to understand the encounter.

Suddenly, he heard the terrified bellowing of his cows and the frightened bleating of the goats. He realised they were in danger so ran across the field in the direction of the sounds as fast as his legs would travel. He saw two creatures leaving with a young goat each being carried in their talons. The talons had grasped the goats across their back and picked them up. The goats were screaming as they were carried off up to the top of the rocky outcrop. Another two creatures held a calf, though this one was carried in their arms, and were also heading up to the rocky outcrop. Carlos was panting when he reached the cow and goat pens. The creatures were no longer there, and the remaining animals were terrified, hiding in a corner of the pen. The mother cow was bellowing and looking around for her missing calf. Carlos realised that the cow was way too large for the creatures to pick up and carry off.

He counted the animals, 22 goats and 12 cows with 5 calves. They couldn't let this happen. They couldn't watch as each animal was taken one by one. Resolved, he ran from hut to hut and asked the villagers to come out for a meeting. Timidly, they crept out of hiding, petrified and clinging to each other with several choosing to stay indoors. Carlos asked them to take a number of the goats and cows into the huts to protect them. One of the village men spoke up.

"No. If we do this, then they will come looking for the animals. We cannot live this way."

"The creatures won't stay here on the island. They will leave," Carlos answered.

"How do you know this? Maybe they will stay here and kill all the animals then kill all of us," said a woman.

"You saw the male creature today when I was in the field. He could have killed me but he didn't. I don't think they want to kill us," he answered.

"When there are no animals left then they will kill us," said one of the men.

The other villagers all murmured and agreed, their voices getting angry.

"We will leave this place today. We will not come back."

All the villagers yelled out in agreement. Carlos sighed. He knew there was no hope now. He also knew that what they said was true. The creatures may eat all the animals and then go after the humans. He raised his hands.

"Yes. Ok. We will leave here today."

Chapter 15
The Strong Female

She awoke as the new day was dawning, yawned and flexed her tired muscles. The last two days had been tough, and they had flown such a long way from their homeland. So much ocean, so much nothing. Sometimes, it had been difficult to concentrate when looking at nothing but continual ocean, and the boredom had started playing tricks with her mind. The hunters were excited when they saw the island in the distance. They had passed a few small islands, but there was no fresh water. The island meant food, water, rest, sleep and rejuvenation. They twittered eagerly as they flew closer and saw the tall trees and waterhole.

They saw the humans as they flew in. Back in their homeland, they would have avoided the humans at all costs, but were too tired, hungry and thirsty, and were forced to accept the humans were nearby and try to ignore them.

She could smell the animals as they circled the field and knew they had chosen the right place to rest. Although hungry, she knew they would not be eating until morning. Rest and sleep would be welcome as soon as darkness fell.

The strong female landed near her on the rocky ledge. She extended her wings and flapped them loudly before withdrawing them. It was a show of strength, and she was too tired to really care how powerful the strong female was or how much she liked to show-off. As they had flown across the ocean, the strong female had flown very close to her and knocked her off formation a few times. No doubt the strong female was exhausted as well.

The new day dawned for the excited hunters. They twittered eagerly until a few of the males decided it was time to bring back food. She watched from the top of the rocks as the alpha male encountered the human. She had not encountered a human before but had seen them from a distance. She wondered about them but had no real interest. Soon, the males brought back baby goats and a calf, and the hunters squealed with delight as they ripped parts from the animals to devour.

Three small animals were not enough for the number of hunters, so it wasn't long before a few other hunters flew down to hunt for more. By midday, they had eaten their fill of calves, goats and chickens. She found it highly amusing to watch one of the hunters trying to catch a chicken from the air. The chickens ran and hid under bushes or in their little shelter and the hunters were not fast enough.

She was watching one of these episodes when she suddenly felt something crash into her, forcing her to fall sideways. Her shoulder stung and she looked up to see the strong female towering over her. She jumped to her feet, hissing and raised her wings in anticipation of flight or fight. The strong female hissed and stood ready to attack. An angry roar filled her ears and the alpha male landed between the two of them. He faced the strong female and used his chest to bump her backwards.

BUMP ... BUMP ... BUMP

The strong female stepped back a few steps and growled. He bumped repeatedly. She tried to counteract the bumps and stand her ground but as he kept bumping, she gradually became submissive and allowed herself to be bumped backwards. She put her head down to show defeat.

The alpha male strode back over to where she stood watching and looked intently at her. He was making it clear that aggression from the strong female was not acceptable and that he would not tolerate it.

She exhaled and felt calmer, then flew down to help catch a chicken. She heard various sounds and watched as the humans left the island in their boats. By the late afternoon, there were no humans left on the island.

Chapter 16
The Break

There were no humans left on the island anymore, the huts remained abandoned, the crops left to wilt and the remaining animals left to fend for themselves. The hunters had killed most of the animals for food and the ones left had bolted into the jungle for protection. She knew they would be leaving this island soon. The flock had landed in this location to feed, water and rest. They had been here for several days now and were well-fed, well-watered and well-rested. There was not much food left, so the flock were keen to move on. She could feel the restless energy in the group and was eager to continue their journey to find a new land.

With a thud, the alpha male landed next to her on a large rock. He towered over her in height and was much heavier in the torso than she was, a magnificent, lean male and a great leader. He looked at her intently for several minutes and she returned his gaze silently. It was a mutual understanding of an attraction between them, and then he flapped his wings and flew off. She knew it was only a matter of time before they would be together and start a family. Nothing would happen while travelling as they could not have a pregnant one among them on such a long trip. She felt such longing for an infant and excitement at the prospect in the near future.

Suddenly, she felt the hair on the back of her neck rise and looking around, realised that below on a rock, the strong female was watching her and breathing rapidly in anger. The strong female had seen the alpha male land near her and was not happy at this or its meaning. She decided to move away where the strong female could not see her as the scrutiny made her uncomfortable. She planned to keep a distance between the strong female and herself until the strong female calmed down and stopped the jealousy. She flapped her wings and rose in the air, turning to head up toward the top of the rocky outcrop. The alpha male was up there as well as other hunters and it felt the safest place to be and out of sight of the strong female.

She was almost to the top when something crashed into her with tremendous force from her right side. The blow took her breath away and knocked her off her position in the air. Her wings buckled and she slammed against the rock face and crumpled.

SNAP!

She felt the main bone in her left-wing snap in two. The pain blinded her and she tumbled down the rock cliff face to the ground fifty metres below. The world tumbled upside down with her in a mix of colours, shapes, pain and confusion. She blacked out before she reached the ground.

Chapter 17
The Death Sentence

She regained consciousness in severe pain and didn't understand what had happened. Gingerly, she opened her eyes and tried to focus. Her head hurt and every part of her body ached, but her left wing throbbed with intense heat and pain. Never had she felt pain of this magnitude and darkness threatened her consciousness. She groaned and again tried to focus.

Other hunters stood around peering down at her sympathetically. She couldn't remember why she was on the ground and why she was in so much pain. As she tried to sit up and stand, the pain almost caused her to black out again. Finally, she managed a sitting position and tried to look over her left shoulder to see her wing. She was aware it was dangling down uselessly at her side, and she couldn't seem to get it to extend or retract, and the pain from it radiated through her being. She stared at the misshapen appendage through pain and nausea and was terrified. She knew what this meant. They all knew what this meant. This was a death sentence.

She looked up at the faces around her and could see the concern, fear and pity on their faces. This frightened her even more. She was doomed and they all knew it. The alpha male was standing back looking down at her. She saw a strange, sad look on his face and she began to whimper.

Her mind cleared and she remembered what had happened. Quickly, she looked around for the strong female, remembering the strong female had crashed into her and knocked her out of the air. Suddenly, she felt very vulnerable sitting on the ground, unable to fly. What if the strong female attacked now? She was a sitting target. She couldn't see the strong female but continued looking between the legs of the hunters around her. Again, she looked at the alpha male and saw his expression was one of sorrow, concern and resolve. She knew they must leave soon and she knew that she couldn't go.

The alpha male turned behind him and charged. The hunters standing around moved aside to let him through. He let out a loud roar and the hunters shuddered at the anger in the sound. She could see the strong female on the outside of the flock, standing quietly and trying to disappear. The alpha male spied the strong female and was after her. He charged at the strong female and banged his chest into her with such force, she fell backwards. Immediately, she jumped to her feet and the alpha male charged again. This continued for some time with the alpha male pushing her further away from the flock.

Everyone in the flock knew what was happening, although it was a rare event. The strong female was being exiled from the flock. The alpha male had made this decision based on the aggressive nature she had shown and the harm she had inflicted on a fellow hunter. When the flock left the island, the strong female would tail the flock but was not welcome in the hunter community again.

She couldn't see the alpha male pushing the strong female from her position on the ground, but she could hear the roaring from the altercation. Everyone standing around her was watching the situation unfold and it took some time before the alpha male returned.

A few days passed.

The flock should have already left but they were stalling not wanting to leave her injured and alone. They all knew that she would never fly again and once the food ran out on the island, she would die. One of the hunters brought her calf meat to eat and another brought her a chicken. On the second day she managed to stand up and walk to the waterhole for a drink. She had black bruises all over her body, but they would heal. The wing just dangled and every step jolted the broken bone and caused tremendous pain.

It was just following a drink of some water that she heard twittering and knew the flock were ready to leave. She sat down on a rock near the water stream and watched them prepare. They were stretching out their wings and limbering up muscles. The alpha male strode over to her. He stood and looked down at her, making low moaning noises. All the other hunters stopped what they were doing and looked at her. She felt tears trickle out of her eyes and down her cheeks, wetting her chest. This was goodbye.

With further twittering, the flock turned, rose one by one and flew off, circling once. She watched them until they disappeared into the sky. She saw the strong female well behind them but following as she would for the rest of her life.

Then they were gone and she was alone and left to die.

Chapter 18
The Carer

I t had been four weeks since his people fled the island, and Carlos was restless and agitated. He knew they had done the right thing by leaving the island under the circumstances. They had no choice. They had been forced to leave and yet, a part of him yearned to know what was happening on the island, his island. Had the creatures left as he expected? Were they still there and taking up residence now? Had any animals survived? He knew he had to go back and find out.

His wife told him he was crazy and swore at him as she did when she was angry. He didn't tell the other villagers as they would think him crazy as well. They had come back here to the mainland and started settling into mainland life. Many of them were happier here on the mainland and would never return to island life. Carlos found it difficult as the island had been his life and he loved the isolated existence and the buildings, crops and life they had built.

On the mainland, it was crowded and everything was already built. All he could do was fish where he could be on his own most of the time. Bringing back fish brought in enough money for them to survive, and he felt that was all he was doing now, surviving.

Word had spread on the mainland about the demon creatures that had invaded the island. The villagers from his community had talked and the stories had become exaggerated and unworldly. None of the mainland villagers would venture anywhere near the island now.

Carlos set out on the trip which he estimated would be two days, with just a small sail on his boat and oars. At the last minute, he decided to bring his ten-year-old son, Andres. He left word with a neighbour to let his wife know that he had taken the boy with him. They would not be back for two and a half days. No doubt his wife would have built up a large amount of anger by then and he would be in deep trouble when he returned. The island had been his son's home too. Andres was not a little boy anymore. He should be treated as a young man. The trip was long and Andres took a few turns on the oars. Fortunately, the wind was in their favour and finally, they could see the island come into view.

Carlos felt a tear in his eye as he sighted his beloved home. He didn't know what to expect coming back, but he had to know what state everything was now in. They pushed the boat up on to the sand and made their way through to the fields and huts.

The island was very quiet and Carlos guessed he had been correct and the creatures were gone. Surely, they would be noisy with their twittering if they were still there. The fields and huts looked the same as if they had just walked away from them that very day. The rock face and outcrop looked empty, and all was quiet. Carlos and Andres wandered around to the huts looking for animals. The huts were untouched. Everything was just as they had left it except for the lack of animals. Andres let out an excited squeal when he found many eggs in the nesting box of the chickens. The eggs would be their dinner.

"Son, it will be night soon. Why don't you see if you can catch a fish in the stream and I will gather some vegetables."

He sent Andres off with the net they previously used for catching fish. Carlos walked around the vegetable garden and found a good amount of vegetables they could also cook for dinner, and took them to the hut. Tonight, they would sleep in their comfortable beds, eat a good meal and tomorrow, they would head back to the mainland. He wondered what chance he had of talking the villagers into coming back to the island, but knew in his heart, there was no way they would ever step foot on this island again.

After a while, Carlos realised Andres had been gone for too long so went to find him and tell him to forget about the fish. He walked down to the fresh water stream and glanced about. He could not see his son anywhere.

"Andres," he called.

No answer. He walked around the edge of the stream and called again. Puzzled, he wondered if his son had fallen in. No. Andres was a good swimmer. A rustling noise alerted him to some bushes on the other side of the stream. He saw some movement and nearly laughed when he realised there were a few chickens running around loose.

As he neared the rock face, he became aware of a terrible stench. He imagined this may be the remains of the animals the creatures had devoured. Slowly, he crept closer and closer. A large rock which was taller than a man hid an opening in the cliff face. Carlos remembered the children liked to play in this little cave and he guessed that was where the remains of the animals were. The stench was strong and he found himself breathing through his mouth. When he reached the opening to the cave, he saw Andres sitting on a rock just inside looking into the darkness of the cave.

"Andres?" he asked, puzzled.

Andres turned to look at him.

"Papa, she is hurt," he said, quietly.

Carlos stepped into the cave and waited for his eyes to adjust to the dimness. Against the far wall, only metres from where he stood was a creature sitting down on the ground with her back to the wall. He knew immediately it was female and she was in bad shape. Her breathing was laboured and she was so thin, her skeletal frame poked out. She was filthy dirty and he could see on her left side that her wing hung down, badly broken.

He let out a big sigh and sat next to Andres on the rock. Andres looked at his father.

"We have to help her."

Again, Carlos sighed and looked at the pitiful creature. She looked like she was dying. He put his arm around his son.

"It looks like she broke her wing and the other creatures had to leave her behind. She can't fly now so maybe she cannot catch her own food. Son, I think she is dying."

"She wants to die," Andres answered, quietly. "But we can't let her. We need to get her food and water."

Carlos looked again at the creature. She had been quietly watching them the whole time, not trying to move, not afraid, not aggressive, resigned to her fate. He looked around the cave. There were carcasses of animals so he guessed the other creatures had left this for her before they flew off. It didn't look like she had eaten for some time and he thought she would be in too much pain to move very far, so not drinking water very often and definitely not able to catch the roaming chickens. Carlos stood up having decided to do what they could.

"Andres, I will collect a pail and bring her water and some eggs and vegetables. I saw some chickens in the bushes across the other side of the stream. I want you to try to catch some of the chickens for her."

"Yes Papa."

Andres had a big grin on his face as he ran off to chase chickens. Carlos shook his head. He was a good-hearted child and Carlos was very proud of him.

By the time Carlos returned to the cave with a pail of stream water, a dozen eggs and root vegetables, Andres had managed to catch two chickens. He had broken their necks and was carrying them hanging upside down by his side. Very slowly and gently so as not to startle the creature, they laid the chickens, food and pale of water close to where she was sitting.

"Son, we will know by the morning if she will live or die. If she drinks water or eats something, then she has the will to live. If she does not, then we cannot do anything about it."

Andres nodded hoping she would eat something. He did not want her to die.

Chapter 19
The Ward

Carlos opened his eyes as he heard a sound and after a few minutes, he remembered where he was. He was in his old hut on the island, and he and Andres had found an injured creature the night before. He realised the sound he heard had been Andres racing from the hut. Carlos climbed out of bed and followed, knowing Andres would be keen to see if the creature had lived through the night or not.

He reached the rock cave and slowly stepped around the large rock and into the opening. Andres was again sitting on the rock staring at the creature.

"Papa. She has eaten a chicken," he said, happily.

Carlos looked down and sure enough one of the chickens was missing, there were less eggs and a good amount of water was also gone. He looked at the creature and was sure she seemed just a little bit brighter. Her breathing, although ragged, was not as laboured as it had been the night before.

"What will we do, Papa?" Andres asked.

Carlos contemplated the situation, unsure what the best course of action was. He sat down on the rock next to Andres.

"Well ... this morning we need to gather lots of food and water for her and leave it here. We will visit again next week and maybe we will bring a goat for her. Then, we will have to visit every week to feed her."

Andres nodded excitedly with a broad smile lighting up his face. Carlos warned him.

"Son. This must be our secret. You must not tell anyone about her, not even your Mama. People would want to kill her. Do you understand?"

He looked into Andres' eyes.

"Yes Papa," Andres answered solemnly.

They would tell his wife that they were undertaking work on the island, father and son, and would be gone for two or three days every week. Other villagers would wonder what work they could be undertaking so they would have to come up with a good project they were working on. He remembered that this rock cave flooded when the rains came each year. The creature would not be able to stay in this cave permanently. He would use materials from the other huts and make a building just for her, but away from the village, perhaps on the other side of the island.

Over the next few hours Carlos and Andres gathered as much food as they could find and spread it around the creature. The pail of water was filled but would not last for a whole week. Hopefully, the creature would be feeling better in a few days and find her own way to the water. They caught fish, killed a few more chickens, found a large collection of eggs and Carlos knew bushes that grew edible berries plus vegetables from the garden. There was a good amount of food surrounding the creature by the time they were ready to leave the island.

Both father and son stood at the entrance to the cave and looked down at their ward. There was a gentleness in her eyes and Carlos wondered if it was gratitude, that she understood they were trying to help her.

"We will name her Viktoria," he said.

Andres smiled. "I like that name."

Chapter 20
The Handover

Carlos was dying. He lay on his bed - tired, worn out and old. His time had come and he was fine with that. His son, Andres, was beside him and his grandson, Juan. His lovely wife, Maria, had left this life many years ago and he had continued with his son's family for support. He looked forward to being with Maria again after so long apart.

In his last hour of life, he worried about Viktoria and her ongoing welfare. She had been part of his life for fifty years and he had looked after her and brought her food, along with Andres and now Juan. He built a hut for her and had done his best to provide for the poor creature, left alone to die.

She was doing well now and was no longer hungry or sick. Her wing never healed that she could fly but it no longer hurt her and she could move around the island easily. In fact, she was incredibly fast at times, adapting where she needed to. He reached out and took Andres' hand in his.

"Son, please remember the promise we made. Please look after Viktoria."

"Of course, Papa," he replied, quietly.

Andres loved Viktoria as much as Carlos did. He had been the one who found her many years ago, broken and starving, on the verge of death.

What Andres could not tell his father was that he worried about his son, Juan. What would happen one day when Juan was the one to look after Viktoria? Would he continue to feed her or let her die?

Juan had a strange way about him, no empathy, and Andres often worried how he would turn out. Juan was already a young man and Andres loved him as any father loved a son, but he was always aware of a cruel and evil side to the young man. On occasion, he had witnessed a younger Juan being cruel to animals and Andres had severely beaten him for this but it made the boy more aggressive and angrier. There was a defiant, built-up anger in the young man, and a nasty streak.

Andres had a bad feeling about how Viktoria may be treated in the future, but he could not tell his father this. He just reassured him that Viktoria would be cared for.

Part Three - The Capture

L.J. Fox

Chapter 21
The Scientist

Dr Clint Marne glanced around the crowded room and wished again that he hadn't come out. His boss, Bill, had talked him into it and tomorrow, he would let Bill know what he thought of this socialising idea.

"Clint, you need to get out sometimes," Bill had told him. "Have a drink, go dancing, find a girl. Other people do it."

Why had he allowed himself to be persuaded? Here he was, sitting alone in a crowded bar, feeling awkward and wishing he could melt into the floor. At least, he had managed to buy a drink at the bar so he had something to sip on. Even then, he had no idea what drink to order. What did people drink? Standing at the bar, he heard the man next to him order a bourbon on the rocks, so he ordered one as well. Sitting and peering at the drink, his scientific mind told him that rocks meant ice cubes even though they didn't look like rocks. His first sip of bourbon on the rocks nearly knocked his socks off. The liquid was strong but after a few sips, he began to enjoy the smooth flavour.

"Hey, are you that scientist dude I read about in the paper?" a female voice asked him. He looked up from his drink and saw a young woman standing in front of him, staring at him. She looked to be in her twenties, with dark blonde hair pulled back in a ponytail.

He put the drink down on the bar table. "Umm ... yes. I guess that's me. I'm Dr Clint Marne."

She raised an eyebrow at the formal introduction as her friend appeared at her side, a girl with loose brown hair who was staggering slightly. "Sal, this is Dr. Clint Marne, you know ... that scientist dude in the paper a few weeks ago."

The brown-haired girl peered at Dr Clint Marne through unsteady eyes. "Do you kill animals?" she asked, slurring her words.

"Well, no. I try not to ... I ...," he started to answer.

"But you do sometimes? You know ... kill animals?" she repeated. "You're a monster!"

The two girls giggled among themselves and moved off. Dr Marne stared after them with his mouth open in surprise. Was he a monster? He looked down at his half empty glass and decided to concentrate on the rocks rather than try to talk to girls. They were just too alien to him and he had no knowledge or understanding of how they thought.

He had always felt socially awkward, as long as he could remember, always the nerdy kid at school, the one bullied by other boys. His energy and passion had been transferred to books and schooling, excelling in his studies which had made the bullying more fierce. He loved animals and his parents allowed him to own a series of pets throughout his childhood, everything from a cat and dog to a few chickens and even a lizard at one point. He studied every aspect of his pets and read every book he could find at the library on scientific information related to his pet. He felt his calling was with animals, research and understanding their thought process.

Clint had studied for over twenty years, to the point where he was now a world-renowned expert on animal behaviour, anthropology and biology. His Ph. D thesis had been the theory that animals thought to be extinct still exist in remote areas of the world. He travelled the world, often to exotic locations to study bones and record legends from indigenous people. Articles he authored were published in various scientific journals and he was often quoted or cited in his field. Requests for him to be a guest speaker were a regular occurrence although he disliked the social interaction involved in attending as a guest speaker. Bill assured him it was a necessary evil so they could obtain grants or funding to further their research.

It was not that he didn't dream of a wife and family and thought about it often, but he had resigned himself to a bachelor life due to lack of understanding of females. There had been a few dismal relationships with research students over the years, but he later realised that they were more interested in furthering their careers than in him.

He knew he looked like a nerd to females with his pale skin and dark curly hair inherited from an Indian grandfather, and his black glasses. The thought of a make-over or change of style never occurred to him and he wouldn't know where to start. Other people he knew from university days were married with children, played sport and indulged in camping, fishing or other hobbies. He was genuinely happy for those associates and wished them well. Other than a fading dream of having his own family one day, he was happy with his life and didn't regret his decision to focus on research.

He looked around the crowded bar at the people chatting, laughing and a number of couples dancing closely on the dance floor. It was time for him to head back to the facility where he worked. By the time he cleared all the security checks and screening, it would be past his bedtime. He couldn't say it had been a fun time and he most likely would not be attempting to socialise at this bar again, but damn, that bourbon on the rocks had been delicious.

Chapter 22
The Aftermath

For Kim, the next few days dragged by in a fog. She remembered the trip back to the mainland had been the longest boat trip imaginable, sitting on the floor of the boat with Jamie's head on her lap, stroking his hair. The police officer closed his eyes and placed a sheet over him, but she moved the sheet from his face. She needed to see his face and touch him. She was barely aware of anyone else around her on that boat ride, just her and Jamie. There was so much blood and with the fading sun, the blood looked darker and his body grew colder. How could this cold and bloodied body be Jamie? Where had he gone?

She glimpsed Juan on the beach when they arrived back at the village even though it was dark. He was hanging back but she saw him and remembered who he was. She watched as he slipped away quietly into the night. She had a vague recollection of Marcos telling Matt in his broken English that he wanted his family to have nothing more to do with Viktoria. At the time, she had no idea what that meant. Shock had set in with the three friends and Kim found it difficult to function, talk or know what to do. She fought and cried when they took Jamie away from her. She didn't want to leave him, couldn't let him go. A doctor sedated her and the next morning someone arranged for the three friends and Jamie's body to be taken to Chile, an hour's drive away.

In the back of a van with Jenna and Matt, the three stared out the window, not seeing and barely communicating. Terror and panic had made way for grief and pain and the events of the day before were too horrific to even tell the officials. Who would believe them? A demon had chased down and killed Jamie?

When the village policeman was asking her questions the night before, she wept and shook her head, unable to speak. Today, she wanted to lie down and not wake up as the pain was absent when she was asleep.

In Chile, there was much activity and the three friends were taken to a medical centre to be checked by a doctor, and where police began asking questions. Matt tried to answer the questions in a jumbled and stammering voice, and Jenna just burst into tears. None of them were in any state of mind to answer any questions.

Kim dozed fitfully until several hours later when two people arrived from the Australian Embassy to assist them. Their passports were lost back on the island where the backpacks had been abandoned, so new passports were organised, and arrangement were underway to transport Jamie's body back to Australia. The embassy made the distressing phone call to Jamie's parents to tell them their only son had been killed. They also had no money, clothes or toiletries as everything they owned had been in the backpacks. The embassy took care of all their needs, including the appointment of a local legal representation who worked diligently to have Jamie's body released for an autopsy in Australia, rather than Chile.

Mr Luis Vidal had spent a few years in Australia when he was younger so his English was fluent and he proved to be a very helpful and kind middle-aged man. He explained to Kim that she must speak with the police. They had been hovering around at the hospital, waiting for the green light to interview the Australians. She realised that they may refuse her permission to leave the country and may even consider her a suspect in Jamie's death. Mr Vidal called them in.

A senior detective and his younger colleague entered the room and introduced themselves as Senior Detective Stefano Diaz and his companion, Detective Lucas Soto. She had no idea if they had spoken with Matt and Jenna yet, or if they were hearing the story for the first time from her. She wasn't even sure how to tell the story or how anyone could possibly believe what they had to say.

Senior Detective Diaz spoke English very well with a strong accent. "Mrs Anderson, I am very sorry for your loss."

Kim closed her eyes and nodded her head, accepting the sentiment.

"I am sorry to ask you these questions so soon after your loss, but it is important that we establish what has happened and I understand you want to go home to Australia as soon as possible?"

Kim again nodded, looking him in the eye to try to read whether he was friend or foe. His eyes were very dark and unreadable.

"I would like you to tell us in your own words what happened yesterday. Can you do that?"

She looked across at Mr Vidal, nodded and took a deep breath.

"The four of us are here from Australia for a camping holiday, you know ... backpacking. We've been here for three weeks, camping and touring the coastline, and we heard there was an uninhabited island. We wanted to camp on the island for a few days so an old man from the village took us there in his boat and was going to pick us up at noon on Wednesday. We arrived on the island at lunch time on Monday and stayed one night."

Her eyes started to fill with tears. She blinked a few times and they spilled over, running down her cheeks.

"When we were exploring the island the next day, we found a green hut and when we walked inside ..." She hesitated, remembering the horrific scene and wondering how she would describe it.

"Yes. Go on."

"We saw a ... thing ... like ... like ... nothing I've ever seen. She looked like a demon. We turned and ran as fast as we could. After a while we stopped and ... Jamie was not with us."

She let out a heartbroken sob and tears continued to fall. As she talked her voice started cracking up until she was openly crying again.

"We went back to look for him ... and he was lying on the ground all covered in blood. Matt and I dragged him to the beach and then the boat came and picked us up not long after that."

She looked up at the senior detective who was studying her as she spoke. His forehead was creased in a frown.

"May I ask you some questions?"

"Yes." She dabbed at her eyes with a tissue.

"How did you find out about this island?"

"Jamie asked the fisherman in the village if they knew somewhere and they all said no except this old man. He told Jamie about the island."

"Do you know this old man's name?"

"Yes. His name was Juan, but I don't know his last name."

"Can you describe him or the boat to me?"

"He looked maybe sixty to seventy years old, skinny, silver hair, brown skin. He wore a white shirt and a white straw hat."

She realised that description probably covered 95% of the men in the village.

"The boat was not very big, had a motor at the back, and ripped vinyl seats that once would have been red but were very faded."

She shrugged her shoulders to indicate she couldn't think of anything else to add.

"Did he go on the island with you?"

"No. He was in a big hurry to get away. He said something strange." Kim struggled to remember. "Umm ... Viktoria will be happy to see you or something like that."

The senior detective repeated - "Viktoria will be happy to see you?"

"Yes, that's right."

"Who do you think Viktoria is?"

"I guess that is the demon thing. I don't know."

"You think he knew there was a ... animal or something on that island?"

"I don't know. I think so."

"So, you think he took you all to the island thinking that you would not be coming back?"

"I don't know."

These were thoughts she had been trying not to think about. It was far too bizarre to contemplate that Juan would have set out to deliberately put them in harm's way.

"Just before we left to go to the island, a man in a black T-shirt confronted the older man and they were arguing. I don't know what they were saying but they kept looking at us, so I guess the argument was about us."

"What did you think it was about at the time?"

"I assumed this man was his son and perhaps he was angry that Juan had agreed to take us a long way out to the island. Maybe he though the old man wasn't up to the trip." She shrugged her shoulders.

"This is the same man who was with the police when they picked you up?"

"Yes. He said his name was Marcos."

"How did he know where you were or to come and get you?"

"I have no idea. I guess the old man must have told him where we were going."

"The trip took 2 ½ hours to get there from the village. You arrived at the island around 12."

"Yes, that sounds right."

"Why do you think he came to get you?"

"I have no idea. Perhaps, he knew the danger and was angry with his father. Perhaps, he didn't want anything bad to happen."

"I wonder why it took him so long to decide to take action then?"

"I don't know."

"This animal you claim you saw … is it possible it was another person?"

"No." She shook her head violently. "Absolutely not. I didn't say it was an animal."

"Could it be someone dressed to look like a demon?"

"No."

"Could it have been an animal of some sort, like a big monkey?"

"No."

"What do you think it was?"

Kim paused and thought about it. She had been thinking about it since the attack and couldn't come up with anything to suggest what that thing was.

"I don't know but it looks like … a prehistoric human … sort of like pictures I've seen of when ape started turning into a man … or a real-life demon. I just don't know."

She shuddered at the memory. She had been trying to get the picture of the demon thing out of her mind and kept seeing those eyes looking at her.

"You called the demon 'she'. How do you know it was female?"

"I just knew. There was something sort of feminine about it in a rough way."

"Do you think you would be able to assist a sketch artist to draw a picture of it?"

Kim shuddered again. Her first instinct was to say no but she did not want to jeopardise her trip home. Would this nightmare never end?

"I can try."

"Good. Now were you and Jamie getting on well?"

Kim looked up at him with eyes wide. She could not believe he was asking her this question. She knew he was just doing his job, but the question was still painful.

"Jamie and I were very much in love. We just married last year."

She sobbed again and wiped tears from her eyes.

"What about your two friends?" He studied writing on his notepad. "Matthew Fines and Jenna Jacobson. They get along well with Jamie?"

"We were the best of friends."

The senior detective stood up and his colleague followed suit. His face was still unreadable. She wondered what he would make of her story.

"Thank you, Mrs Anderson. Again, sorry for your loss. I will send that sketch artist in this afternoon."

"Ok"

She lay back on the bed and closed her eyes.

Chapter 23
The Return

The hair on the back of Kim's neck stood on end and cold shivers ran down her spine as she witnessed the likeness of Viktoria emerge on the artist's paper. She was sure the artist thought her image had come from a horror book and was not real and in truth, she was worried the finished sketch would end up looking like an evil cartoon drawing.

Eventually, she looked at the finished picture and knew it was as close as she could possibly remember, having only been in the presence of Viktoria for a few minutes. The image of that creature would burn in her mind forever. She wondered how Jenna and Matt were doing and if they had been interviewed or asked to work with the sketch artist as well. Would all the sketches look similar, or did they all see something different? She was beginning to question her own mind whether this was real or not, and she had begun referring to the being as Viktoria.

What would happen if the autopsy was performed here in South America? How did she feel about that? Could she trust the local officials? How many other tourists had been fed to Viktoria? How many were missing? How many of the bones and remains in that hut were human and how many were something else? How did all those animals end up on the island? Judging by the bones and remains in that room, it must have taken a considerable amount of time to build up. Had Juan been feeding Viktoria for some time? Again, she shuddered when she thought about how close Matt, Jenna and herself had come to becoming a meal, not to mention the body of Jamie. Now she just wanted to go home and hug her mother.

Kim didn't see Jenna or Matt for a few days and that was ok, as she felt seeing them would open up the rawness of what happened. She just wanted to grieve on her own. Detective Sato, the younger detective, came back a few times with questions. He told her that Juan and Marcos were being held in custody pending further investigations. She didn't ask if he believed her story or whether they would look for Viktoria. There would be time to think of that later.

Finally, she was informed that she could leave, along with Matt and Jenna, plus Jamie. The police would continue the investigation and work with the Melbourne police to keep everyone briefed. They were allowed to leave but were informed that should anyone be prosecuted, they may be required to fly back to Chile as witnesses.

Their arrival in Melbourne was a sad affair with everyone's parents at the airport to meet and comfort them, including Jamie's parents waiting for his coffin. She hugged her mother and Jamie's parents, promising them she would call in to see them soon. None of the parents really knew the whole story and she was not look forward to telling Jamie's parents how he had died. They would all think she was crazy. The trip of a lifetime had become Jamie's life trip.

Although seated together on the plane, Matt, Jenna and Kim didn't talk about the fateful day. All were quiet, lost in their own grief and torment. They had both given her a hug when they first saw her and did the same when saying goodbye at Tullamarine airport. Permanently bound together by what had happened on that god-forsaken island, and yet, the trauma had also ruined their friendship. Kim knew she could not talk to them about what they all lived through and what they witnessed, and she was sure they felt the same.

Her mother offered to stay with her, but she wanted to go home alone. Home to the house she and Jamie had saved to pay a deposit on, where they had planned to raise children and live a long life. She wanted to be alone, grieve alone and learn to accept that Jamie was gone. She had already been staying somewhere else for weeks now.

Kim walked around the silent house, stopping and touching everything that Jamie had owned. Her tears flowed freely and she wondered if they would ever stop. How many tears can one person possess? As far as she was concerned, her life was now over at twenty-five years of age. What did she do now?

The next few days were spent wandering around the house, looking at photos, and adjusting. Her mother phoned multiple times and dropped by to see her each day and she spent time with Jamie's parents. She wasn't sure what Jamie's parents or her mother thought of the story of how Jamie had died. It was too outrageous. Who would believe it? She knew they tried to believe it and thought possibly some type of animal had killed Jamie. It really didn't matter if they believed a demon had killed Jamie or not. It didn't change anything.

The autopsy results were as expected, heart failure due to blood loss from deep laceration to the jugular vein. They were unable to identify what had caused the laceration but had recovered hairs and fibres, which had been sent away for forensic testing. There were other minor lacerations on the outside of his left arm which Kim surmised was where Viktoria had initially grabbed him. His body was released to Kim and she organised the funeral.

The Melbourne detectives introduced themselves to her. They were Senior Detective Karl Lay and Detective John Jameson. They were sympathetic to her situation but must have wondered what had been dumped in their lap with talk of monsters and demons. They could not contribute other than relay information from the South American authorities.

They informed Kim that the three artist sketches completed in Chile were remarkably similar. The detectives had been sent copies and said all three statements were basically the same. They kept straight faces, not revealing what their thoughts were and she didn't care whether they believed her or not. They also told her that Marcos had been released pending further investigations, but Juan was still in custody. They didn't really know much at all. Kim hadn't expected anything else and was sure the entire matter would just fade away now. In some ways, she desperately wanted authorities to find Viktoria so this would never happen to anyone again, and to prosecute Juan, but at the same time, she never wanted to step foot in South America again.

Chapter 24
The News

'*South American sources are reporting that a prehistoric animal has been captured on an island off Juan Fernández not far from the coast of Chile. Information is sketchy but it is believed the animal is larger than a human and aggressive. It is thought to be the animal that recently killed Australian tourist, James Stuart Anderson. South American authorities have not confirmed the information, but our source claims the animal is being taken to a research location in the United States. More information as it comes to hand.*'

Kim had been resting on the couch watching the news on television when a breaking news bulletin flashed across the screen. She bolted upright, quickly turning the volume up. This was the last thing she had expected – that the authorities would investigate her story and capture Viktoria. How on earth had they managed to capture her? Perhaps, the autopsy results were alarming enough for them to investigate the type of animal that had killed him. They never would have expected to come across a living being like Viktoria. She almost wished she could have seen their faces the first time they saw her.

Her first thought was to pick up the phone to call Jenna and Matt and tell them the news, but put the phone down again. She still couldn't bring herself to talk to them about Viktoria. She placed her hand on the phone to call her mother, or Jamie's parents and then withdrew her hand. What would she say? I told you there was a monster. I didn't imagine it. The phone rang in her hand and it was her mother. At least she could talk to someone about Viktoria now.

Months had passed since Jamie's funeral and Kim had been working toward moving on. She still had sad moments where she found herself in tears, but slowly the grief was transitioning to a deep sadness and acceptance. It was difficult enough to lose a loved one, but to lose one such in a violent manner was a very hard pill to swallow. She had just commenced packing up Jamie's belongings and was trying to decide what to do with them. Originally, she had planned to sell the house as it held too many memories for her, but she realised these were good memories and she didn't want to forget them. She wanted to remember the happy times they shared and the dreams they had nurtured. If she sold the house and moved away, it would be new and would feel as if she was trying to forget Jamie.

She had not heard from Matt or Jenna since the funeral where both had appeared thin, pale and miserable. For the three of them to have once been so close, it was distressing they could no longer communicate with each other. Whenever she had thought of them, all her mind could see was Viktoria and perhaps, it was the same for them.

A dozen journalists from newspapers contacted her by phone and there had been a few knocks on the door. Politely, she informed them she had no intention of telling her story to the press. An Australian national killed overseas was always going to attract attention and the journalists could sense a juicy story and were persistent. One journalist left his card and said he would be happy to speak to her whenever she was ready.

One recurring thought that tormented her in the past few months was that Viktoria was still loose on that island. She was concerned other tourists may be taken to the island whether deliberately or by mistake. Did she have an obligation to try to prevent this from happening? If she did talk to the press, would she even be believed? It was a dilemma that righted itself when she heard the news announcement on television. Viktoria had been captured so other tourists were now safe. She felt a weight off her shoulders and made a mental note to call the Melbourne detectives to ask if they had any news on the case with Juan and Marcos. It had been months since the tragedy and Viktoria had been captured, which meant the authorities had found the hut and the room of bones.

She felt sorry for the people having to sift through the debris and clean up that room.

Kim had returned to work one month ago and her colleagues at the office had been supportive. She did not elaborate on Viktoria but summarised that Jamie was killed by a type of animal. Surely, they would lock her up in a mental health facility if they heard what had really killed Jamie. Although not a strenuous job, she found it difficult to summon the energy to get through the days and guessed she may have a form of depression or a post-traumatic stress disorder. Grudgingly, she visited a doctor, accepting that she may need some medication to pick her up.

"Mrs Anderson, you're pregnant."

The lady doctor smiled cautiously watching Kim's face, aware of Kim's story. Kim stared at her for several minutes trying to absorb this news.

"How is that possible?" she finally asked.

Through working the dates, it appeared Kim had become pregnant in the fishing village the night before the four of them left for the fateful trip to the island. The lethargy, absence of periods and nausea she had been attributing to the stress of losing Jamie, and of her own terror, a type of post-traumatic stress disorder. Although on birth control pills for many years, with her illness in South America just prior to the island visit, she had either missed a day or vomited up the pill and Jamie and Kim had made love two nights before he died.

It was so bitter-sweet to be having Jamie's baby and sad this was not a child he would ever meet.

"Are you sure?" she kept asking.

Once the initial shock was over, she found she was so excited and happy about this news, she felt she could burst. For the first time in many months, her heart had thawed and the future suddenly looked like a bright place to be.

"Yes, yes," the doctor said grinning. "We ran a few tests."

That evening, curled up on the couch to watch the news and patting her tummy affectionately, the South American news update had broadcast. Two huge events in one day. A new baby and the capture of Viktoria.

Life was finally starting to look up.

Chapter 25
The Journalist

For several weeks following the South American announcement, the press camped outside Kim's house, calling, knocking and shoving notes under her door. She unplugged her landline phone and muted her mobile phone, temporarily shut down her social media accounts and instructed her mother not to visit. She felt like a prisoner in her own home, unable to step outside without being harassed.

Suddenly, the young Australian tourist was not only killed in mysterious circumstances or by an animal, but by an aggressive prehistoric animal! This was a career-making story for a journalist, and each desperately wanted to be the one granted an interview.

Kim wondered if Matt and Jenna were suffering the same fate. Jamie's parents had received a few offers for interviews, but they refused. Gradually, the door knocks and phone messages slowed one by one, though not completely. She began to feel she would soon have her own life back.

One morning, she was placing rubbish in her wheelie bin, softly humming a tune that had stuck in her head, when a voice startled her.

"Hello Mrs Anderson. I bet you thought you'd got rid of us all."

She turned, startled and was face-to-face with the same journalist who had left his card with her a few months previously. She couldn't remember whether she kept his card or not, but recalled him to be likeable at the time. He was standing in her driveway, smiling gently at her, waiting to see if she would tell him to get lost.

"Catchy song, eh?"

Usually, she would have felt threatened being approached unaware, but the fact that he heard her humming made her blush furiously and then she laughed. She hadn't laughed for ages, and she laughed louder and longer than what the situation warranted. He grinned, finding humour in the situation.

He appeared to be around forty years old, soft brown hair worn quite long in a ponytail that hung halfway down his back. His face, although not classically good looking, presented a pleasant appeal with sparkling, intelligent eyes and a quick, easy smile. His clothing was neat and casual, if not a bit retro. She assessed him as a little eccentric and imagined he was good at what he did.

"Sorry to startle you. I know we journalists are the last people you wish to see right now."

Kim looked at him and waited for the spiel she knew was coming. After catching her humming and then laughing about it, she couldn't very well tell him to fuck off. She remained polite and looked at him expectantly. He cleared his throat, aware of what she was thinking.

"You may remember me. My name is Miles Cooper, but everyone calls me Coop. I'm sort of a freelance writer, so I don't have to answer to anyone."

He gave her a quick smile, almost apologetic for thinking she may remember him. She waited.

"I have a proposition for you that I hope you will listen to and consider."

Her first response was to say she was not interested but something about his gentle voice made her wait.

"Go on. I'm listening."

"I think one day this story should be heard ... Jamie's story and what happened out there on that island. No one knows except the three of you who were there. One day, a rogue journalist will make up and embellish a story if they can't get access to the truth and there will be false and misleading information published. For Jamie and his family, one day his story should be published so it is true and fair. The latest news that this animal has been found will make the whole story more intriguing. The public will want to know what happened. I would really love to represent you and Jamie with this story, but only when you are ready for it to be released. My proposal is that we talk and I write, and one day when you tell me it's ok, then the story is published. I don't think this story is finished yet."

She looked at him, assessing his words and looking for a connection in his eyes, something that made sense to her. She didn't feel the story was finished either. Maybe it would never be finished. She didn't have closure yet.

"What if I never want the story published?" she asked.

"Then it will never be published."

Kim studied him as the response was said with such finality and determination. Was he telling her the truth, that he wouldn't publish a story if she did not want him to?

"How can I trust you?" she asked.

He smiled and shrugged his shoulders, putting his arms out, palms upward.

"Ah, that is up to you to decide."

The weird thing was that she did feel she could trust him, this complete stranger. She trusted him somehow. She believed him.

"Why talk to you now? Why not wait until a time when I do want to go public, if ever?"

Coop nodded his head to indicate that it was a good question.

"Well, everything is fresh in your mind and untainted at the moment. There has been no court case, and the creature they caught has not been detailed to the press. You have not been influenced by other people, or the authorities in any way. Your story is straight and clear to you right now. It is a good time to get it down on paper, even if you never wish to use it."

She contemplated him, tossing the idea around in her mind before agreeing.

Over a few days, he conducted several interviews with her, and she found the more time she spent around him, the more she could trust him. The interviews were very relaxed in her lounge room, at the dining table or over coffee in the garden. He felt relaxed and comfortable too, happily making them both coffee in her kitchen as if he'd been doing it for years. He was a big coffee drinker, and she guessed that was a necessary part of being a journalist. He even brought over his preferred brand of coffee.

Coop talked about himself and it worked to relax her and help her feel more receptive to discussing her own life. He'd been married at twenty-two years old and still at university, until two years ago when they had separated. His wife decided she had married too young and needed to go out and see the world. He was upset about the marriage breakdown but remained on good terms with his wife. They had two teenage daughters he saw regularly, particularly when they were seeking pocket money. He proudly showed Kim selfies with the girls where they were pulling faces at the camera.

Now he lived in an apartment in Richmond with a good view of the Melbourne Cricket Ground. It turned out he was also a keen supporter of the Carlton Football Club, which caused Kim to wrinkle her nose in mock distaste. Collingwood supporters historically disliked Carlton supporters.

She recited the story of South America from the beginning and Coop wanted details such as where Kim met Jamie and how they had become a couple. She found herself telling him stories of their life together and pointing out photos from albums retrieved from a cupboard. It impressed her that he wanted the big picture and not just the grisly horror of the incident itself.

Kim explained how Matt and Jenna had become such close friends with herself and Jamie in recent years, and how the South American trip had been a dream for the two guys since their time together at university. She clarified with Coop that she did not wish to impinge on Matt or Jenna's privacy, and if the story was ever to be published, she would be seeking their approval.

With permission, Coop recorded their conversations, but she noticed he still used a notepad and pen to write notes and referred to his notes often. Discussing her life with Jamie had not been the ordeal she had anticipated and had filled her with sweet memories, nostalgic moments and a cleansing.

The story of the island and the death of Jamie had been tough and there was a copious amount of tears and sobbing, as she had known there would be. Coop sat very still during this retelling, not asking questions, and let her tell the story in her own way and in her own time. At one stage, when her emotions became too much, he suggested they stop for a break and reached over to give her a gentle hug. She let her head rest gently on his shoulder and allowed the soft embrace of comfort.

He was very interested in the artist sketches completed by the three friends in Chile and would try to track them down as well as speak to the detectives in Melbourne, and hopefully, Mr. Vidal and the detectives in Chile. She confided in him about not being able to communicate with Matt and Jenna. How guilty she felt that she could not contact them and felt she had abandoned them. He told her they would feel the same way and were probably feeling guilty. He suggested that time heals, and the three of them may be ready to catch up again shortly. He told Kim he had approached Matt and Jenna, but they were completely incommunicado and he felt they were not going to talk to him any time soon, so he had left them alone.

Kim found that she could confide in Coop the bottled-up feelings that she couldn't tell anyone else. This complete stranger was suddenly her confidant. Finally, she shared her news of Jamie's baby she was carrying, and how this little miracle was bringing such joy in the short time she had been aware of the pregnancy. He was delighted and she caught the glimpse of a tear in his eye. After hearing the story, he understood what this baby meant for her, her mother and Jamie's parents.

When they had covered as much of the story as she was able to relay, Coop left to finish his investigations and write up the piece. Kim admitted she was sorry to see the end of their interviews. They had been a welcome release and a cleansing of her soul in a time she really needed it, and she admitted to enjoying Coop's company. She had even switched coffee to his brand.

A few days later, the Melbourne detectives arrived to update her on latest events in South America, and the past few months had seen a flurry of activity. The old man, Juan Rojas, had been officially arrested and charged with murder. Other charges were still pending as no one had experienced anything like Viktoria before or even knew what she was. They were waiting for the scientists to define whether she was classified as a human or an animal. There was still discussion on whether Marcos would be charged. The analysis of the hut of bones and remains was still underway so they did not yet have a tally of animal verses human remains which would also affect the charges against Juan. The detectives understood that there was certainty that human remains were involved.

Juan told authorities that the oldest son in his family was tasked with caring for Viktoria and bringing food to the island. No one knew where she had come from, but he understood she had been left behind by her kind well over one hundred years ago. Juan was 71years old and his father had cared for Viktoria for most of his life, and his grandfather had also been her carer. It was his father and grandfather who built the green hut to shelter her many years earlier.

The detectives explained it was unknown how many humans had lost their lives on the island to Viktoria. Her main meal was goat or other smaller animals, but unsuspecting tourists may have found their way there, assisted by Juan. The scientists were working with Viktoria and examining her, but she was prehistoric, a relic from a by-gone era.

The detectives shook their heads in disbelief at the outlandish story. They informed her that when it came time for Juan Rojas to be tried in court, Jenna, Matt and herself could appear via video link as witnesses. This came as a great relief as she didn't wish to face South America again or look into the face of Juan Rojos, the man who had deliberately sent them to slaughter.

Chapter 26
The Demon

C lint couldn't believe the excitement he felt and other than the occasional dinosaur bone discovered in a remote location, nothing could compare to this. Today was the day the prehistoric creature from South America was due to arrive at the facility. This was a dream come true, a once in a lifetime opportunity and he was the lucky scientist chosen to run the project and research this creature.

A lifetime of dedication to becoming a total nerd was about to pay off and how sweet it tasted. His excitement was palpable and he felt like a child ready to somersault up and down the hallway. He poked his head out of the office door to check if anyone was in the hallway, and whether it was possible for him to somersault, but alas, too many people.

Forever, he would be known as the scientist who studied Viktoria, who categorised her, examined her, psychoanalysed her and wrote a book on her, but his excitement was so much more than the fame associated with the research. It was the challenge and love of working with a previously unknown species and possibly, related to man.

He assembled a research team of specialists in their field to study this creature, and they would be arriving in the next two days, though some had flown express to be present on the arrival of Viktoria. This was the most exciting invitation they had ever received. Usually, the object being examined was bones, remains or frozen, not a live specimen.

Housed in a rural area in Wyoming, United States, Clint often wondered why the authorities had built the facility in this location, but logically, it was cheap land, quiet, beautiful, close to railway and airport, and most of all, secretive. No one could travel anywhere near this facility without security being alerted. The facility was a fortress, well built with huge, electrified fences for miles around the concrete buildings. Several scientists lived on the premises in little units but most of the workers lived in the local towns with their family. Clint lived on the facility ... of course.

On super short notice, a huge, cavernous room had been repurposed to house Viktoria without knowing her preferences or what environment was best suited. The scientists could only base the room on a habitat similar to that of the island. Viktoria had been a captive on the island, so it may not have been a preferred habitat, but she had adapted over time. The elements had been suitable enough to ensure her survival.

This room was incredibly high, using the full height of the building, four floors tall with reinforced tinted glass skylights to let in light and sun. Rumour was she had wings which seemed incredible, and Clint wondered if that rumour was a mistake. If this information was true, they needed this extra height. There were ledges in various locations up the sides of the wall in case she wished to land and roost at a height. There was a small freshwater pond around ten feet deep with running water from a waterfall and a good number of fish in the pond to observe her catch and eat them. The walls were made of huge rocks which could be partially climbed, and a few large boulders formed a small cave for a hideaway, with cameras inside to monitor her every move. Blankets had been placed in the cave for her use. The banks around the pond were grass and large trees in pots had been placed around the room. There were bushes with berries on them scattered around, again sitting in pots. A long horizontal rail had been placed across one corner of the room replicating the perch she was sitting on when found by authorities. At each floor level were windows made of reinforced glass and people could see into the creature room, but Viktoria would not be able to see from her side of the glass. A large sliding reinforced door at the bottom floor was the entrance for food to be brought in and where Viktoria could be taken out for tests.

Clint sighed and scanned the room again, hoping everything was in place and ready to go according to plan. He hadn't been provided with much information in advance of her arrival. The brief summarised she was human-like in appearance but had some animal characteristics, had killed and eaten humans, was abandoned on an isolated island in South America, and appeared to have a broken wing. Based on this scant information, he had designed this room for her and couldn't wait to view the creature.

The gate guard phoned to announce the truck had arrived at the front gate. Clint left his office to meet the truck in the creature room. He stood behind the reinforced glass at ground level so he could view from a safe location. The creature was to be unloaded inside the room for safety and security. No one quite knew what to expect so the most stringent precautions had been taken.

An old, battered truck with a reinforced crate backed slowly into the room. Clint could see a large padlock and heavy chain holding the crate closed. He was shocked to see the ancient transport they were using for this incredibly special occupant and realised it was the same truck used to transport cattle decades earlier. Logically, he realised that in a small village in South America, this may be the best truck they could locate at short notice. Once they had the creature in the truck, there was no way they could risk trying to swap her over to a more appropriate transport vehicle.

With dismay, he realised that there was no simple way of feeding or watering her in that crate and groaned at the thought of the creature suffering dehydration, hunger and her own filth. His thoughts were interrupted by the sound of crashing as Viktoria continually threw herself against the gate of the crate in an attempt to free herself. The force of the blows spoke volumes as to the strength of the creature. Clint wondered if she had been doing this the entire way from South America or was she aware she was nearing the end of the journey? He hoped she had not injured herself with this show of strength. He could hear her heavy breathing from the exertion of crashing into the gate. Was she doing this out of fear? From the very little he had heard of this creature, her number one instinct was for survival. Did she feel her survival was currently threatened?

The truck came to a halt and slowly the tray lifted so the crate was leaning on an angle before sliding gently onto the ground. The truck drove out of the room and Clint imagined this was one load the driver would be relieved to be rid of. A security guard unlocked the padlock and removed the chain from the gate on the crate. He exited the room at a fast pace and the reinforced doors closed behind him. Viktoria was alone in her new room.

Aware of movement behind him and whispers, Clint turned to see the room had filled with other scientists, his boss, Bill, other managers and even the administration staff. Everyone was anxious to see the aggressive creature famous for killing an Australian backpacker on an isolated island in South America.

Sensing this new situation and the sudden silence, Viktoria stopped fighting and sat quietly waiting to see what would happen. After a few minutes, she gently pushed against the crate gate, and it opened, slowly swinging on its hinge. The sound of inhaling from the crate was audible and Clint realised she was sniffing to detect the environment, an animalistic trait. Cautiously, she peeked out the side of the gate, looking around the room. Clint held his breath as did everyone in the secure room. All eyes and ears were on the crate where a dark face was scanning left to right.

Although it felt like hours, it was only a few minutes before Viktoria emerged from the crate. This was the first time the scientists and colleagues had seen her and there was a collective gasp of astonishment. Nothing they had been told could prepare them for the real thing. Clint felt the hair on the back of his neck prickle, and later he would discover that everyone in the room had the same reaction upon first sighting Viktoria.

She inched down the sloped ramp of the crate until she reached the dirt floor of the room. There was another gasp as the scientists realised she had wings on her upper back. One was terribly misshapen and hung at a strange angle. The scientists breathed in her strong physique, talon-like toes, powerful haunches, wings and dark eyes.

Clint turned to his colleagues who stared, speechless at the apparition in front of them.

"Ladies and gentlemen, you are now looking at a real live demon."

Chapter 27
The Baby

Senior Detective Kevin Lay visited Kim with results of the analysis from the hut of bones. Forensic anthropologists identified twenty-three human remains and hundreds of remains of goats, sheep, calves and a few dogs and exotic animals. Although this news was expected, the sheer number of humans was staggering, and Kim enquired how so many people could disappear in the area without attracting attention. The identity of the human remains was still being processed with DNA matched against missing person records, and in some cases, using ancestry records as not all missing people are recorded as missing.

Juan Rogos was charged with qualified homicide, attempted homicide and conspiracy to commit a crime, and would never see freedom again. His trial was not yet scheduled but expected to be held in six months' time. Marcos was not charged and on conditional release as he had knowledge of the deaths - of Viktoria and what his father was guilty of. He was also the person who had brought the killing to an end, reporting the situation to authorities.

The detective returned the backpacks belonging to her and Jamie, retrieved from the island when Viktoria was captured and no longer required by the forensic team. Her first reaction was to toss them both in the rubbish bin and have nothing to do with them but later, she realised she needed to unpack the backpacks and this may be the closure she was seeking. It wasn't.

Information on Viktoria was scant, and the detective didn't have any further news of her or where she had been relocated to. On a news channel, she watched video footage of a truck with a stock crate on the back, being loaded onto a ship and tried to imagine Viktoria locked in the back of a cattle truck. She struggled with this thought and obsessed over where the authorities were taking her, needing to know the details. These thoughts occupied her relentlessly and she wondered if she would ever have closure from her ordeal. Perhaps, Coop had been correct when he stated that he didn't feel her story was over yet.

Kim's baby boy was born five months later after a long and difficult labour. She named the child, James Keith Anderson, but decided to call him James rather than Jamie. This child made her feel hopeful about life again and she considered him Jamie's final gift. Jamie's parents were in raptures over their grandchild and Kim thought it beautiful to see them with the baby. Jamie had been their only child and now they were recipients of Jamie's final gift as well.

Coop maintained his visits to Kim at least once a week, calling in at various times for coffee and a chat. She didn't ask him about how the story was progressing or whether he'd managed to source the artist sketches of Viktoria from South America and knew he would inform her when it was finished and he was ready. As well as writing the article, Kim felt that Coop had become a genuine friend to her and was keeping a watch that she was ok.

Jenna visited the hospital after James was born with a card and gift for the newborn. Kim hadn't seen her since Jamie's funeral and thought she looked thin and pale with bags under her eyes and a strain on her pretty face. She was delighted to see James and held the baby tightly to her chest, whispering what a little miracle he was. Tears slipped down her cheeks as she held him and breathed in his baby smell. The two of them had spoken together many times of their future hope for children but they never could have guessed it would start with Kim as a single mother.

They chatted easily on baby topics, pregnancy, breast feeding, giving birth and the joy of a newborn child. As she relaxed, Jenna confided her concern about Matt and his mental health. Although never officially living together, she had stayed full time at his apartment since before the South American trip and found it difficult to continue attending her job as she was afraid to leave Matt alone. He resigned from his job, didn't attend football and sat at home all day, watching movies, playing computer games or sleeping. His sleeping was plagued with nightmares, and he often woke screaming and crying. Doctors diagnosed him with a post-traumatic stress disorder and depression and prescribed various medications. Jenna worried about him self-harming and didn't know how she could help him. He wouldn't talk about it and she struggled with her own trauma from the events.

Tears ran silently down her cheeks as she spoke of seeking support from Matt's parents and sister, and how they visited him regularly and tried to engage him in activities or sat with him for company and support. Both girls knew that Matt idolised Jamie and had since school days. The trauma of the island and Jamie's death hit him hard and Kim didn't know what to suggest. They all carried their trauma and grief in different ways. The two girls hugged and felt close at that moment as they hadn't in a long time, promising to keep in contact.

Kim planned to visit Matt with baby James and hoped the sight of Jamie's baby would help lift his spirit. Unfortunately, with a newborn and lack of sleep, she never made it to visit Matt. Two months later, Kim received the devastating news that Matt had taken his own life with a drug overdose. She felt incredible guilt, wondering if seeing the baby would have brought Matt back from the edge. She felt incredibly sad for Jenna, for Matt's family and for the partnership the four of them had once shared, the doomed trip and the collapsed dream.

Viktoria had now claimed two lives.

Chapter 28
The Recovery

Dr Clint Marne's entire days were filled with Viktoria and he thought of her every waking moment and went to sleep thinking of her. If his body allowed it, he would have worked all night. They had learned so much about her and yet, knew so little. She was an interesting being and so human-like most of the time.

He'd been deeply disturbed and angry when Viktoria first arrived at the facility, dehydrated, starving and filthy. She was the most important discovery in history, and the authorities had mistreated her to the point where they could have lost her. One of the first things she had sought when released from the crate was water, lying on her stomach at the water pond and frantically drinking water. For the first two weeks, she hid in the cave area, peeking out regularly but only venturing out for water. She ate the mangoes and other fresh fruit they left near the cave but wouldn't touch meat. The scientists just watched Viktoria during those first weeks as she interacted with the environment, eating, drinking and resting.

Spiking a mango with tranquiliser, they were able to move her to an examination room and perform a number of tests. Clint conducted a manual examination, recording his voice as he processed her extremities. She was terribly emaciated and malnourished, with protruding bones, mild hair loss and gum disease. There were a few scars present on her body that were well healed and x-rays showed a malunion fracture in her wing which would need osteotomy surgery to break and reset the bone with a rod and screws to hold it into place.

It was difficult to estimate her age but the broken bone in her wing suggested it had happened as an adult and it was known that she lived on the island for over one hundred years. Clint couldn't believe that she physically was still capable of reproduction.

Her DNA showed her to be a previously unknown species but with a possible common ancestor to modern man. Clint could see the Neanderthal resemblance with the low heavy brow, deep-set eyes, strong and slightly, masculine features, coarse hair lightly covering parts of her body yet, she was more human-like than *Australopithecus africanus*. What set her apart from the bones and partial skeletons found of archaic man were the wings, horns and talon-like toes. Her horns were small bumps on either side of her head, barely visible. Clint envisaged that the male of the species had larger horns and like any species with horns, were used in combat. The skull was thicker than a human and her fingernails were sharp, coarse and strong, as were the talon-like toes. She was the stronger, fighting version of early man.

A few scientists were sceptical that she could be real, an anachronism, as no skeleton or bones had ever been found belonging to one of these creatures. Clint argued that not many of the original creatures would have survived the ice age, and with low numbers and based most likely in remote parts of Africa, no remains had been uncovered to date. The scientists named the new sub-species, *Homo nike viktoriaensis*.

Despite the vast amount of animal and human remains found on the island in the green hut, the scientists were confident she had eaten large amounts of protein because there had been no choice. Her physique, teeth and make-up suggested she was similar to humans in regard to diet. On the island she had sourced all edible vegetation and a few health conditions suggested she was lacking in fruit and vegetables. Clint did not believe humans were her preferred food choice, but she had hunted them so as not to starve. Her survival instincts were incredibly strong to have survived over 100 years alone on an island without food. This hypothesis was based on watching Viktoria's behaviour and documenting every movement.

Over time, she was offered a variety of food in various forms including a live goat, butchered lamb, cooked meat and fruit and vegetables. She was more content eating the butchered meat and cooked meat in preference to killing the goat. She only killed the goat after a few days without food. She refused to catch fish, and Clint was curious whether she had ever eaten fish on the island, contending that she wouldn't have been starving had she eaten the abundant fish. When offered cooked fish, she gorged it down including bones, seeking more when finished. She particularly liked melons and mangoes but did eat other fruits when offered. Her weight increased dramatically in a short time period once she had access to food.

The temperature in the room was set to warm as she would have experienced on the island for most of the year. When they turned the heat down, so the room was getting close to freezing, she still did not light a fire despite having wood and rocks. She relocated to the rock cave and wrapped herself in the blankets that had been left there.

Clint used two adjoining rooms with reinforced glass close to Viktoria's room. When he opened the sliding door, Viktoria learned to immediately enter the room. It had taken a few months to achieve this but was now an easy task. He offered her treats passed through a drawer opening in the glass similar to what is used in prisons. She loved the mangoes and cooked fish treats he prepared.

In the room, he performed tests to study her intelligence and behaviour, sitting close to her through the window, watching her reactions and trying to communicate with her. So far, she refused to communicate with him at all. When Clint talked to her or gestured, she stared at him and was silent, although he was sure she understood everything. He also placed a large screen on the wall on his side of the room where he could play videos to her to judge her reactions. Through footage of humans, cars, cities, animals, aeroplanes, trains, water, mountains, gorillas, birds flying, and insects, she sat quietly, watching the screen. The only reaction she exhibited was when footage of baby humans or baby animals were shown. Her eyes lit up and she threw herself at the window making loud exhaling noises which Clint took to be acute interest and perhaps, longing. She refused to participate in any tests he attempted but would sit on her haunches and quietly watch him. He was patient.

It was also frustrating that she refused to fly. Her wing healed beautifully and x-rays confirmed the metal rod had been successful and the bones knitted. The rod would stay in place for the rest of her life to strengthen the wing. Viktoria spent much of the day spreading out her wings flapping and then withdrawing them. Clint could see she was testing the strength of the damaged wing and trying to build up the muscle, but he did wish she would try to fly. The wings had a bat-like appearance but stronger and coarser. When they were extended, the skin was pulled taught and looked almost translucent in places.

Viktoria was a terrifying sight with her wings fully extended, the perfect demon from ancient literature..

Chapter 29
The Decision

Coop had become a regular visitor at the residence of Kim and James, even running errands for them on occasion. Jenna questioned if Kim was romantically interested in him and she vehemently denied it. The question shocked her as it was something she had not considered but admitted this stranger had become a huge part of her life and she was fond of him. Jamie had been the love of her life and there would never be anyone else. How could there be?

Jenna planted the thought that perhaps Coop was interested in Kim. She didn't think that was the case and was certain Coop felt paternal towards her and James, a protector. Kim wondered if listening to her story during the interviews, he had felt pity and a responsibility to look after the wounded. It didn't matter to her as she enjoyed his company and was content with their relationship.

When James was four months old, Kim took Coop by surprise one afternoon, explaining that she wanted to see Viktoria again. Over one year had elapsed since the incident on the island and despite trying hard to forget Viktoria, she was haunted day and night by visions. She questioned why she had never been asked to view Viktoria to identify her, then laughed, realising what a ridiculous thing it was to think there could be more prehistoric creatures with wings available for a police line-up. The fact was that Kim felt a strong need to see Viktoria for closure. Closure couldn't happen knowing Viktoria was held somewhere in the US being examined and she was in Australia with no knowledge of what was happening. She felt discarded and left out, eagerly scanning headlines each day, anticipating updates or photographs. She wanted to know if Viktoria remained as she remembered, looked the same and behaved the same. She wanted to look into those brown, intelligent eyes she remembered so intimately looking into her soul and understand why her husband had been killed. Was it for nothing?

The court date for Juan had been postponed pending the examination and research being conducted on Viktoria.

Kim knew her chances of visiting Viktoria were remote but wondered if Coop would help her in this quest, help her to visit the location where Viktoria was being held. Surely, Coop would think she'd lost her mind, wanting to view the murderous creature again, and maybe she had lost her mind. She needed to talk to the scientists who were studying her, view her, understand her and search for the end of her story.

This request rattled Coop and she watched him pace up and down the lounge room, head down, deep in thought. She had never witnessed the intense, working, journalist Coop as all she had seen was visitor Coop. Not wishing to interrupt his pacing as she could see he was contemplating the situation, she quietly sat and watched him.

Eventually, he stopped pacing and sat down on a lounge chair facing her.

"We have to go public with the story," he stated, looking at her solemnly.

His eyes searched her eyes to gauge her reaction. The thought of going public didn't shock her as it would have twelve months earlier.

"Why?" she asked.

"I don't think there's any way they would let someone in to see Viktoria. Not even you."

He paused, stood up and commenced pacing again.

"If we go public, the world will know exactly what happened, and we may be in a position to pressure the authorities. Never underestimate the power of the people. We'll run a campaign, and the authorities will have no choice but to allow you to see her. In the meantime, I'll communicate with my contacts, the police and the US authorities and see what we can do."

He sat again and looked at her, waiting.

"Tell me about the story being made public," she asked him.

"I'll revise and update the story I wrote some months back now. You read it and approve it."

She nodded, relieved that she would be able to approve it.

"Then, it will be published in major Australian newspapers, plus distributed to international news outlets, and with media releases. It'll go out with a big bang."

Coop was still pacing at this stage, pumped with his plans. Kim briefly wondered if he was like this with every story.

"Be prepared for media out the front again I'm afraid, plus phone calls and requests for interviews and television spots."

"Really?" she asked, taken aback by this thought.

"You need to do this. If you are serious about visiting Viktoria, then we go all the way, saturate the media and create public awareness. Are you sure you want to do this?"

The more Kim thought about it, the more determined she was to see Viktoria, without really understanding why.

"Yes. Let's do it!"

Kim looked up at Coop to see he was pacing again, deep in thought. Was she doing the right thing? Would she regret this decision?

Maybe ... but she had to do it.

Chapter 30
The Campaign

A few weeks later the story went live, and she cried again reading the story Coop had written. It was well-written, powerful and provocative. Triggering so many emotions from the depths of despair through to acceptance and finally, hope for the future. How had Coop managed to compile all these emotions into his article? He'd nailed it, but she was not the general public. Would they feel the same?

Even the artist sketches of Viktoria from South America were included with the story, along with a photograph of the four backpackers before they left for the trip of a lifetime, and a photo of Kim with James in her arms. She was reluctant to have her own photo appear, but Coop stressed it was important for the reader to connect with her, the grieving widow with a small baby. The photographer had captured Kim in a soft light gazing into the camera lens, not smiling but exuding a genuineness, her soul on display.

From the time the story was published, her life became chaos, with media parked outside her house and relentless. She received requests to appear on well-known television shows to talk about her experience, weekly magazines approached her for her story, international papers and shows sent requests and the phone never stopped ringing. She stopped answering it and let callers leave messages. Even her parents and Jamie's parents were inundated although still happy for the story to be published.

Kim preferred Coop to make the decisions regarding interviews and the direction of the story, trusting him with her best interests as per his planned campaign. The story went wild on social media all over the world, trending on various platforms. Websites appeared dedicated to Viktoria, as well as forums and groups, with everyone theorising on her origin, including expert scientists. Some decided she had been engineered in a laboratory based on the movies of *Jurassic Park* fame. Many believed she was not real and a hoax, designed to create unrest in the world. One company designed an iPhone game where Viktoria fought the backpackers. Demon images and memes appeared all over the Internet and television networks ran tales and legends from the dawn of time. A few religious cults claimed this was the work of the devil who had sent a demon to earth to begin the apocalypse. End of World Preppers began preparation for the end of the world, protests and rallies dominated many of the major cities with people calling for the death of Viktoria. Gun sales soared in the United States and the world felt it had descended into chaos.

The worldwide interest in Viktoria was much more extreme than Coop or Kim could have imagined, and Kim was forced to hire security staff to keep the public and media away from her home and a bodyguard for when she left the house. Fortunately, she received money from a few interviews to pay for the security.

Kim appeared on the Friday Night television program along with Jenna. The story was also for Matt, a second victim of the Viktoria tragedy. Friday Night did a great job with the story and showed the same artist sketches and photos that Coop had already published, and showed footage from the funerals of Jamie and Matt. The interviewer, Sarah Parr, was gentle with the two girls and yet still managed to elicit enough emotion that the girls and the film crew ended up in tears.

Meanwhile, Coop with cooperation from the Melbourne police department, sent off requests to the US authorities for Kim to visit Viktoria. A few weeks passed before there was a response. Surprisingly, it was positive and they accepted Kim's request to visit provided she was accompanied by Coop. There was a ton of legal paperwork and restrictions, including that authorities must approve all written material before publication, photos were permitted but must also be approved prior to publication and there was to be no unauthorised recording of the visit. The scientist in charge, Dr Clint Marne, had questions he hoped Kim could answer. Coop ran a check on Dr Clint Marne and the two of them studied his impressive resume so they would know what to expect. Consent forms were signed and various security forms were sent back accepting the agreement and conditions. A passport was arranged for James Keith Anderson and their trip was scheduled for the following week. Coop and Kim were elated that the strategy had worked, and this trip would be happening.

Kim felt incredibly excited in the knowledge that she had this opportunity to see Viktoria in the flesh again, but also dreaded the encounter. She tossed and turned for many nights wondering if she was doing the right thing.

Chapter 31
The Meeting

Two weeks later, Kim, Coop and James flew to Wyoming, United States via Los Angeles. Kim felt a mixture of emotions preparing for this trip. She was no longer the frightened and grief-stricken widow who returned from South America. Somehow, she felt different, older, stronger and wiser. She was a mother now, a protector of a little being, and she had the support and friendship of Coop. She felt committed to this trip and was clear on the outcome she wanted.

They stayed at a hotel in a small town near Wyoming. Coop in one room and Kim and James in the next room, and hired a rental car, exploring the Wyoming area the day before they were due to see Viktoria. The countryside was an attractive green with scenic mountains surrounding them. People were friendly and the restaurants served good meals. With the research facility so close to the small town, it improved the economy as could be noted by the multitude of cafes, eateries and shops.

"Now we're here and it's happening tomorrow; I don't know exactly what I'm expecting." Kim put her knife and fork down and looked up at Coop. "Maybe it'll be an anti-climax and we'll go away disappointed. I guess I'm wondering why I'm here."

"This is something you needed to do. Maybe once you've seen her, you'll be able to put it behind you," he suggested.

"I'll be interested in your first impression of her. You know what a shock it was to me and the rest of us. At least you know what to expect but I'm still curious to see how you'll react."

Even though Kim knew what to expect, having seen Viktoria before, would the reality of viewing Viktoria in detail in a safe environment make a difference?

The sky threatened to rain the next morning as they drove to the facility where Viktoria was located. The facility was imposing from the outside with the large fences stretching into the distance, armed guards at the gate and miles of massive, concrete buildings. The countryside was green and pretty and this massive structure blotted the landscape and Kim felt she had landed on another planet. She wondered what the locals really thought of this monstrosity in their midst.

Getting through the main gate was an experience, with a ton of phone calls, ID checks and more phone calls. Once, this would have intimidated Kim, but she just felt annoyed as they knew she was coming. After a few more stop points, they reached the door to the main building and were escorted to meet the scientist in charge.

The man who jumped to his feet to meet them was not what Kim had expected. From his extensive resume, she had expected the stereotypical Einstein-like scientist with crazy, long, grey hair and wild, goggle eyes behind thick black glasses. This scientist was quite young, late thirties she estimated, with dark, curly hair, honey-brown coloured eyes and black glasses. His face lit up into a broad smile and he seemed excited as he raced over to them and shook each person's hand in a welcoming gesture. She smiled at the exuberance of him and immediately found him likeable.

"I'm Dr Clint Marne, overseeing the research of ... Viktoria."

He paused and looked at Kim waiting to see her reaction to the name. Kim smiled and nodded her head.

"Pleased to meet you. I'm Kim and this is Coop." She gestured towards Coop who shook the doctor's hand.

"Miles Cooper, but please call me Coop."

The doctor nodded. "This must be the young James." The doctor looked down at the sleeping baby in Kim's arms and Kim found it heartening that he had taken the trouble to find out the name of the child and acknowledge him.

"I thought we would have a chat first in my office." He signalled with his hand for them to follow him into an adjoining office where they sat in two very simple chairs. The doctor stood leaning on the edge of his desk.

"Can I offer you coffee, tea or water?" he asked.

"No, thanks," they echoed. They were keen to get down to business. The suspense had been building for some time, and they were keen to see Viktoria. Kim looked around the plain office without personality or personal touches.

"Dr Marne, what exactly is Viktoria?" Kim started.

The doctor clasped his hands together, happy to talk about his special project.

"Well, what can I say? We've never come across anything like her before. Never! Not even bones or fossilised remains. It's as if she's appeared from nowhere. She's a new species or sub-species to us - humans. I would say unique; however, she is only unique to us as we have not seen her kind before. There must have been or possibly still is, others like her in the world. She was born to parents and has common ancestry with early man."

That thought was too repulsive for Kim to accept. The doctor noted the sceptical look on her face.

"It's true. She has Neanderthal-like traits but millions of years ago, there was a mutation where her type evolved with wings and other features, most likely from the *Australopithecus africanus* group. Man evolved differently and in a different continent. Viktoria is typically what we think a demon looks like. Man has obviously seen her species many years ago and drawn illustrations and written of the encounter. The stories and images became more horrific over time and more diverse until we have man-goat demons and supernatural demons. Viktoria is not a supernatural ghoul. She is flesh and bone, with DNA, a blood group and human-type injuries. She's more human than animal."

Kim shook her head, not wishing to accept that she could be human-like in any way.

"But she eats humans."

"Only for survival. Tests performed show that her diet in a perfect world is pretty much the same as humans. She eats meat, vegetables, fruit and nuts. She prefers cooked meat to raw meat but cannot light a fire or use tools. To the best of our knowledge, she never attacked any of the family who brought food to the island. There was basically no food on that island, so she had no choice but to eat what was offered to her. Her teeth are similar to ours with sharper incisors, but she also has molars appropriate for grains and vegetables."

Kim was still shaking her head in denial. This was not possible.

"Plane crash survivors in the snow have resorted to eating their dead companions when they had no choice. There have been numerous reports of cannibalism in survival situations, even in your own country, I believe there was a convict in Tasmania known to eat his friends when he had no other choice. It's not a pleasant thing to think about, but I believe she did it to survive. I think she's been on that island for well over one hundred years, having been left behind by her kind when she badly broke her wing."

"Over one hundred years? That's ridiculous," Coop snorted in disbelief.

"Yes, but true. The family have been feeding Viktoria for many generations – three generations I believe. I estimate she was already mature when she damaged her wing, and that was over one hundred years ago. She's still of a reproductive age."

Kim and Coop looked at each other, eyes wide.

"Wow!"

"Are there other creatures like Viktoria out there?" Kim asked.

The doctor shrugged his shoulders.

"I don't know. Over 100 years ago, there must have been, but they may now be extinct or functionally extinct. There are different levels of extinction. The world is a big place. It's possible there's a small group or small groups in their own remote location. Man would be their biggest threat. I'm sure they keep away from civilisation. They are like the strong, predator version of man but they lack the intelligence that man has, which is why their species is not the dominant one."

"What will happen to her?" Kim asked.

"Well, she can never be released. She is too dangerous, or the public would see it that way, anyhow. She will be in captivity for the rest of her life, which will be a darn sight longer than any of us. She will be tested and researched, and we can learn from her."

"So, she will be a circus animal," said Coop.

The doctor stood up and started pacing.

"I realise that discovering Viktoria was due to a terrible tragedy with the loss of your husband."

He stopped and looked at Kim momentarily, then resumed his pacing. His voice animated as his excitement for the topic increased.

"But what an opportunity this find is for mankind. She is so unique, so unexpected. She fills the gaps in the evolutionary family tree. If only we had a male as well."

He stopped his pacing and sat down again, then turned to face Kim.

"May I ask you some questions, Mrs Anderson ... err ... Kim?"

Chapter 32
The Questions

"Sure." Kim sat up straighter and nestled James closer to her chest. He'd been quietly gurgling away.

"I don't wish to upset you, but we didn't receive adequate information other than Viktoria was discovered on a remote island, in an old hut, sitting on a perch with bones around her, and she killed a man. That is about all we were told. I would like to know more if you are able," he said, smiling at her gently.

"Yes. That's fine. Let me know what you need me to tell you."

The doctor sat back in his chair but was totally focused on Kim and what she was saying.

"Did you hear her make any sounds at all the whole time you were on the island?"

Kim thought back, remembering them entering the hut, Viktoria sitting watching them, the frantic run from the hut.

"The only sound she made was when the boat came to rescue us. We climbed in and as we were leaving the island, she made this really loud mournful sound, like a cry."

The doctor was listening intently.

"Like a cry of sorrow or anger? Was she upset you were leaving?"

"Yes, I think so." Kim remembered the haunting sound.

"Do you think she was upset that her food source was escaping, or do you feel she was upset being left alone?" he asked.

Kim frowned, puzzled by the question. She closed her eyes and thought back to that time.

"Umm. It started as an angry sound but slowly turned into a long, sad cry."

"Can I ask you ... how she killed your husband?"

The doctor was nervous about asking this question, but he needed to know. Kim nodded slowly and looked across the room so she could focus on an object. It was easier to relive the scene if she could focus on something and not look at the person asking.

"We ran from the hut, four of us, and Jamie was behind me. He was slower due to an old football injury. After a while, we realised he was not with us, so walked back to look for him."

She paused for a few minutes and concentrated on breathing, then continued.

"He was lying on the ground with blood everywhere. His throat had been slit, but not slit across, it was slid downward, you know ... vertical. He also had some minor cuts on his arm which is where I guess she grabbed him first."

The doctor didn't voice his thoughts but imagined that she could have inflicted the fatal wound with her sharp fingernails but most likely, her talon-like toes. He envisaged she grabbed his arm to stop him running and knocked him off his feet before inflicting the fatal wound. He had seen her do similar with a few live animals they had put in her enclosure.

"So, she tried to make the death quick. Was there any sign of her near your husband ... after the attack?"

"Yes. I think she ran off when she saw us coming."

Kim shivered remembering the fear they had experienced at that time.

"Do you know if she was running on two legs or using her arms as well?" he asked.

Coop and Kim looked at the doctor, puzzled.

"Do you mean like how an ape runs?" Coop asked.

"Viktoria has the ability to run like a human or use her arms like an ape. She has longer arms than we do. I imagine she interchanges to suit the situation."

Kim shook her head negatively.

"I never saw her run."

"Can you tell me about when you first saw her? How she was sitting on the perch, your thoughts on the room, anything really," he asked.

Kim shuddered, remembering that horrible moment when they stepped into the room. Coop closed his eyes and imagined himself in that room with Kim as she described the event.

"The room was dark and the stench was terrible ... heaving with insects. I was trying to breathe out of my mouth. Viktoria was so huge right in the middle of the room, staring silently at us. She had her back claws and feet wrapped around the wood pole like a bird sits on a perch. She didn't move. She just watched us. All over the room were bones and carcasses. It looked like she had just tossed them aside when she finished."

Kim looked across at the doctor to see if he wanted more information. His face revealed he didn't feel the horror, fear or revulsion that other people would feel in a room full of bones and carcasses, with a demon sitting in the middle of it. His face showed wonderment and fascination. He was enthralled. He sat up suddenly, snapping out of his momentary trance and asked if there was anything else notable on the island. Kim thought about it for a few minutes

"There was no animal life at all. The four of us commented on it. No birds, nothing. The whole place had no sound other than the wind and waves. Also, she watched us when we were camping the night before and when we went to bed, she ate the fish bone scraps and took a blanket with her. We saw it later in the green hut."

The doctor nodded remembering how Viktoria liked to wrap herself in the blanket they had left in the large room for her.

"Time to see her. Are you ready?" he asked.

Kim took a deep breath and nodded.

Chapter 33
The Visit

Walking down the corridor, the doctor turned to Kim and Coop and asked them a question.

"Have either of you heard of Nike, the Greek Goddess of victory?"

Kim and Coop shook their heads.

"She was known as the Winged Goddess of victory. The Roman equivalent is Victoria. Interesting, isn't it?"

Kim found it too creepy and coincidental not to be devised after seeing one of these creatures.

"Viktoria's species is now referred to as *Homo nike viktoriaensis*, but I think we will always just call her Viktoria."

Coop and Kim followed the doctor through a few connected rooms until they found themselves standing in a room with a large window, so large it filled the entire wall. Through the window was a massive room. The room was well-lit and the two of them scanned the contents of the room; rocks, cliff faces, water, grass, plants ... and then they saw her ...Viktoria.

Involuntarily, Kim sucked her breath in and held it. Here was Viktoria in front of her, sitting on a grassy knoll with a cliff face behind her and a water pond beside her as if she was enjoying a picnic. She appeared to be pulling apart a melon and only fifty metres away. Kim could still make out her features and she felt the hair on the back of her neck stand on end.

"HOLY SHIT!" exclaimed Coop. He had jumped back at the sight of her, a natural flight reaction.

"Nothing prepares you for the reality of seeing her," the doctor said, enjoying the reaction of Coop.

The scientists had faced the same reaction the first time they saw her, except for Dr Clint Marne, of course. The three of them stood at the window watching her, no one moving, no need for words. Coop couldn't take his eyes from this creature. He took in all her features and then turned to the doctor.

"No tail?"

For some reason, he expected a creature with wings, horns and talons to have a tail as well. Illustrations of demons usually displayed a tail.

The doctor smiled, impressed with the question.

"No tail, but there is an extra vertebra in the tail bone of the spine suggesting that an earlier species may have had a tail."

Coop raised his camera.

"No flash," reminded the doctor.

Coop agreed and snapped a few photos, zooming in to see the finer details. He had written the story of the four backpackers and Viktoria and knew the story inside out. He had seen the artist sketches and knew what to expect and yet, nothing could have prepared him for what he was looking at. He had also felt the hair all over his body rise and a strange primal urge to flee. He reasoned that this is what humans had been doing for centuries when confronted with one of these creatures. To him, it seemed strange that this species was the one almost extinct, but as the doctor had indicated, they did not have the intelligence of modern man and hence, their decline.

James made a small whimpering sound. He had been happily looking around and sucking his fingers but was almost due for a feed. Viktoria raised her head and looked straight towards the window where they were standing.

"Can she see us or hear us?" asked Kim, suddenly alarmed.

"No," replies Dr Marne.

Kim could see Viktoria flaring her nostrils as if trying to catch a scent. She held very still as if listening. Purely coincidence Kim decided. After a few minutes she went back to peeling her melon.

The doctor told them how Viktoria had been quietly testing her boundaries, the windows, the doors and the walls. She had been doing it by stealth, hoping no one would realise what she was doing.

"She's a lot more intelligent than what we think," he explained.

"She may not be able to light a fire, or maybe she wants us to think she can't light a fire. I don't wish to underestimate her."

The doctor told them that although her wing was now fixed, and she flexed it and flapped it, she had not flown. The doctor wondered silently whether Viktoria did not want them to see her fly. It all seemed to point to a creature acting dumb and letting the enemy underestimate it.

The doctor was keen for Viktoria to see Kim. He wanted to know if Viktoria would remember her at all and how she would react. All the humans Viktoria had encountered at the facility had been male. He was curious if this would make a difference and explained to Kim that they had the two adjoining rooms with reinforced glass between so Kim would be safe on one side. She would be able to get up very close to Viktoria without any fear for her safety. Kim was terrified at the thought but felt she needed to do this. This is why she was here, to see Viktoria, to try to understand.

He pressed a few buttons and a panel slid across a wall in the next room. Viktoria looked up at the sound and immediately headed towards the opening. He explained that they had done this so many times that she was happy to enter the room, seeking treats. Kim took a deep breath as she watched Viktoria heading into the room and straight toward her.

Chapter 34
The Escape

Kim stood close to the glass within a few metres of Viktoria with the doctor and Coop at the back of the room. She could barely breathe through the fear she felt but was determined to conquer it. Prickling rippled up and down her back, settling in her neck and scalp. She must have clutched James too tightly as she felt him stir in her arms and murmur. She whispered to him, "Please be good".

Inside the room next door, Viktoria approached the glass and spied Kim. She froze and stared at Kim, her face surprised. She had been expecting to see the doctor as she usually did. Kim focused on her eyes and could see the same eyes she remembered from the island in the hut of bones but with a different expression. Viktoria looked left and right, seeing the doctor and Coop standing at the back of the room behind Kim.

Slowly, she approached the glass, ready to flee at the smallest hint of danger. Her eyes flew back to Kim and she seemed mesmerised, sitting back on her haunches just metres from the glass. The doctor had never seen her behave like this before and wondered if the fascination was because Kim was female or whether she recognised this person from the island.

After a few minutes, she inched closer and stopped again, her eyes not leaving Kim. Kim could see the dark depths of her eyes and the expression on her face and had to admit, she felt she was looking at a human and she felt certain Viktoria remembered who she was. Viktoria was exactly as Kim remembered although she had not been this close to her on the first encounter. She thought of what the doctor informed them that she only hunted humans for survival. Was it true?

Kim stared into Viktoria's eyes, wanting to know, needing to know. What was Viktoria thinking? Did she remember Kim from the island and was puzzled why she was here? Did she have any empathy for the people she had killed? Was she thinking how tasty Kim looked?

Behind her, Coop was madly taking photos, and the doctor was scribbling notes. All was still and quiet, with everyone lost in their own agenda as this strange greeting took place.

A few more minutes passed, with Kim and Viktoria lost in a mutual staring episode before Viktoria broke the spell by looking down. She looked down into Kim's arms where baby James lay. Kim saw the expression on her face change in a split second. Her eyes widened and her entire face changed, as if her face was melting in real time. Her mouth and face dropped, and her eyes looked haunted and forlorn.

Without warning, Viktoria slammed her forearm against the glass.

CRASH!

Everyone jumped in fright and Kim let out a terrified scream. James started crying in fright and hearing the baby cry, Viktoria opened her mouth and let out a loud sound, somewhere between a scream and a moan. She repeated this mournful sound a few times, anguish on her face.

CRASH!

She slammed her forearm again on the glass. In fear, Kim backed away from the glass looking at the doctor for reassurance as he was the one who had said they would be safe behind the glass. The doctor looked stunned as if he couldn't believe what was happening and wasn't sure what to do.

CRASH!

This time, Viktoria used her shoulder to ram the glass panel, then again.

CRASH!

CRASH!

Her muscles rippled and she used sheer strength to batter the glass. Kim reached Coop and he wrapped his arm around her shoulder, leading her away. She was sobbing in fear and James was crying loudly as they headed toward the door to leave the room. Reinforced glass or not, they didn't wish to stand by and watch Viktoria so tormented and desperately trying to break the glass. The doctor seemed to snap out of his stupor.

"Yes. Yes. I think she's upset about the baby. I'm sorry. I wasn't expecting this. She has reacted a little to films with animals and their young, but never like this."

The baby's presence hadn't registered with the doctor. Now he kicked himself he hadn't thought of how she may react. He was the expert in behaviour. How could he have missed this possibility?

CRASH!

CRASH!

Viktoria slammed again and this time there was a cracking sound as the glass started to splinter down the centre with fine cracks jagging outward. Quickly, the doctor raced for the door and hit a red button on the wall. A loud alarm filled the building, the sound deafening in their ears as the three of them raced out of the room with the doctor turning to lock the door behind them.

CRASH!

Racing down the corridor, the sound of the alarm was piercing with people running out of offices and heading down the corridor as well. A swell of people filled the corridor and Kim realised the alarm must be an 'evacuate now' siren. Coop held Kim's arm firmly, not wanting to lose her in the crowd.

The doctor stopped and spoke to a few people, and Kim and Coop halted, waiting, unsure whether to follow the crowd or wait for the doctor. James was screaming now, which only made the piercing siren more unbearable. They could still hear crashing from down the corridor where Viktoria was slamming into the glass. The doctor was now on the phone and they imagined he was frantically trying to get security to the room.

"COME ON," Coop yelled to her over the noise.

She looked back at the doctor and decided they couldn't wait. They didn't want to be in the building if Viktoria managed to escape the room.

The people running down the corridor had thinned out as the initial rush was over. The place was a maze and in the rush to evacuate, they were no longer sure where they were. Behind them there were more crashing noises, the siren and now they could hear someone screaming.

"SOUND'S LIKE VIKTORIA'S OUT," yelled Kim to Coop as they raced down another hallway.

"COME ON," Coop urged as they turned a corner. He had her arm and was supporting her as they raced down the corridor.

Finally, they were at a door which looked like one they had entered previously but couldn't work out how to open the door. James was screaming, and Kim jiggled him, as she looked frantically for a way to open the door. Spying a green button against the right wall, she pressed it and the door slid open. Before the door automatically closed behind them, they could see the form of Viktoria at the far end of the corridor. She was running and using her arms to keep her balance on the floor. She was racing straight toward them. Kim screamed and the door closed, separating them from Viktoria.

"Oh God!" Kim said, bending over and trying to get air into her lungs.

This could not be happening again, running from Viktoria.

"Come on. We have to go."

Coop grabbed her by the upper arm and propelled her toward the car. They were outside in the daylight and not a security guard in sight where there had been many only hours ago. The evacuation siren was still ringing in their ears, blaring through external speakers. As they headed toward the car park, they heard crashing and realised Viktoria was trying to break down the door.

"OH GOD!" Kim screamed, not aware of what she was saying anymore.

They ran toward the car as the grey sky opened up and rain fell. Crash after crash reverberated behind them, each sounding louder than the previous. Kim hoped fervently that Viktoria wouldn't work out the green button. How smart did the doctor think she was again?

As they ran, both Coop and Kim continually glanced back over their shoulder at the door, hoping it was as strong as it looked. The car seemed so far away, and James was still screaming, wet from the rain, his face red and distressed. The siren blared its deafening alarm and when the crashing stopped, both Kim and Coop looked at each other in a panic. Why would she suddenly stop?

Out of the door which had slid open, raced Viktoria. Coop glanced back and let out a stifled scream. Kim didn't need to look over her shoulder to know what was coming. They were still too far from the car to reach it, and a car wouldn't offer them any protection from Viktoria, they both knew. Knowing how hopeless the situation was, in unison they stopped and turned to face what was coming.

Viktoria in full flight was an incredibly intimidating sight and Kim knew why humans had drawn illustrations of demons from long ago. Her wings were not fully out and not retracted either. They were out to her sides as if ready to fully extend if needed, and she moved with an incredible speed now on two legs. Coop wrapped his arms around Kim in a protective shield and Kim pulled James tightly against her chest.

They stood as lambs to the slaughter and watched Viktoria approach.

Chapter 35
The Flight

As she neared Kim and Coop, Viktoria slowed to a slow walk and stretched herself up to her full height. Her wings, which had been carried sidewards, slowly stretched out and upward, giving her a tall, wide appearance. It was a spectacular vision, higher than her head and well out to the sides and reminded Kim of giant bat wings. At full height and with her wings extended, Viktoria was a truly fearsome creature. She stood well over two metres tall and towered over Coop. This stance aimed at intimidating, and it did - not that either of them needed any further intimidation. This was how Viktoria's kind had terrified humans many years ago.

Viktoria looked down at the humans in front of her. James was still crying and Kim gently rocked him back and forth, kissing his forehead and breathing in his smell. She didn't look up at Viktoria, fearing she would lose her mind and courage if she did. She imagined they were all dead ducks, and it was just a matter of time. Was there anything she could do to protect James? The thought of Viktoria taking James away as a meal nearly made her fall to the ground in despair and horror. She would do her best to protect him at all costs and if that meant sacrificing her own life, then she would. Decision made, she felt calmer, and taking a deep breath, she looked up at Viktoria and saw that she was inching her way toward them.

Viktoria turned her head slightly to look at Coop and she pulled an expression, a frown. She reached out her arm and seized his shirt front with her strong fingers, her fingernails ripping his shirt as she yanked him toward her. Coop let out a gasp of fright and released his hold of Kim. Viktoria held him close to her and exhaled her breath audibly straight into his face. If ever there was a sign of utter disdain, that was it. She flung him to the side like a discarded piece of rubbish. Coop's body flew through the air for several metres and landed heavily on his back. He didn't move.

Kim looked at the crumpled Coop and then back at Viktoria. It was her turn now. Would she do the same to Kim?

The frown left Viktoria's face and she gazed at James in Kim's arms. He was still crying and starting to toss around wanting to be fed. Viktoria relaxed and slowly folded up her wings like a concertina door. They neatly withdrew into a relaxed state still visible over her shoulders. She was listening to James, cocking her head to one side and then to the other. Her nostrils flared as she drew in his smell. Kim waited for what was going to happen next. Would she rip her throat out like she had with Jamie? Would she toss her flying like she had with Coop? Was this the last minutes of her life?

Kim looked down at her crying baby and prayed to the universe he would be spared, even if she would not be. She didn't want her last sight of him to be where he was distressed, crying and hungry. Slowly, she moved her right hand and pulled up her shirt, placing James against her breast where he latched on immediately to her nipple. The crying stopped instantly as he started suckling.

She saw Viktoria's eyes widen at the sound of the suckling and pull a few strange facial expressions which Kim couldn't decipher. She stepped closer, gazing down at James, then closer. Kim could smell her breath and her musky body odour. Viktoria sighed and made a few more strange facial expressions as if her face was collapsing. She slowly held out a large hand toward James. The hand moved closer and closer to the baby, until she was almost touching him.

"NO!" Kim shouted with as much aggression as she could muster, fiercely staring into Viktoria's eyes.

Viktoria pulled her hand back in shock as if stung by a flame. Again, she reached her hand out toward the baby.

"NO!"

Viktoria made more strange sounds and sighs and Kim realised she was crying. She could see watery tears in Viktoria's eyes as the creature moved back a step and made a few loud moans. Kim could see the pure anguish in her eyes. Viktoria stretched both arms out toward James and then drew her arms to her chest as if holding a baby to her breast. She looked down at her boy-like breasts and moaned. She rocked her arms to her chest as if holding a baby and lifted her head, looking up to the sky and let out a very loud anguished moan. It was the saddest sound Kim had ever heard. Suddenly, Kim realised she wasn't afraid anymore and knew Viktoria wouldn't harm her. Viktoria wanted a baby of her own and was grieving for a baby that she would never have.

Kim became aware of her surroundings when she heard loud noises and shouting. She'd been so absorbed in Viktoria that she had blocked out the incessant siren and what was happening around her. Looking around, she saw security people carrying rifles which she guessed must be tranquiliser guns. They would not kill their prized specimen, but they couldn't allow her to escape and kill civilians either.

Kim would later wonder what was going through her mind at that moment, but she stepped toward Viktoria and looked up, pointing to the sky with her right arm.

"GO!"

Viktoria looked at her and frowned as if trying to understand. She seemed oblivious to the activity around her as her focus was just on the baby.

Again, Kim pointed up to the sky.

"GO. HURRY," Kim yelled at her.

Viktoria looked up where Kim was pointing, then turned and saw the men approaching. She made another strange sound, quickly extended her wings and started flapping them. Kim remembered the doctor saying she had not flown yet. Maybe she couldn't fly and had lost the ability. Kim held her breath, glancing back at security as they levelled their rifles.

Viktoria faced Kim again as her flapping increased and made a sound like a loud grunt. Kim would ponder that sound afterward but wondered if it was a goodbye. Viktoria increased the intensity and speed of her wings flapping and Kim could feel the air from them blowing in her face. She saw the strain on Viktoria's face and the determination. Suddenly, Viktoria ran to the right as if in slow motion, her feet left the ground, large wings furiously beating and Kim watched as her body rose and drifted over the car park. The men with rifles ran up to Kim looking up and trying to aim at the flying creature. Kim watched as Viktoria's shape became smaller and higher, moving away from them and out of range of the rifles.

Viktoria gained height and Kim could see her heaving downward with her wings to gain more height. She held her breath and watched the figure as it grew smaller in the sky until she couldn't see her anymore.

Pulling James from her breast, she looked around for Coop and her heart sunk as she remembered his crumpled body on the ground. Terrified that Coop was dead, she gingerly made her way over to him. He was motionless and she stood above him, looking down, remembering finding Jamie unmoving, and unable to face finding another dead body. Tears ran down her face and she let out a sob. It couldn't happen again. Looking over at the gathering crowd of people to see if anyone could come and help, she saw the doctor on his phone in a frantic call with someone. Others stood staring at the sky and talking in shocked voices. Finally, someone killed the siren and the silence was more deafening than the alarm.

Kim sucked in her breath and knelt down beside Coop. He was lying in the same position that Jamie had been, on his back with his face facing the sky, except Coop's eyes were closed and he was not covered in blood.

She reached out gingerly and touched his forehead. It was warm and wet from the rain. She let out a little sob of relief as Coop opened his eyes and those honey-brown eyes looked up into her eyes. His eyes scanned her face and she realised he was concerned about her and James. She smiled down at him and let out a big sigh of relief. He was alive and he was going to be fine.

"Let's go home. You have a story to write."

Part Four - The Chase

L.J. Fox

Chapter 36
The Tracking

"**S**O, WHERE THE HELL DID SHE GO?"

The boss was angry and his voice matched his anger. The older, red bearded man paced up and down the office, glaring at Clint from time-to-time just in case Clint forgot how angry he was.

Clint sighed, resigned to his fate and sat up straighter in his chair. He knew he was in for a grilling and he knew he deserved it.

"I don't know, Bill," he said, quietly and apologetically.

"Well, a lot of bloody good you are. What have we been paying you for this past year?"

He stopped to glare at Clint again. Viktoria's escape from the facility had become Clint's fault, his omission, his mistake and he knew ultimately, he was responsible for the welfare of Viktoria, but damn it - he had not built the place. He had been told the reinforced window could withstand a gun blast, a bomb explosion or an elephant charge. How was he to know how strong the walls, doors or windows were, or how weak in this case? It seems the glass was weaker if attacked in one place continually. What about the damn main door? The security of the facility should not be his concern.

"Do you realise what's going to happen when the public find out about this?" asked Bill, his voice raising a few notes.

Clint nodded his head and grimaced. Oh, he could imagine.

"It will be mayhem. MAYHEM! People will panic and we will have anarchy, not to mention the destruction that your animal may cause." He again glared at the doctor.

Clint thought it mildly amusing that suddenly Viktoria was HIS animal.

"Where is the woman from Australia and the journalist?" Bill asked.

"They're on their way back to Australia now. Still in the air."

"Lucky for us they were not harmed." Another glare.

Still pacing, Bill ran his fingers through his red thinning hair. Clint couldn't agree more with that thought. The thought of Viktoria harming his guests would have been an insurmountable catastrophe.

"We will never get another government grant after this. This was our big chance to be noticed in the scientific world, to showcase our facilities and attract more funding. We will be the laughing stock of the world. We will have to cancel next week's announcement. What exactly happened yesterday?"

He stopped in front of Clint and waited, tapping his fingers on the desk.

"Well ... umm ... the Australian woman had a baby with her and that upset Viktoria. She became very agitated and smashed through the reinforced glass window plus a few doors. We gathered tranquiliser guns and chased her out to the carpark but by the time we got there, she flew off."

"Flew off! Like a fart in the wind! FLEW OFF! FLEW OFF WHERE? I thought she couldn't fly yet." He glared at the doctor.

Clint shifted in his chair, uncomfortably.

"We don't know. We have had emergency services trying to trace her but there have been no sightings so far."

Clint chose to ignore the jibe about her not being able to fly yet. He had wondered if she was playing them and indeed, she had.

"That's a lucky thing. We are facing full scale panic here. There is a good chance someone will shoot her as it is. What is your best educated guess as to where she would go?"

Clint sighed and thought for a few minutes. He'd been thinking of this ever since Viktoria escaped.

"She wants a baby so ..."

"What do you mean she wants a baby? Are you saying she will kidnap a baby?" Bill's face had reddened and his voice went up an octave.

"No. No. I don't believe so. If that was the case, she would have taken the Australian baby yesterday. She had the opportunity. She wasn't aggressive toward the mother and baby."

"Damn well seemed like an aggressive thing to do, smash through the reinforced glass and a couple of doors," said Bill, not convinced.

"Viktoria has been testing the boundaries of the room for months, looking for weaknesses and a way out. It's been in my reports."

Bill nodded.

"I think seeing the baby yesterday triggered her emotionally. She lost control and decided to force her way out. You know ... the viewing room is the only place where she hadn't had an opportunity to test the boundaries."

"She seemed to be after that baby, even when they were outside," said Bill.

Clint sighed. "She's an intelligent creature. She would know she couldn't keep a human baby alive. I think she desperately wanted to touch the baby and see it up close but I believe she wants her own baby and will look for more of her own kind."

"Her own kind? But they are extinct."

"Are they? We don't know that. The world is a large place. It's possible there are some left somewhere. I just don't know, but I do think she will try to find them."

Bill settled a little and sat in the chair opposite Clint. His large weight filled the maximum width of the chair.

"I'm not sure who we get involved here. As mentioned, if the public find out she's on the loose, it will be mayhem. The military will no doubt shoot to kill due to the threat to the public. You have to remember ... she has already killed humans before, and not only that, but eaten them."

Clint nodded unhappily.

"In a perfect world, we would handle this ourselves and reacquire the asset. What a shame you did not think to implant a tracking device in her. We could have tracked her and reacquired her quickly."

Clint stared into space for a full minute, then his eyes widened. He sprung out of his chair and to his feet so fast the chair tipped over backwards. Bill jumped in fright at the sudden movement and waited for the doctor to speak.

"But we did!"

Chapter 37
The First Night

Viktoria landed with a thump in a crop field and toppled over a few times. She was panting from exertion and total exhaustion. Her repaired wing ached with a pain she hadn't felt in a long time and all the other muscles in her body were tired. She had flown for the first time in over one hundred years and although well-healed, the wing was weak from lack of use and there had not been time to build up the muscles required for such strenuous use.

It would be dark shortly, the best time to fly long distances with less chance of detection, but she had been flying all day and urgently needed to rest. Ahead in this field, she glimpsed a large shelter and her body didn't give her much choice but to crash-land in the field.

She was not sure what the crop was where she landed but it was taller than her and still very green. She didn't care what it was, provided it hid her from the prying eyes of any humans about. The ground was moist under her feet where the crops had been irrigated and she contemplated lying down in the field to sleep but needed more shelter. It may rain tonight and it would become too cold for her. She had lived her entire life in warm climates and would not survive in a cold environment. Survival was number one.

Slowly, she trudged through the crop and found the tall plants moved aside easily to let her pass but it was almost dark when she reached the large farm building at the top of the field. There were no animals nearby and the shelter was deserted. The nearest human building was quite a distance away so she felt safe to take refuge in this shelter for tonight and possibly, the next day as well. She had flown all day today but that was foolish as she may be seen by humans in daylight. It would be best to rest during the day and fly at night. Hopefully, this building would shelter her for tonight and tomorrow as well.

Inside the open door, she found soft straw on the floor and strange objects with large, rounded wheels. She walked around and smelled everything, noting that the objects with wheels smelled similar to the boats the humans came to the island in. She could not detect any immediate threats here and feeling exhausted, curled up in the corner and fell into a deep and peaceful sleep.

Chapter 38
The Farmer

Viktoria awakened and knew immediately something was not right. The sun was not shining where it is supposed to at daybreak. Confused, she stretched and stood up, listening and watching. Striding over to the shelter door, she looked around and realised it was no longer morning. It was halfway through the day with the sun above which explained her confusion. She couldn't remember ever waking up later than daybreak and this confusion had thrown her off guard. Even with her plans to spend the day resting in this location, the late awakening had stressed her and made her uneasy.

She paced up and down the building contemplating what to do. She was hungry but knew it was unwise to hunt for food during the daylight hours in an area with humans. Noticing a long length of wood hanging horizontally across the shelter between two posts with a smell of chickens on it, she decided it looked solid enough so jumped up and perched as she had for many long years on the island. This stance relaxed her and felt right for her frame.

Viktoria knew she needed to fly across another ocean. She was too far north where it was cold and she would never survive here. She must find a way back to her original homeland where it was warm enough for her kind to survive. She had no idea where the flock she had been travelling with ended up or if they found Utopia, or whether her family of hunters were still alive, remembering the terrible drought when she had left. She just knew that she must head toward the most likely place that she could survive and the only one she knew.

She was also aware she was not currently capable of flying across an ocean or any long distance. Flying the day before had severely exhausted her and her wing still ached. The humans had repaired the broken bone in her wing, but she had not used it until yesterday and her muscles were weak from underuse. She needed to become well-muscled and develop strength in her wings, especially the repaired wing. From her time in captivity, she had gained weight and been well-fed, her health was good, her mind sharp and her motivation was strong. She just needed muscle strength and fitness to enable a search of her own kind.

Falling asleep perched on the horizontal wood, as she had done for over one hundred years, was easy and restful. Many hours passed and it was late afternoon when she was suddenly awakened. Her eyes snapped open, listening, smelling, paying attention to what had awakened her. Detecting nothing for a while, she began to think she was imagining things or dreaming when suddenly, two small terrier dogs burst through the shelter door barking frantically and bouncing up and down. She was wide awake now. What was happening?

They were looking up at her and leaping up and down, trying to nip at her but were unable to reach. The yapping dogs were annoying and she pictured picking them up and tossing them to stop their incessant barking. The scent of the dogs had been masked by the smell of the objects with wheels which was disturbing as she realised it could be masking other smells.

Suddenly, she heard a human voice.

"What are you guys up to?"

A man walked in the shelter door, a man with longish hair and a large amount of hair on the bottom of his face ... a very hairy man. His clothing sported bright coloured checks, reminiscent of a blanket she remembered from the island. The shock of seeing him without detecting him alarmed her and she held on tightly to the perch, unsure what to do. Should she make a fly for it? The hunters' first instinct was always to flee or fly in most cases. She held rock still hoping this human would take his noisy dogs and leave. The dogs continued yapping and looking up at her.

Eventually, the human looked up and he and Viktoria stared silently at each other, eyes meeting. Viktoria had already started to stretch her wings out, in case she needed to flee quickly. To the human, Viktoria would have appeared huge, silhouetted, perched on a chicken perch which was head height and been terrifying. He stared open mouthed, stunned, dumbfounded and paralysed. Viktoria also felt paralysed, unsure what to do.

Suddenly, the human yelled out and stumbled backwards, falling over his own feet as the dogs continued their endless yapping. The human scrambled to his feet and ran. The dogs continued barking for a few minutes then took off after their master.

It was time to leave this place. Although, not what she had planned, the human had found her and he may return and bring more humans. She would be forced to risk flying in daylight and instinct told her to head south.

First, she needed to eat.

Chapter 39
The Miss

C lint stared at the little green blip on the monitor he was holding on his lap, a device held as if it were a treasure map.

"Where is she?" Bill asked.

"Looks like she's stopped a few miles south of the barn where she was seen."

Clint was annoyed that Bill had insisted on coming along on this trip. He had deployed a small unit of scientists and security specialists equipped to handle anything. Bill tagging along complicated things more than it needed to.

Clint estimated Viktoria was stationary at present and may be feeding or drinking. If they could reacquire her now, it would end the nightmare, the public wouldn't know much, nor the press, not to mention other scientific communities. This incident could be categorised as a small accident to learn from. A farmer had seen Viktoria in his barn and nearly wet his pants. Now, the police and authorities knew she was in the area and Clint hoped to find her before a hot-headed authoritarian or red-neck farmer shot her.

The green blip started moving again slowly. Clint estimated they may have a visual shortly. He picked up the walkie-talkie and spoke to the other vehicle to let them know. Travelling on a tarred road with only a narrow lane for traffic in both directions, it was fortunately quiet with barely any vehicles out. Acres of fields on both sides of the road, and a scattering of trees with the occasional farmhouse or barn. Viktoria was giving all buildings a wide berth and sticking to the quiet country areas.

On the right side of the road, Clint saw the remains of a calf. They slowed down to take a closer look and noted, it was in a field where a herd of cows cowered in a corner where the fences met. The walkie-talkie crackled as John Temper in the other vehicle notified him of the find. Viktoria had been here only moments ago.

They moved on again and within minutes he could see the form of Viktoria flying above the field on the right side of the road and watching her in full flight took his breath away. Her wings were large and she flapped them to gain or maintain height but mostly, glided. Clint knew that many people would think of her as ugly, a demon, an abomination, but to him, she was a thing of sheer beauty.

He watched as she became aware of the vehicles following her and increased the flapping, her head swivelling around regularly to see where they were.

Clint spoke into the walkie-talkie.

"Any chance of a shot while she's in the air?" he asked.

"I can try."

John Temper loaded the tranquiliser into the rifle and aimed out of the front passenger window. He tried to rest the rifle on the car door but the road was too rough and it bounced the rifle around. He found it was more stable if he simply held the rifle and tried to still it himself. He could see Viktoria slowly rising higher and knew in a few minutes she would be too far away for the tranquiliser to reach. They also didn't want to risk her falling from a huge height and harming herself.

His finger moved on the trigger with the sights set for the dart to land in her torso. He was on the verge of pressing the trigger when the vehicle hit a pothole in the road, throwing him forward with the released dart embedding in the roof of the vehicle.

"Damn," he swore.

Quickly, he aimed the rifle in the air again but realised the opportunity was lost and Viktoria was now too high. He relayed the bad news to the doctor.

Chapter 40
The Trooper

As darkness fell, Clint knew they could not continue much longer. They had been driving all day, not even stopping to eat, other than packets of potato crisps hurriedly purchased at the convenience store when stopping for a bathroom break and fuel. All were tired and hungry, so a plan was devised to stop at a motel for the night, eat a good meal and sleep. If they left early before daybreak, they could find Viktoria before she flew off. She would be stopping for the night, having flown all day.

They planned five hours sleep then all up by 3am and on the road. A suitable roadside motel was booked where they could park their vehicles in front of the units and eat at the small diner next door. The crew thought the food had never tasted so good, hunger making everything taste better. Even the cheap bed felt comfortable and warm. All the men fell into a deep sleep within minutes of their heads hitting the pillow.

Clint's phone rang and rang. Sleepily, he fumbled around trying to locate it on the bedside table. Disoriented in a strange place, he cursed that nothing was where he thought it was. Finally, he answered the call, glancing at the digital alarm clock which showed 2.30am. A deep voice introduced himself as Chief of Operations, Police unit. Clint was wide awake in an instant.

"We have your ...umm ... animal thing ... in a barn at Northmede at 23 Yellowstone Road. A farmer saw it fly into his old barn."

"Is she harmed? Has anyone approached her?" Clint asked, alarmed.

"Nope. No one's been near it yet, but we've surrounded the building. The system tells us we are to contact you immediately."

"DON'T APPROACH HER. REPEAT, DO NOT APPROACH HER. My crew are not far from you. We'll leave immediately. Please wait until we get there." Clint pleaded.

He had no idea how far Northmede was from the motel but thought he'd seen the name on the map.

"Well. We'll wait a little while, but we can't have that thing out in public now, can we?" Abruptly, the chief hung up.

Clint was out of bed and in clothes in record time. He ran along the verandah knocking on all the doors of his crew. It took only five minutes for the entire crew to be in vehicles and on their way to Northmede. Clint was sweating with apprehension, knowing what could happen with the police. With all the publicity Viktoria had generated, they may see this as their chance to be heroes and protect the public by being quick to shoot. He swore his crew to secrecy regarding the tracking device and could just imagine the possibilities if the police got hold of it.

Although the trip felt like hours, they were driving in the gates of a field with a mass of headlights within fifteen minutes. There must have been twenty police and emergency vehicles surrounding the barn, along with private farm vehicles. Headlights blazed against the wood of the old barn. The huge barn doors were open and the inside was in darkness. He could see farmers standing against their vehicles with shotguns in hand and police scattered everywhere, with guns drawn. He grimaced as he thought how frightened Viktoria must be with all this commotion.

They pulled to a stop and the crew jumped out. He quickly located the chief and headed over to find out what the current situation was. All assembled were staring at the old barn motionless.

"I'm Dr Clint Marne. What's going on?" he asked the chief.

The chief turned and stared at him, summing him up with a brief snort.

"We got a man in there," he said and turned back to the barn.

"YOU WHAT?" Clint asked, incredulous.

"I sent a trooper in there, just to check that thing is still there." The chief wouldn't look at the doctor.

"I told you to wait," Dr Marne said, exasperated.

Suddenly, the air was filled with the sound of a blood-curdling scream which ended as suddenly as it had started. Everyone froze, staring at the barn. No one knew what to do. There was a moment of silence, then a faint noise could be heard.

WHOOSH. WHOOSH. WHOOSH.

Viktoria appeared in the headlights at the barn door. She was flying low, straining to get height. Clint could see her wings frantically flapping and pushing and he saw she had the trooper hanging from her talons. The bottom half of the trooper was dragging along the ground as Viktoria frantically tried to lift him and gain height. Clint heard the clicking of guns engaging.

"DON'T SHOOT, DON'T SHOOT, DON'T SHOOT!"

The chief screamed out to the assembled group, having spied the trooper. Viktoria struggled to lift the weight of the trooper. Clint saw she only had a short runway to gain enough height to lift above the circle of vehicles. If Viktoria was the only one to exit that barn, she would have been shot dead but having the trooper with her would save her life. He held his breath hoping she would be able to lift high enough to clear the vehicles. He also hoped that trooper was alive because he couldn't see any flicker of movement from him. If the trooper was dead, Viktoria had no hope.

Everything seemed to be happening in slow motion. He saw her gaining height and he could see the trooper's shirt ripped where Viktoria's talons were trying to grab hold. All guns were aimed on her. He exhaled as he saw her fly over the vehicles but the trooper's legs crashed into the windshield of a police cruiser, shattering the glass.

"DON'T SHOOT. DON'T SHOOT!"

The chief screamed out again as Viktoria disappeared into the dark night with the trooper hanging limply from her talons, legs dragging in the dirt.

Chapter 41
The Obsession

Panic ensued after Viktoria flew away with a trooper in her talons. In the darkness of the night, no one knew what had happened and the farmers and police were beside themselves with anger. Clint knew they would shoot her on sight from here on. He also knew she could not fly with the trooper, due to his weight and the state of the trooper's shirt almost in shreds. He suspected they would find the trooper just beyond the gates to the field and while the police were regrouping and discussing a search plan, his team slipped away. Their last sight of the field as they exited the gate were zig-zagging spotlights pointed up at the sky, voices yelling into radios, bets on who would be the first to shoot the animal and truck engines roaring to life. Clint was relieved that the monitoring device had not been detected.

Not far down the road, the driver in the front car slammed on the brake and framed in the bright headlights stood a ruffled and dirty looking trooper without a shirt and a ghost-white face. The crew jumped out of their vehicles and rushed to see if the trooper was injured. Amazingly, he did not have a scratch on him. His recollection was that Viktoria had been sitting in the rafters of the old barn and picked him up by the shoulders of his uniform shirt. Of course, he had fainted from the shock. What a story he would have to tell his grandchildren one day. Clint let the chief know via radio that they had the trooper, he was unharmed and he would be dropped off at the nearest hospital for a check-over.

As they drove through the night watching the monitoring device blips, Clint wondered how Viktoria was feeling now she knew the danger was real. He was extremely worried she would be shot by a farmer or a police officer and hoped she was as smart as he expected and be on her guard.

It seemed unlikely his crew would get close enough to tranquilise her now that she had experienced such a close call. He was unsure what the right thing to do was, but he couldn't go home and forget she was in danger. Clint had to admit he didn't care if they never captured her, provided she was safe.

She flew all night and the following day. The crew took turns driving so they could keep going. Fortunately, they were in a rural area with not as many people and she seemed to be heading towards Texas. Clint knew she needed the warmer environment to survive and instinctively was flying towards the warmer areas.

Two weeks later, he sent the crew home. This method of attempting to capture her was not going to work and after speaking with a disappointed Bill, it was decided the doctor would continue the search on his own. He could call on more resources if required. In recent weeks, Bill turned a corner with the search for Viktoria. Initially in favour of shooting her, he was now adamant that Viktoria was not to be harmed. He fully supported Clint's quest and happily signed for expenses to continue the search.

Over the following weeks and months, Viktoria flew through Colorado, Oklahoma, Arkansas and Mississippi. Clint slept rough, often in his vehicle, ate take-away and enjoyed too much bourbon without the rocks. Occasionally, he stopped at a hotel, showered, shaved, ate at a restaurant, slept in a comfortable bed, and washed his clothes. More often, he was dishevelled, unshaven, unshowered, dirty and not eating well. Sometimes, he realised it was an obsession and he probably needed professional help to move on but convinced himself this was the most important work he had ever undertaken and a once in a lifetime opportunity.

Keeping a distance behind Viktoria's blip on the monitor, he never seemed to catch up with her. A few reports came in over those months including one from a lady who had seen Viktoria looking in her house through glass doors. A few farmers reported missing lambs, calves, goats and chickens, and one farmer reported seeing her in his barn. One man asserted she had taken his dog, a group of children claimed to have seen her perched in a tree and a roadside worker shot at her as she flew past.

Maybe it was the warmer and more humid environment, but Viktoria decided to stay in Alabama for a few weeks. Clint felt he knew her well now and his theory was that she knew she was getting closer to the coast and the trip across the ocean would be difficult. She had achieved it many long years ago and wanted to build up her strength before tackling the trip.

It was sunrise one morning when Clint finally saw Viktoria. He was on a dirt road in the middle of nowhere with fields on each side of the road and several large trees, a few of which had died and displayed ghostly structures in the early morning. There she was - sitting on a branch of a dead tree. He could see her silhouette with the sun rising behind her and the sight took his breath away. He lifted his iPhone and snapped a photo.

Within minutes, she had stretched her body, stretched her wings and flew away into the sunrise. Clint followed, of course.

Chapter 42
The Storm

Viktoria shook the water off her face as she struggled to remain level in the air. She had known for a few hours that rain was coming. She could sense it but was flying over woodland where there were no shelters or caves. The hunters always hated the rain. They understood rain was necessary for food, water and growth, but they disliked the feel of water on their body, and especially their face. The wet trickled down, penetrating the skin, crept into the nostrils and blurred the eyes. She growled low in her throat in anger with herself for being caught out in the downpour. The downpour had been striking sideways in a torrential burst for at least fifteen minutes now. More than the dislike of water, the rain made flying very difficult. The water infiltrated her wings until they felt heavy and she started losing altitude.

To add to her misery, she was starving, not having eaten for days due to the heavy woodland and her desire to leave the woods behind her. Now she realised she had made the wrong choice and should have eaten and found shelter somewhere ... anywhere.

Her legs grazed the top of a pine tree and she realised she was descending too fast. She couldn't see where she was or what was below due to the ferocious nature of the storm so braced herself as she was about to crash into trees.

Viktoria's head and upper chest hit a large trunk of a tree, knocking the breath from her. She gasped for air and attempted to wrap her arms around the tree to hold on, sharp fingernails searching for a grip. The memory of her fall from the sky on the island many years ago terrified her as she had broken her wing. Her grip faltered and she slipped down with branches whizzing by as she frantically dug in with her nails and talons. Eventually, the falling slowed and her talons found a grip in the bark. Everything was still for a few minutes as she tried to breathe and settle her fear. She couldn't see how high she was due to the heavy rain but guessed she was still too high to jump. Just to be safe, she retracted her wings and held them close to her body. No broken wings for her today.

The rain was relentless and she shivered with cold now she was no longer flying and creating heat. Eventually, she moved one leg further down the tree and grasped with her talons, feeling secure she moved the other leg down. This would be a slow process, but it was the only way she could descend without injuring herself.

Viktoria was never so glad when she felt her legs hit solid ground. It was still raining heavily, and she could hear thunder in the distance which terrified her. In her homeland, the hunters always took shelter in caves when they saw lightning or heard thunder. Nowhere to hide now and for the first time since she left the island, she felt utterly miserable. There would be no flying now. She would have to walk.

Lightning and thunder occurred irregularly over the next few hours, but the rain was constant and torrential. Walking kept her body warm and her instinctive compass told her which direction to head in. She could feel bruises and scratches from her crash landing which stung.

Suddenly, Viktoria found herself in a clear and open area. She recognised the hard grey surface with white lines that she'd seen from the air for many months now across the land. This was where the humans sat in shelters with wheels and chased her. She trembled at the sight and began to back into the woods. She couldn't hear any sounds so she stopped and listened. There were no little shelters with wheels tonight in the dark. If she followed this hard grey surface, she would find shelter. At this stage, she felt desperate for shelter, for warmth, for sleep and food.

Walking along the hard grey surface, her talons clicked as she walked but it was easier than trying to see in the woods and dodge trees and logs. As she walked, she dreamed of a time when she would be with her family again. Would she see the alpha male again? Would she be accepted back in the fold? Would she have youngsters? She uttered a little sob as she always did when thinking of youngsters. She so desperately wanted to be a mother and had so much to look forward to. Lightning snaked across the sky and she flinched in fear. Not long after, the big boom of thunder. She jumped and shuddered but kept walking hopeful the lightning would go away.

Suddenly, she could hear a noise. She halted on the hard grey surface, squinting and shielding her eyes from the light. Movement and wind pushed against her and the loudest boom noise she had ever heard. She cried out and tried to run away then became aware of something where the trees of the woods started. She tried to see through the rain what was happening, moving closer. She was very close before she realised there was a shelter with wheels pushed up against a tree with a hissing sound and a smell that made her nose wrinkle. Why was this little shelter with wheels banged into a tree? Did it crash land like she had a few hours ago into the tree? That made sense to her. Was there a human in this little shelter with wheels?

Cautiously, she crept up close to the little shelter with wheels and peered through the glass. She remembered glass from the laboratory where she had been locked up. A female human was lying very still and not moving, and Viktoria was unable to touch her due to the glass in the way. She banged on the glass with her hands remembering the glass at the laboratory had broken, allowing her to walk through. She knew now that she could bang this glass and break it, but did she want to do that?

She looked in at the female human and wondered what to do. Why was the female human not moving? Flashback came to her mind when she fell from the sky and broke her wing and woke to find other hunters around her. Maybe it was similar and this female human would wake up as well. She banged lightly on the glass, but nothing happened. She banged again and the female human moved slightly. Viktoria jumped back, unsure what to do.

After a few minutes of thinking, she moved forward and hit the glass firmly. The glass shattered and collapsed everywhere. She saw the female human move again just slightly and now she could smell the odours from inside the little shelter with wheels. She could smell the human, other strange smells and some type of food. On the island there were times when she had been so starving that she had eaten humans. She shuddered as she remembered those times. She may be hungry now, but she was not starving like she had been on the island. That was a different type of hunger.

Still, she could smell food and leaned in through the broken glass to try to identify where the food smell was coming from. Her stomach growled at the thought of food and on the floor, she could see a black object that felt soft when she touched it. The food smell was inside this object. She lifted the object and items fell to the floor. She sensed the female human moving and groaning. Viktoria had to lean right over the female human to reach the items on the floor on the other side. She touched several objects squeezing them with her fingers and lifted them to her nose to smell them. She found an apple and joyously bit down and devoured in in seconds. It wasn't enough and she frantically groped through the items on the floor looking for more food items.

A piercing shriek shocked her and in fright, she threw her head up, hitting the roof. She roared in fright and pulled back out of the glass. Stepping back, she realised the female human was awake now and screaming, frightened by Viktoria leaning across her. Now she understood why the female human was upset, she felt calm and lifted her hand up to settle the female human. She wasn't sure how to communicate with her or how to reassure her, making noises as she would to reassure a youngster. The female human kept screaming. Frustrated, Viktoria stepped back and after a few minutes she walked away and back down the hard grey surface searching for shelter.

Chapter 43
The Social Media

VIKTORIA CAUSES CAR CRASH – ASSAULTS WOMAN

Clint read the headline and sucked in his breath. Frantically, he scanned the newspaper item looking for more information. He was annoyed he had not been contacted as soon as the authorities realised they were dealing with Viktoria. According to the article, a woman had been driving home from a long trip interstate and a storm hit just after dark. She found it difficult to see due to the heavy rain when suddenly, Viktoria materialised on the road in front of her. She swerved and crashed into a tree and when she gained consciousness, the creature was leaning through a broken window rummaging around the car. She screamed and the creature left.

Clint sighed and closed the newspaper. He signalled for the waitress to bring him another coffee. He was at a typical breakfast venue, an anonymous roadhouse in the middle of nowhere, serving bacon, eggs and hash browns with strong coffee which helped his hangover. Scratching his two-week old beard, he pondered how to handle this new situation. Should he jump up and down and demand to be kept in the loop, or should he just keep quiet and head to where the latest incident had happened? He didn't feel he had the authority to be demanding anymore. Somehow, his months of sleeping rough and eating poorly had taken a toll on his state of worth. The obsession with finding Viktoria did not wane but he no longer wished to negotiate or communicate with the police or government authorities. He was becoming a committed nomad.

Checking his phone, he already knew that social media was on to the Viktoria story. There was now a dedicated Facebook page for Viktoria and people were encouraged to send in information on her where-abouts and their photos of sightings. Every day he spent time scanning through the photos and trying to identify which were real and which were generated by artificial intelligence. It was not always simple to identify the difference. There was an Instagram account by someone claiming to be following Viktoria which Clint found extremely unlikely. Hashtags containing Viktoria were often trending on popular platforms and most of the younger generation were excited about Viktoria and were out in force trying to obtain that exclusive photo of her that would make them famous. They were pro-Viktoria or team-Viktoria, and he heard rumours of food being left out for her at night. Viktoria-watchers with binoculars scanned the skies day and night, and even the authori-ties were under fire from the pro-Viktoria public. If the authorities did ever shot Viktoria, he guessed there would be riots.

The older generation were afraid, not at all sympathetic and had their hands on their shot guns ready to take her out if the opportunity presented. Word was that some people were laying traps for her in their barns or old buildings and there were neighbourhoods taking turns guarding their area with guns in hand.

Clint had come to the attention of the media and the public knew that a scientist was on her trail though no one knew of the tracking device. He was very careful to hide any evidence of the device every time he left the car. He'd been recognised at a few diners and even been asked for his autograph, but most people were curious and wanted details about Viktoria.

He wondered about Viktoria in the wild storm the night before and pictured her out there - wet and cold, looking for shelter. Sure that she would have found a safe place out of the rain, he was saddened to read the papers the next morning and discover she had been out in the rain on a road in the middle of nowhere.

He retrieved a local map from the glove compartment and worked out where the car accident had happened. Tracing his finger along the direction she was heading, he estimated she would be hitting a small town not far away. Usually dodge towns, he just knew, she would be seeking food and shelter.

He finished his coffee, left money on the plate and headed out to his vehicle. He felt confident that he could catch up with her in this town.

Chapter 44
The Boy

Viktoria stood motionless, staring through the glass at the family in the shelter. The rain was still falling heavily and dripped down her face, making it difficult to see clearly. She had been shivering for so long she felt she would never be warm again and approached the first shelter she came to attracted to, the lights. She had never seen inside one of these shelters where the humans lived. As she edged her way to the side of the building, she could hear noises coming from inside. Voices, laughter and a clinking noise. Peering through the glass, she saw a male sitting in a large chair and a young male human on the floor playing with little colourful objects. They looked warm and happy and well-fed. Viktoria felt so envious watching this human family. She watched for a few minutes and then slowly turned away.

Next to the shelter stood a smaller shelter and the door was open. She walked through hoping she would find a place to rest. A shelter with wheels sat in the building but it was sleeping and there were no humans in it. She walked around the front of the shelter with wheels and saw in the corner, blankets of soft material. She lay down on the soft material and wrapped it around her, desperate for warmth. Within minutes, she was asleep.

Her eyes fluttered open slowly. Where was she? Daylight shone through the open door and she could hear a noise. She had slept past dawn again which meant humans would be up and about. Carefully, she sat up aware of the bruises and scratches from her crash landing the night before. What was the noise?

Then she saw him, a young male human standing at the open door watching her. He was talking in a quiet voice. She looked at him wishing she could understand. Was he afraid? Was he happy? What was he saying to her? He didn't move but held his hand out and kept talking in a quiet voice. The material on his chest was a very bright colour and almost hurt Viktoria's eyes. She didn't feel afraid of this little male human as he didn't look like he wanted to hurt her. He pulled something out of his pocket which made a strange noise as he fiddled with it with his hands. She could suddenly smell food and leaned forward, uttering little grunting sounds. He walked forward slowly, bent down and placed the food item on the ground near her, then stepped back. Viktoria put her hand out and took the food item gulping it down with one swallow.

The young male human talked again and then slowly moved out of the open door. Viktoria moved out of the soft material she had been lying in and sat up. She stretched her limbs and scanned her body for injuries. She felt well enough to continue the journey today and was pleased the rain had stopped and she could see sun through the doorway. She wondered where the young male human had gone and hoped he would bring back more food.

Before long, he was back and she could smell he had brought food. He placed the food at her feet and sat back in a crouch, watching her eat. Fruit, half a cooked chicken and soft food items she had tasted a few times before that the humans liked. It was not enough but she was so pleased to have something to eat.

After a few minutes, he stood up and left, closing the door behind him. Viktoria sat in the soft material, stunned. She had not expected him to close the door and wondered how she would get out now? She walked around the building examining the walls and door and saw this was a shelter that made a lot of noise when you touched the walls. If she tried to force her way out, the noise would attract humans. That was not what she wanted to happen, so she waited for the young male human to come back and open the door.

Chapter 45
The Secret

Ryan could not wait to tell his friends what was going on at his house. They would not believe it. He could hardly believe it himself. He had Viktoria in his garage. How exciting was that? He would be the star of the neighbourhood once this news got out. He would be the star at school. He would be famous, maybe even on television! How lucky could one boy be?

He had gone out to the garage just after breakfast planning to ride his bike to Jay's house. They had organised to spend Saturday morning making bike jumps in the park near Jay's house. Once he saw Viktoria, his plans changed. He knew straight away who she was, having seen a video of her on the news. Everyone was talking about her and the whole world was looking for her, but he was the one who had Viktoria.

She did look a bit scary, but he knew she wouldn't hurt him. It was just something he knew. She smelled bad, like a wet dog and needed a good shower and some deodorant. Maybe he could keep her forever, like a pet. His parents would find out sooner or later. Would they let him keep her? Should he tell them? He shook his head. Not yet. She would be his secret for now, except for Jay and Terry and Ken. He had to tell them. They were his best friends and how could you keep a secret from your best friends? He would be such a hero.

His mother caught him in the kitchen rummaging around in the refrigerator looking for food.

"Hey, didn't you just have breakfast and take a muesli bar with you?" she asked in her stern mother voice.

"Yes, but I'm really hungry," he answered, stuffing whatever he could find in his pockets.

He pocketed a few cookies, some bread and when she left the room, the rest of the cooked chicken from the refrigerator plus an apple and banana from the fruit basket. Filling his pockets, he ran back out to the garage to feed his new pet. He was so thrilled to see her eat the food and told her of his plans for her and how they could be great friends. He didn't know if she understood or not, but he hoped she did. He shut the door as he left, not wanting her to leave or others to find her. It was Saturday morning and he didn't think his dad planned to go out. Luckily, because if his dad went in the garage to get his SUV then he would see her. He couldn't hide Viktoria from his dad forever and they would need to find another place for her. Maybe she could stay in his bedroom.

He raced to Jay's house in a great state of excitement. Within an hour, he had confided his secret to Jay, Terry and Ken. They didn't believe him and wanted him to prove it. He smiled to himself. Wait until they saw her. They would never doubt him again. Ryan couldn't wait to see their faces when they saw Viktoria. He excitedly brought them back to his house, swearing them to secrecy.

Ryan hesitated before he opened the garage door. He couldn't hear his parents, so assumed they were busy in the house. He looked at his friends and took on a serious tone.

"Now don't be afraid. She does look scary but just keep quiet and walk slowly," he instructed.

Slowly, he opened the door and the four of them slipped inside with Ryan closing the door behind them. The inside of the garage was dark until their eyes adjusted. Viktoria was standing on the other side of the SUV, standing up and still, watching the boys. He heard a few of his friends gasp when they saw her.

"See, I told you I was telling the truth," Ryan said.

The boys stared at the vision in front of them before Ken made a strange noise and wet his pants. Urine splashed down his leg and formed a puddle on the concrete. The other friends did not even notice.

"She won't hurt you," Ryan repeated as he stepped closer to Viktoria. His friends stayed back.

"Do you have any food on you?" he asked them. No one answered.

"Guys. Do you have any food on you?" he asked again, firmer.

Jay looked at Ryan and pulled a sandwich out of his pocket.

"Put in on the ground in front of her," Ryan instructed.

"No, you do it," Jay responded, not wishing to get any closer.

Ryan took the sandwich, removed the clingwrap, and placed the sandwich on the ground in front of Viktoria. She stepped forward and picked up the sandwich, eating it quickly.

Again, Ryan heard his friends gasp.

"She sure is hungry," said Terry.

Ken couldn't contain himself any longer. "I have to go home now," he said quickly and turned, opening the door and ran off down the street.

The other boys watched him go, shrugged their shoulders and turned their attention back to Viktoria.

"Does she understand what you say?" asked Terry.

"I don't know but I talk to her anyway," Ryan replied.

His friends were full of questions for him, and he was feeling ten-foot-tall as he answered them, the expert on Viktoria.

"Are you going to tell your parents?" Jay asked.

Ryan thought for a moment. "I will have to because they'll find her. I hope I can keep her," he answered.

The boys left, gently closing the door behind them. The three of them decided to hang out at Ryan's house for the day so they could keep an eye on Ryan's parents and to keep peeking in the garage at Viktoria. They took food from the kitchen a few times when Ryan's mother wasn't looking and took it out to her.

As the afternoon ended, Ryan's mother called him in and told the other boys to go home. Reluctantly, Ryan came in for dinner. He watched his mother put the left-over casserole in the fridge and decided to take it later for Viktoria. He found it increasingly difficult not to tell his parents about the surprise in the garage. He was bursting to say something. They would be surprised, but they would be proud that he had captured Viktoria and was caring for her.

"Dad. If I wanted a pet, could I have one?" he asked over dinner.

His father frowned. "Well, you've had a few pets before and you haven't looked after them. Look at Nino the rabbit and Fluffer the hamster. We had to find another home for them because you didn't look after them."

"But I'm older now. I would look after a pet now," he answered, confidently.

"Are you after a puppy?" his mother asked.

Ryan smiled. "I was thinking of something bigger than that."

"Bigger?" asked his mother. "No ponies, goats, cows, sheep or any dog larger than a Labrador."

Ryan sighed and sat down. Hmmm, that put Viktoria out of the question but maybe after they saw her, they would change their mind.

After his bath and snuggled into bed, he was determined to wait until his parents were relaxed and watching a Saturday night movie with a bottle of red wine, and then he would sneak into the kitchen, steal food and go see Viktoria. She must be hungry again by now. He could hear his parents moving around the house for ages. Would they never settle down and be quiet?

The house phone rang and he hoped he wouldn't fall asleep before he could carry out his mission. He could feel his eyes drooping. Don't fall asleep. Eyes drooping again. Don't fall asleep.

Suddenly, the light in his room was switched on and his parents were standing in the doorway. Ryan blinked away the sleepiness and tried to focus on them. They both had their serious and angry parent faces on.

"Ryan," his father spoke. "That was Ken's father on the phone. You've been telling stories and scared Ken badly. He's too scared to go to sleep tonight."

Ryan looked at his father, not sure what to say next.

"Ken says you've been telling your friends you have a monster in the garage and it's your pet."

He glared at Ryan, waiting for a response. Ryan couldn't work out what response to give. He waited for what his father would say next.

"Ken says you showed them the monster." This sentence was spoken in a loud and grumpy voice. "Ryan. What's going on? Did you tell them you have a monster as a pet?"

A lot of different excuses came to mind, but he discounted them and decided to tell the truth.

"Yes. I have Viktoria." He looked up at his parents to see their reaction, but they just stared at him. He jumped out of bed, voice raised in excitement. "You know, Viktoria. From the news."

His mother spoke. "Ryan. Are you saying that you have that prehistoric animal and it's your pet?" she asked and he could see her eyebrows go high like they did when he was in trouble.

"Yes. She's in the garage."

His father sounded angry. "That's enough. It's really cruel of you to scare your friends like that. I expected more from you. Why would you tell stories and scare people?"

"It's true, Dad. I have Viktoria in the garage. I have been taking her food and she slept in the pile of sleeping bags last night."

His parents looked at each other. Ryan wasn't sure what the silent signal meant, but he was pretty sure he was in deep trouble now. Damn Ken. It was supposed to be a secret.

"Ryan, I'm going to go out to the garage and then I'm going to come back in here. When I don't find anything out there, you will be punished. It will be extra chores for a month and no playing with your friends."

Ryan sighed. "Yes, but can I come with you?"

"No!" His father said with a finality and left the room while his mother stayed at the door staring at him.

"Really Ryan, I'm very disappointed in you," she said.

Ryan didn't answer. He knew they would soon realise he had told the truth. The minutes stretched in silence. Ryan waited. How long did it take to walk out to the garage? His mother stayed at the door watching him.

Suddenly, there was the sound of the side door opening and closing, and the sound of footsteps racing through the house. His mother turned and left the room.

"John, what is it? What's out there?"

Ryan could hear his father mumbling and his mother repeatedly asking what was wrong. He tiptoed out of his room and down the hallway. He could hear his father on the phone and he was sure he was calling 911. That was not good. The police would come and they would take Viktoria away. He couldn't let that happen.

Quietly, he sneaked out of the house and to the garage.

Chapter 46
The Dart

Viktoria had been settling into the soft material for another night in the little shelter when the door suddenly opened. In fright, she jumped to her feet and found herself staring into the eyes of the human father. Seconds ticked by as their eyes locked before he closed the door and left.

After a few minutes, the young male human entered and she could tell something was wrong as his breathing was rapid and movements, fast. She didn't know what was wrong but the hair on the back of her neck stood on end and she tensed, waiting for something to happen. He talked in a fast voice and she wished she understood. He opened the door and was telling her something in his fast voice.

"GO!"

She recognised that word. She had heard that word before when she escaped from the facility. The human mother had told her to 'GO'. She understood now that the young male human was telling her to go through the door and escape.

She made her way toward the door when the human father appeared, blocking the escape. He had a long item in his hands, and she remembered seeing other humans with this long item previously. It made a big bang noise that hurt her ears and she knew to be afraid of this long item.

The human father spoke to the young male human and the young male human yelled back in anger. The father spoke again and the young male human answered in anger. The father lifted the long item and pointed it at her. She drew in her breath and raced to the far side of the shelter. There was nowhere to run or hide so she turned to face the human father, unsure what to do.

Before she realised what was happening, the young male human raced up to her and wrapped his arms around her. She sucked in her breath with the shock of the action and held still. The young male human's arms reached just below her waist and he held tight with his face against her skin. She looked down at him, at the top of his head and then looked across at the father. The father had a complete look of horror on his face and was calling to the young male human. The young male human ignored his father and continued to hold on to her with all his might.

She heard the loud, blaring sirens as they approached, and had heard them before, remembering bright, flashing lights. There was a screeching noise and she could hear lots of shelters with wheels arrive outside, along with voices, yelling, and a clicking sound the humans did with the long item. They were coming for her. She knew it and she had nowhere to run. She couldn't even try to escape with the young male human holding on. Would they hurt the young male human? She didn't know. Should she take the young male human with her?

The human father stepped back, and other human faces appeared in the door looking in at her. She could see the long items in their hands. There were lots of voices and she knew the father's voice was worried and afraid. A different human stepped into the shelter and aimed his long item at her. The young male human looked over at the different human and yelled a sound, holding tighter to her. Without thinking, she placed her arms around the young male human's shoulders to protect him. He felt warm and soft. She patted his head and felt his hair, so smooth, so soft.

A few more humans entered the door, all with long items in their hands. One of them was calling to the young male human and he replied but didn't let go of her. The stalemate dragged on as they remained in this position, the humans with their long items pointed at her, and she, with the young male human in her arms. She heard more noises and voices.

Suddenly, at the door was a human she recognised. It was the male human from the facility where they had locked her up. She had spent many hours in this human's company, and knew his voice, his walk and his mannerisms. He wouldn't harm her and she felt more relaxed. He stepped in through the door and the other humans moved aside to let him through. He also pointed a long item at her, and this threw her off-guard. Did he want to hurt her too?

She held the young male human and bent her head down to smell his hair.

BANG!

Something hit the wall behind her. She jumped and held her breath, glancing back at the wall. On the ground was a strange object with a pointed end. She had no idea what it was, but it had come out of the long item and was supposed to hit her. She worried about the young male human, that they were trying to hurt him. She turned her body to the left to shield him from the humans. The human was fiddling with the long item, getting ready to aim. Again, she bent her head down to smell the young male human's hair which smelled a sweet fragrance. She gave a little shushing sound to tell the young male human that he would be safe and she would look after him.

BANG!

A sharp pain hit her right shoulder. She cried out and let go of the young male human to pull out the object stuck in her shoulder. A trickle of blood ran down her shoulder. She pulled out the object and threw it across the building to get it as far away from her as she could.

The young male human cried out but still held on to her. He was crying now, sobbing and she could feel his wet face. She placed her arms around him again and shushed him, twittering into his hair. The humans at the door didn't move. What were they waiting for? Would they aim another object at her? She knew she had no place to hide and couldn't stop them, so she waited. The young male human kept crying and talking.

A strange sensation washed through her body and she remembered this feeling from when the humans captured her on the island and the same feeling when she was in the facility. She knew she was about to fall asleep. She didn't want to land on the young male human and hurt him, so she loosened her hold on him and slowly sank to the floor, leaning her head back against the wall. She was aware of the young male human throwing his arms around her neck and holding her tight. She twittered again and then all was black.

Chapter 47
The Breakout

Clint watched Viktoria slump to the floor and close her eyes. This should be a time of elation as she had finally been recaptured, and he would be able to continue his research back at the facility. Why did he feel so guilty, then? Why did he feel he had betrayed Viktoria. It was the strangest feeling.

He watched the little boy throw his arms around Viktoria's neck, and saw her eyes flutter open and heard the soft murmuring noises she made to him. Anyone in the garage could have no doubt that Viktoria tried to protect the boy from the police and the guns. She was gentle and tender with him and would not harm him. The boy's parents had been paralysed with terror tonight and he wondered if it was the age of the boy that brought out Viktoria's maternal instinct.

The boy was crying and Viktoria was now sedated. He cautioned the other police to wait while he felt the pulse in her wrist. He indicated that she was out cold and the police moved in. He could hear the mother crying out for Ryan as a policeman forcibly pulled the child from Viktoria's neck and carried him over to his waiting parents. The mother was sobbing and kissing the boy. The father looked incredibly relieved.

It soon became apparent there was an issue with authority and who had it. The police chief insisted Viktoria come with them and be placed in lock-up which he was confident was safe and strong enough to hold her. Clint didn't have a problem with that as a temporary holding area, but it irked him that the police chief was pushy and intent on asserting authority over the doctor. Clint planned to arrange a secure vehicle from the facility to pick up Viktoria from lock-up as soon as possible.

He informed the police that the tranquiliser may only work for thirty minutes or so. It was the same dose they had used on the island, but she was carrying more weight now than she had been then so the dose may wear off faster. He suggested they transport her to lock-up as quickly as possible. Two police officers took one of Viktoria's arm each and two took a leg each and they lifted her up. The roller door was opened for ease of carrying her straight out to the waiting van rather than fit through the small side door.

"Phew. She does smell," said one officer, wrinkling his nose.

"Not your type, eh?" joked another.

The jokes quickly dried up when they realised she could wake up while they were carrying her. Each man breathed a sigh of relief when they reached the van, and the doors were locked behind her. Clint hoped she wouldn't wake up before arriving at lock-up. Although the van looked solid and safe, he had seen her break out of a supposedly secure facility, so he knew what she was capable of. He decided to follow the van just to be on the safe side.

Already on the radio, the news station was reporting that Viktoria had been captured, the fastest grape vine he had ever heard of. The media would be all over this house and family before morning and the young boy, Ryan, would be famous. He made a note to regularly communicate with Ryan, send him photos of Viktoria and news.

As he followed the van, Clint phoned Bill.

"Bill, we got her!" he announced when the phone was answered.

Bill's excitement echoed through the phone, and arrangements were made for a secure vehicle to leave the facility immediately for the retrieval of Viktoria. Clint smiled as he hung up the phone. Bill's excitement was contagious and he started feeling the excitement that Viktoria had been caught again. So much research left and so much to learn.

He had been driving behind the van for ten minutes and was drifting off in his little fantasy of researching the secrets Viktoria had to offer; setting up a fund to raise money and sending a team to Northern Africa to try and locate other members of her species. If they could locate a male, that would be the ultimate dream for a scientist such as Clint.

Viktoria could fulfil her need to be a mother and they could breed offspring.

Stopped at a red light with Clint in his little dream state, he realised he could see Viktoria's face through the back window of the van.

WHAT?

She was no longer asleep and in the dark of the night, her face looked back at him, lit up from the van's interior light. He could tell by her movements she was crashing against the back doors. He slammed his fist on the steering wheel and honked the horn. It seemed pointless as Clint knew the driver of the van would have felt the crashes as Viktoria slammed against the doors. He'd probably wet his pants in fright.

SLAM!

SLAM!

It was only a matter of time. What should he do? He was sitting in his seat staring and not believing this was happening. Did he have any tranquiliser darts left? Should he find them and try to tranquilise her again?

Before he'd had a chance to put his hand on the tranquiliser gun, the van door slammed open. He had suggested this possibility but didn't expect it to happen. One door remained closed and the other slammed back. Viktoria stood, staring straight at him. In a flash, she jumped and landed on the hood of his car. The shock took his breath away and he was immobilised by the sheer suddenness of it. For a moment, he could see her looking through the windshield at him and then, she was gone, off into the sky.

Quickly, he scrambled to open the car door and stepped out to watch her fly off. She was frantically flapping as fast as she could, to increase her height and speed. Clint guessed she was concerned about being shot or tranquilised again. He stood and watched until there was nothing left to see and she had disappeared into the night sky. He turned and saw the two police officers were doing the same thing, staring up into the dark.

He smiled weakly at them and climbed back in his car, staring at the steering wheel. He was completely dumbfounded and for the first time in his life, had a blank mind. Tears threatened to spill and he fought to keep them at bay. The phone rang and absently, he answered. Bill's voice rambled with plans for Viktoria. Clint stopped him mid-speech.

"Bill ... we lost her."

Chapter 48
The Shot

It was close to Jacksonville in Florida when Clint heard via the car radio, there was a commotion going on at a small town called Becker. The news reported that a creature believed to be Viktoria had been captured in a barn and people were warned to stay away. Clint groaned, aware that this warning would attract every person within a fifty-mile radius to come along and watch the spectacle.

Clint called Bill, asking him to obtain details including where the barn was. Meanwhile, he sped up the car and headed for Becker. In recent weeks, Viktoria had managed to increase the large head start on Clint and he had been unable to make up the distance. He was at least twenty miles behind her all the time. It hadn't mattered when they were inland, but now they were getting closer to the coast. He had to catch up soon or she would have left, across the North Atlantic Ocean and he would never see her again.

Bill rang back with more information. Locals had locked Viktoria in a barn after a farmer had become alarmed by his restless chickens and barking dogs. He saw Viktoria in the rafters of his barn and locked and padlocked the doors. Now, there were police everywhere and the military were involved. Bill had let them know Clint would be there shortly and had pleaded with them to wait for his arrival.

When Clint arrived, the police were armed and ready for battle and he could see military personnel and a black helicopter sitting neatly behind the vehicles. His pleading to allow him to tranquilise her fell on deaf ears and he was curtly reminded how the last tranquiliser episode had turned out a few weeks earlier. The authorities meant business this time and were determined to shoot to kill.

Clint could hear Viktoria crashing on the barn door and knew she could easily break out. It was only a matter of time. Could she fly away before being shot? Probably not.

CRASH!

The barn door rattled. All rifles were aimed at the door.

CRASH!

The door rattled again. Then, there was silence and everyone froze and waited. Minutes and minutes ticked by slowly, and Clint could see the frustration on the chief's face.

"LOU," he yelled out to one of the troopers. "Go take that padlock off the door."

Even from where Clint was standing, he could see Lou's face turn ashen. The trooper approached the barn door gingerly. He opened the padlock and pulled the chain out. Relieved, he sprinted back to the line of vehicles. Everyone waited. Nothing happened.

"LOU, go open the door." the chief yelled out.

Lou gulped visibly and hesitantly walked over to the door. The door was a sliding one, so he grasped the handle and pulled the door to the right. He achieved it very fast and sprinted back to the vehicle before anything came out at him.

Nothing happened. A few more minutes ticked by.

"Alright boys. We have to go in there and finish this."

A group of police with rifles stepped forward. There were clicks and shuffles as everyone prepared their arms. Clint groaned and slumped to the ground next to his vehicle. He buried his face in his hands in anguish. This was out of his hands now.

The men made their way to the open barn door step-by-step, guns at the ready and aimed in front of them. Clint could see at least ten men in the posse. At the opening of the door, the chief cursed.

"Damn, it's dark. Can't see a thing."

The men walked into the barn and Clint waited for the rifle shots. The men knew that Viktoria liked to perch in the rafters, so guns were aimed high and a few straight ahead. Again, the chief spoke, "I can't see it. Can anyone see it?"

There were negative murmurs. Clint heard a familiar sound.
WHOOSH. WHOOSH. WHOOSH.

He looked up to see Viktoria exit the barn door flapping her wings frantically. Smart girl had hidden beside the door and let the men walk into the darkness of the barn, then slipped out the door behind them. She was already gaining momentum before they realised she had escaped.

He heard himself praying that she would get away.

"Please, please God. Please God."

A few men outside yelled in fright at the sudden sight of her. No one outside had their rifles primed and ready to fire as they'd expected the posse to be successful. There was a flurry of activity as men quickly remedied the situation.

The men inside the barn ran out cursing and aiming their rifles in the air. There was a volley of shots and Clint saw Viktoria flinch, as a shot hit her in mid-air. She continued her frantic wing flapping, and he hoped it was not a serious hit, holding his breath as she rose higher until she was out of gun range. He exhaled and realised he had been holding his breath.

"Right. We'll take it from here."

A commanding voice belonging to one of the military personnel called out and there was arguing where neither side was prepared to relinquish control. Finally, the chief bowed to pressure and the military climbed into the helicopter and with a whirring of blades, the helicopter rose and disappeared in the direction Viktoria had taken, followed by military vehicles.

Clint watched them leave, checked the bleep on his tracking device, then turned his vehicle to follow the trail Viktoria had taken.

Chapter 49
The Helicopter

Clint sped along the road keeping one eye on the helicopter and trucks ahead of him, and one on his monitoring device tracking Viktoria. He hoped she had a large enough head start and the helicopter wouldn't see her. It had taken close to fifteen minutes after Viktoria left, before the helicopter followed due to arguments over control. Clint hoped if they were relying on a visual only, they wouldn't see such a small target as Viktoria.

Another concern he was becoming aware of - Viktoria was flying straight into the town of Becker. She never flew into towns, and he wondered if she had accidentally done this in a panic and he could feel himself starting to panic.

He played with the frequency on his radio until he found the police band. Although the helicopter and trucks were military, they would be cooperating with the local police. He hoped he would be able to gain information by eavesdropping.

On the monitoring device he could see Viktoria had stopped somewhere. The little green blip on the monitor was not moving. He hoped this was not an ominous sign and she wasn't injured.

Ahead and to the right, he could still see the helicopter moving forward so they had not spotted her. When his vehicle seemed very close to where the green blip was, he slowed down to a crawl and opened his driver's side window. This was a residential area with tidy houses, backyards and parks, very suburban and not at all a location he would have expected Viktoria to stop.

Cruising along slowly, he saw her. She was perching on a fence rail in a children's playground. He wondered why she would have stopped here and then he realised she was touching her thigh repeatedly and looking down at it. He could see blood running down her leg. She had been shot in the thigh when escaping from the barn and had stopped to see how badly hurt she was.

He could hear the helicopter, but it was still a distance away. What should he do? Should he try to tranquilise her now? What if he missed and she flew off? What if he didn't miss and knocked her out? She was too heavy for him to lift into his vehicle, and then the military would claim her or kill her. He had no idea what to do as he sat in his car, watching her and contemplating a solution.

A dog barking furiously very close to where he was, startled him and then a woman screamed. He spun around and saw a woman with one hand holding a young child and the other hand holding a dog on a leash. They had been heading into the park and spied Viktoria sitting on the railing.

He leapt out of his car and ran toward them with his hand up.

"WAIT! It's alright. She won't hurt you."

The woman continued screaming and let go of the dog which bolted toward Viktoria, furiously barking. The woman clutched the child to her, backing up and still screaming.

Clint heard the helicopter and turned to see it heading toward them over the top of houses. The screaming and the noise of the helicopter brought other people out of their homes, and he could see movement and faces start to appear.

The helicopter hovered while the crew scanned the situation. The military trucks had not yet arrived. Clint spun around to look at Viktoria. She had stood and was balancing on the railing with her wings out and expanded but was not yet flapping them. What was she waiting for? Standing like that, she was wide open, a sitting target.

Clint knew the helicopter crew would not want to fire bullets with the woman and child and others within such close proximity. They would want Viktoria to fly off where they could get her in the open. He quickly ran back to his vehicle, rummaging around in the back seat to locate the rifle and tranquiliser. Perhaps, there would be an opportunity to tranquilise her and it had to be better than letting them shoot her.

As he scrambled to load the tranquiliser, he could see the helicopter creeping closer to Viktoria. It looked like they were hoping to spook her into flying off and away from this suburban area. She held her ground, watching the helicopter as it became nearer. He dropped the darts on the back floor of his vehicle.

"FUCK!" he screamed as he fumbled around to locate another.

Viktoria was staring intently at the men in the helicopter and Clint wondered if they were trying to get close enough so they could shoot her with one clean shot without risking the public. He could hear the distant sound of sirens and knew the cavalry was on the way. He could see one of the men in the helicopter with a rifle aimed at Viktoria. Clint drew in his breath, waiting for the fatal shot.

With frightening speed, Viktoria leaped to the ground and raced over toward the helicopter. She was so fast it caught everyone off guard, even the sniper who failed to fire. The pilot screamed in fright and the helicopter moved sharply up and to the right. Clint dropped the dart again and stood staring at what was unfolding in front of him.

Viktoria ran toward the open door of the helicopter where the sniper had lost his balance due to the sudden manoeuvre of the helicopter and toppled over backward. There were screams and yells of fright as the pilot quickly engaged the helicopter to ascend to the right to move away from her.

Viktoria engaged her wings, flapping them as she left the ground. As the helicopter moved up and right, Viktoria turned in an arc, heading away. A strange crunching noise sounded and sparks flew. Clint watched dumbfounded as he realised the helicopter had just hit power lines. He screamed out, his voice lost in the horrendous sound of whirring followed by an explosion. The helicopter nose-dived and the rotor blades broke off as they hit the ground, flinging off against a neighbouring fence, and then the helicopter burst into flame.

Clint sprinted over to the flaming wreckage to see if he could drag anyone to safety, but the fire was too fierce. He shielded his face with one arm and reached to touch the helicopter, but the flames beat him back. He could see some movement from within the cabin before it ceased and all he could see were flames. Reluctantly, he backed away and watched the flames, crying for the loss of lives.

Reaching his truck, he slid down to sit on the ground with his back against the vehicle. Tears ran down his face and he could feel burn on his skin from the flames. The military vehicles arrived and chaos ensued.

Looking away he could no longer see where Viktoria had gone, but he knew there was not much time left and he needed to know when she left the coast. Calming himself, he stood, climbed in his vehicle and drove off with eyes on his monitoring device.

Chapter 50
The Goodbye

Glancing in the rearview mirror, Clint saw his eyebrows were singed and his face was red from the fire. He was feeling traumatised by what had just happened, and that somehow, he should have prevented it, though he could not think how he could have. The pilot had panicked - a prehistoric monster charging at the helicopter was not covered in the pilot training curriculum. The sniper had not fired, perhaps caught off-guard and then off-balance. It was a tragic incident and Clint knew he would be having nightmares of the men burning in that helicopter for a long time to come.

Why had Viktoria charged at the helicopter? It was baffling and he wondered if the charging was how her species tried to frighten predators and enemies away. Extend to full height to intimidate and charge if all else failed.

Clint wiped tears away from his cheeks and decided he had cried many times since his involvement with Viktoria. He was passionate about his job and protecting her, and being passionate came with its downfalls. He really felt like a bourbon on the rocks right now. He could almost taste it.

What would he do once Viktoria was gone? She had taken up the best part of twelve months of his life, first at the facility and later, with tracking her. How could he go back to life in a laboratory or behind a desk? How could he go back to nothingness, when he had lived and breathed Viktoria for so long.

He pulled into the empty car park overlooking the beach at Fernandina Beach and stopped the car. Viktoria was perched on a horizontal rail staring out at the beach. She didn't even turn to see who was coming.

She knew. He stopped a short distance from her and watched her for a few minutes. It was late afternoon and she would only have a few hours left of daylight. That didn't matter to her as she could fly at night or in daylight.

Slowly, he opened his door and exited the vehicle, moving slowly so not to alarm her. She turned her head to look back at him and he noticed she looked down at his hands, no gun. She looked back at his face then turned back to gaze at the beach again. Slowly, he made his way toward her and stopped a little way to her left.

He could see the wound on her thigh and fortunately, it didn't look too bad. A grazing wound with no embedded bullet. It would still hurt considerably but she wouldn't have lost much blood. He could see a line down her leg where the blood had dried.

"I hope you find your family, Viktoria."

He spoke quietly and calmly, looking across at her. She turned and looked at him intently as if trying to understand what he was saying. He was pleased she was not afraid of him due to the tranquiliser incident. In her eyes, he saw intelligence, understanding, gentleness, longing and centuries of the history of her species. She could not be the last one. He could not accept that it ended with her. It would be so cruel for her to be the only one left in existence. Would she search forever and the search be fruitless? Would she end up a ghost flying over the earth on her mission?

"HOLD IT RIGHT THERE!"

A loud voice startled them and Clint spun around. Viktoria turned her head, her eyes wide from fright. Standing near Clint's vehicle was a tall, bearded man. He must have walked up quietly from the beach as neither of them heard him and there was no sign of a vehicle nearby.

With a sudden movement, he pulled a revolver out of the inner pocket of a denim jacket and pointed it at Viktoria. His hands were unsteady and his whole body was tense.

"WAIT!" Clint cried out. "Calm down. She won't harm you."

"Damn right it won't."

The bearded man waved the firearm in the air in a threatening manner still aiming at Viktoria and stepped a few paces closer. Viktoria glanced at Clint to gauge his reaction and then back at the stranger. She didn't understand what was happening but knew from the voices that it was not good.

Clint appealed to the stranger, holding his hands in the air in a surrender motion.

"Please. She just wants to leave the mainland. Please let her go."

The stranger aimed the firearm at Viktoria and squinted to focus, turning his head slightly for a better view.

"No, I don't think so. I bet there's a reward out for killing this thing."

The firearm clicked as he readied the gun to shoot. Viktoria heard the click and recognised what that sound meant. She inhaled sharply and grunted.

"There's no reward. Please let her go. PLEASE!" Clint pleaded with the stranger.

He saw the stranger's finger move on the trigger and he knew the man was about to fire the weapon. With a sudden thrust, he threw himself across the front of Viktoria, shielding her body with his own.

"NOOOOOOO!" he yelled.

BANG!

The gun fired, hitting Clint's right shoulder. The impact threw his right shoulder back and he landed heavily on the ground. Although aware he'd been hit, there was no pain yet. All he could think of was Viktoria. Would the stranger now shoot her? He struggled to get to his feet but kept falling back down.

Looking up, he could see the look of horror and terror on Viktoria's face. He glanced back at the stranger expecting him to be aiming at Viktoria. The stranger was frantically fumbling through his pockets. What was he doing? Looking for more bullets?

He'd had only one bullet and it had been discharged. He had not expected to miss the target. With resignation, the stranger looked up, realised he was out of luck. His face showed fear as he looked at Viktoria and the man he had just shot.

Viktoria was still sitting on the railing but had turned her body to look down at Clint. She was making a whimpering sound and Clint realised she was looking at the blood drenching the front of his shirt. He still couldn't feel pain, more of a numbness. Now he could see the stranger was not going to shoot Viktoria, he stopped his unsuccessful struggle to stand.

Viktoria looked across at the stranger, her face creased in an angry scowl. Clint could hear a low growling sound coming from the back of her throat. He hadn't heard her do this before. The growling became louder and fierce. The hair on the back of Clint's neck rose at the sound.

The stranger suddenly turned and fled, tossing the firearm as he ran. He bolted across the car park heading for the road ahead. Viktoria sprang from the railing; wings extended and ran after him. She was roaring as she raced after the man. Clint could not think of any other term for the noise she was making but an angry roar. She was fast even with a wounded thigh as she chased the man. He tripped and fell at one stage and in record time, was on his feet and running again. Clint realised that Viktoria was not trying to catch him because if that was her intention, she would have caught him quickly. She was scaring him away. Viktoria stopped and watched him run into the distance.

She walked back to where Clint lay on the ground. He was examining the wound and noted that there was no exit wound, so the bullet was lodged in there somewhere. He knew the bullet had not hit an artery or his lungs so he felt he would survive. It was bleeding heavily and the pain was starting to kick in. He held his hand against the wound, pressing as hard as he could to stem the flow of blood. He was aware that Viktoria had returned and was standing above him looking down. Her face showed concern.

"I'll be ok," he told her.

She squatted down on her haunches, looking at his wound, a frown on her face. Gently, she held out her hand touching the blood on his shoulder. She made little shushing noises and he remembered the sound she had made with the young boy, Ryan. She looked down and touched her thigh where the blood had dried on her skin. Clint realised she was making the connection that they were both injured in the same way.

She looked down at Clint and he could see her eyes widen, her attention drawn to sirens in the distance. The stranger had reached the road and summoned the authorities. He looked up at Viktoria.

"You have to go, Viktoria. Go find your family. Go make babies," he firmly told her.

She put her head slightly on the side as if trying to understand. He spoke louder and firmer.

"GO, Viktoria. GO!"

Her eyes widened and he knew she understood. She looked up and around. The sirens were getting closer.

"GO ... GO ... GO VIKTORIA!"

He yelled the words to her and she looked at him, making a twittering noise. Slowly, her wings extended and she started flapping them. They stared at each other and Clint felt they were truly communicating for the first time. Like the prehistoric creature that she was, she rose above him, all powerful, hypnotic, terrifying and beautiful. She appeared to hover for just a moment and then she was gone. He watched her until he could no longer see her.

He let his body fall back against the fence and lay, waiting for the police and medics. Tears streamed down his face, untouched. A million thoughts crossed his mind, including a suicidal one. What would he do now? Viktoria was gone. How could anything at work compare to having studied Viktoria? He didn't want to go back to the facility. He didn't even want to go back to a normal home life. He wasn't sure he even knew what normal was anymore. Viktoria had been his life's work, his inspiration and his great passion. What would he do?

Suddenly, he laughed and slapped his thigh. He knew what he was going to do with his future. Like a bolt of lightning had hit him on a clear day, he knew what his future would be. No more lab, no more desks, no more paperwork and no more triviality. He was going to continue tracking Viktoria. He wasn't ready to give up yet. He didn't want to capture her. He just wanted to study her, to research her and to discover if there were others like her. He knew his monitoring device only worked within a certain range but that was ok. He roughly knew where she was heading. He would go to Africa and continue to shadow her.

He would devote his life to her species and finding them.

Part Five - The Flock

L.J. Fox

Chapter 51
The Vessel

Viktoria knew she couldn't continue flying much longer. Night was falling and the sun seemed to sizzle as it touched the water in the distance. She couldn't remember how many nights she had been flying but it had been several. Her eyes were heavy and dry; her arms and wings ached from fatigue and the bullet wound on her thigh stung every time she flexed her muscles. It was no longer bleeding, but the newly grown-over skin tore open from time to time.

After leaving the coast, she had felt shock over the injury, the suddenness of it and the damage, but now she just looked forward to reaching land on the other side of the ocean and continuing her search for her own kind. After suffering a badly broken wing all those years ago, no other injury could ever compare to the pain and sense of impending doom, and being trapped on an island unable to fly.

At times, she was the recipient of a tail wind and all she needed to do was glide and save her energy. Unfortunately, they didn't always last or pushed her away from the direction she was heading. There had even been a storm that battered her with wind and rain for a few hours. That had been difficult and her thigh wound had been very painful during that time. How she hated rain and water! She shook her head remembering the most recent experience.

Hopeful of finding an occasional small pocket of land in the ocean as she had many years ago, kept her alert The flock she had been with at the time stopped at one of the tiny islands to rest for a few days. How she wished for one of those tiny islands now. She was hungry and thirsty but was no stranger to this, particularly hunger. She could fly for days without eating or drinking but falling asleep in the air or being unable to fly due to fatigue were death sentences.

The realisation hit her that she may not make it to the other side of the ocean. This was a terrifying thought, and she felt her heart sink. After struggling to exist for over one hundred years, she could not falter now and let death take her. She took a deep breath and shook her head to clear the fatigue. She must continue. She could not let those big thrashing fish get her. If she landed in the water, she would never be able to take off again, unable to get high enough to flap her wings. The water was a certain death.

A glitter caught her attention, and she turned her head to the right to see a huge vessel in the distance. With the setting sun, the outline of the vessel stood out and that meant there were humans inside. Without hesitation, she turned and headed toward the vessel. This was the closest thing to a potential rest stop that she had seen in days. As she neared the vessel, she could see there was a tall pole on the top, like a tree trunk. No humans were on the top so she guessed they must be inside the vessel as night was approaching.

She circled the vessel, checking it from all angles and nothing seemed concerning or frightening. Slowly, she flew down to a suitable perch at the top of the tall pole. She couldn't believe her luck. She landed, gripped the perch with her talons and after stretching her wings, retracted them neatly behind her, relaxed her muscles, took a few deep breaths and fell into a deep sleep. Sleeping sitting vertical on a perch was the most natural thing in the world to her.

When she opened her eyes, dawn was breaking. She could feel the tingle of light on her skin. The ocean was still dark and black, and the vessel was silent and empty of humans. She stretched her muscles, noting how sore and weary they were. Slowly, she opened out her wings, flexing them and stretching.

Below her in the vessel, she could hear noises and guessed the humans were awake now and ready to come outside. Time for her to go. Slowly, she started flapping her wings and with a sudden leap, jumped from the perch and flew onward and upward, seeking the direction she had been following.

The crewman stopped the video on his phone and continued staring at the speck in the distance as it became further away. He couldn't believe what he had just seen.

Chapter 52
The Flock

"**F**UCK! FUCK, FUCK IT!"

The nurse raced into the hospital room at the sound of the loud swearing she could hear down the corridor, just in time to prevent her patient from trying to get out of bed. He was sitting on the side of the bed with legs on the ground and was fighting with his IV drip which had tangled around his arm in a sling.

"Dr Marne," she said sternly. "What on earth are you doing?"

Clint scowled at her as he continued to disengage himself from the IV drip.

"I'm leaving. I have to go. I have things to do, places to be ..."

The nurse put her hand out and pulled his hand away from the drip.

"You are not going anywhere. In case you've forgotten, you were shot only three days ago. You've lost blood and still need surgery to repair the damage."

As she spoke, her voice softened and she gently guided him back into bed, placing the covers over him. She checked the drip was still working and checked his bandages for bleeding. She noted an iPad lying on the bedside cabinet with the cover open so guessed he had seen something on the iPad which had upset him.

"Now, I want you to rest. Do I need to take this tablet away from you?"

She spoke like a stern schoolteacher who had caught a schoolboy being naughty.

"NO. I'll stay in bed. Promise." He smiled at her and she left the room.

Clint sighed. Damn being shot. Damn being in hospital. Damn. Damn. Damn. Viktoria was getting further and further away. With each day that passed, the chances of finding her again decreased. He had just watched a video on YouTube and TikTok using the hashtag #findViktoria, of Viktoria perched high up on the mast of a large container ship. The sun was rising and she was silhouetted against the dawning sky. In the footage, she stretched her wings out, flapped them and flew away into the distance. One of the crew had seen her and filmed it though it. Clint was pleased she was ok and had found somewhere to rest, but it killed him that he was not out there following her.

It would be some time before he would be able to go after her. Who knew how far away she could be by then? There had been considerable damage to the shoulder joint from the bullet, and the bone had been smashed. The surgeons had operated on him when he first arrived at the hospital, removing fragments of shell and bone, plus stopped the bleeding. Now, he was scheduled for surgery next week to repair the joint with either a replacement or pins. With recovery and rehabilitation, it could be months until he was in a fit state to re-commence his search for Viktoria. Maybe he would never find her and she was gone forever. The thought filled him with depression. Would his entire life be filled with chasing a ghost?

His boss, Bill, had been on the phone with him a couple of times in the last few days. He wanted Clint medically flown to a hospital near the facility, but Clint refused. He wanted to stay in Florida where Viktoria had left the country. From Florida, he could jump on a plane and head across the ocean to follow the direction she had taken. Bill had assured him that they would track every sighting of Viktoria and when Clint was fit, he would have a trail to follow. This had calmed him and seemed logical but seeing her in that video footage had driven him crazy. Damn. He had been following her for so long now and felt she was safer with him tailing her as he could stop authorities from shooting her ... or try to. How would she fare on her own? There was nothing he could do about it, and he had no choice but to accept it and heal.

His phone rang on the bedside table and he picked it up.

"Dr Clint Marne," he answered.

Bill's excited voice yelled into the phone.

"You will never guess what?"

Clint could hear his accelerated breathing.

"WHAT? You found Viktoria?" He was starting to get excited, too.

"No. Better than that," Bill answered in a quieter, secretive voice.

"Better than that? What is better than that?" he asked, puzzled.

"YOU'VE CAPTURED HER?" he yelled.

"We found a whole flock!" Bill left his statement hang in the air.

The nurse had only left the room of Dr Clint Marne five minutes earlier, having calmed him down and convinced him to remain in bed. She was in the nurse's station checking on rosters when the loud swearing reached her again from down the corridor.

"FUCK! FUCK! FUCK IT!"

She headed back to the patient's room, knowing this was going to be one difficult patient.

Chapter 53
The Camp

Jacks threw another large stick on the campfire, and it flared for a few seconds. The night was dark with only one quarter of the moon visible, giving just a small amount of light. Jacks laughed at the story Arthur had just relayed. He certainly knew how to tell a good story, fully embellished and of course, he was always the hero.

She was out on the station in the middle of nowhere with the two station hands, Stewart and Arthur. Stewart was the senior and had been the overseer of the property's cattle for the past fifteen years, and Arthur was a younger indigenous man from the local town. Arthur had worked for the family for the past five years and was a comical storyteller.

"Oh Arthur, you are so full of shit," she said, laughing.

Arthur dissolved into giggles. He loved a good reaction from his storytelling which was half the fun. He reached for his guitar, the old, battered instrument caught the light from the fire and he gently strummed and hummed a soft tune.

Jacks sat back and closed her eyes. How perfect this was. Nothing around for thousands of hectares, big dark sky full of stars, a campfire and soft music. She relished these weekends when she had the opportunity to camp with the station hands in the middle of nowhere, ride horses and work with the cattle. The weekdays saw her living in an apartment in town while she studied at the university for a Bachelor of Agriculture and Land Management, but the weekends were for her enjoyment. She considered herself fortunate that her parents owned a large cattle station in outback Queensland. She had grown up here as her father had. She would be the third generation of Fosters to run the station. They had thousands of hectares and thousands of heads of cattle. During the weekdays, her father managed the station with the help of Stewart and Arthur, but the weekends were hers. Her father took time off and she was able to do what she loved.

Today, they had ridden out to the far west of the property and rounded up a herd of a hundred or so cattle. It was early spring and many cows had young calves on them. She loved this time of year, seeing the babies. This part of the station had small holding yards with a crush where they regularly yarded the cows for worming, branding, immunisation or tagging. They called this area, Cattle Yard Camp.

The cattle were currently in the larger of the yards waiting for worming and immunisation in the morning. She could hear their sound every now and again when a mother couldn't find her calf and called out. The old bull was in one of the smaller yards as he was also due to be immunised and wormed tomorrow.

This part of the station was beautiful with its red dirt, scattered trees and huge rocks and cliffs. Close by was a natural waterhole and the grass grew a little sweeter in this area which is why the cattle often visited here. Surprisingly, other parts of the property were very different from this including areas of dry plains, arid desert and even one part that looked tropical with palm trees and lush vegetation. The scenery was never dull on the station.

"Hey Jacks, you got a boyfriend yet?" asked Arthur, grinning. He loved teasing Jacks about boyfriends.

"Nope. No one will have me." She shrugged her shoulders. "What about you? Any girls interested?"

Arthur showed a big white toothy smile and stopped strumming the guitar, momentarily.

"They won't leave me alone. I got too many after me."

Stewart let out a "HAH" and threw a saddle bag at him. "That'll be the day."

"Shh. Guys."

Jacks signalled for them to be quiet and she sat up, turning her head to listen, sure she heard something. Arthur halted and the three of them listened intently. After a few minutes, they heard the cattle restless.

The three of them were experienced enough to know the difference between the noise that cattle make in general, and when the cattle are restless for a reason.

Jacks stood up slowly, looking around for where she had placed the shotgun. The light from the campfire captured concern on her face. On the station, the primary predators were wild dogs, dingoes and snakes. Wild dogs congregated in packs, having once been domestic dogs and turned feral, attacking calves or sick animals. They rarely touched the larger cows but sometimes chased them for sport. Wild dogs were a real problem for station owners and had less fear of humans.

Dingoes were unlikely to attack a calf when there were people around, but if starving, would kill a newborn calf. She would also not expect to see a snake at night-time. Snakes were cold-blooded and needed heat to survive. She pondered why the cattle were restless, and knew not to ignore gut feeling, and she had a strange feeling that something was wrong.

Another possibility was people creeping around looking to steal cattle, but that seemed unlikely as they would have seen the campfire. They would not be attempting to steal cattle with station hands camping next to yarded cattle.

Stewart and Arthur slowly rose to their feet as Jacks found her gun and stood still listening, every muscle tense and on alert. Stewart retrieved his gun and silently prepared to engage it. Arthur placed his guitar down on the ground and stood listening.

They heard the cows becoming more restless and more distressed with sounds of them calling and banging into the pipe fences. These were older cows who were familiar with pipe fences and being yarded. These cows would only crash into the fences if threatened or attacked.

The three looked at each other and stepped forward heading toward the yards, full alert. The yards were one hundred metres away and the path was dark once away from the campfire. All Jacks could make out were the dark silhouettes of the trees and bushes and the dark object of the yards.

The three of them were only fifty metres from the yards when they heard a calf bleating in panic, and the other cows crying out in fright. Jacks bolted toward the yards hoping she wouldn't fall over anything in the dark. She had no idea if Stewart and Arthur were behind her or not, but the urge to protect the cattle was so strong, she gave no thought to her own safety.

In the dark, she ran straight into the pipe fence, the pipe hitting her forehead. Her head jerked back and she fell backwards into the dirt. Shaking her head and blinking, she tried to jump back to her feet when she was aware of something standing above her. Dazed and with her forehead stinging, she looked up and standing at her feet was something she first thought was a man. Wondering how Arthur or Stewart had managed to get in front of her so fast, as her brain cleared, she realised it was not one of the station hands.

Despite the darkness, she could make out the man was naked as she could see male genitals, but something was not right with the picture. She couldn't see his face and his body was in silhouette, but she could see large wings out to the side of his body. These wings were flapping. She could feel the breeze from the beating wings touch her face and dirt filled her eyes and mouth. Briefly, she wondered if she was dreaming or had hit her head so hard that her brain was addled. Was she hallucinating? Had she hit her head so hard that she had died and this was an angel?

It never occurred to her to scream, not being the screaming type. Fascinated and awed by the sight, she stared in wonder at the strange sight above her. She didn't feel the man with wings wanted to hurt her and she didn't feel fear. Scrambling, she tried to move her feet under her to lift her body and get a better look.

BANG!

The sound of a gunshot startled her and she jumped. The man creature rose and flew into the dark night sky and disappeared. One minute he was there and then, he was gone. She jumped to her feet and could see Stewart and Arthur ten metres to her right with Stewart firing into the sky. When she looked up, she saw two male creatures flying and between them, a newborn calf. There was just enough moonlight for her to see the shapes of them in the air above. The calf was still calling for its mother.

The three of them stood silently and watched the incredible events happening above them. The sound of the calf crying became quieter as the creatures moved away into the night. There was nothing that could be done and nothing that could be said.

Chapter 54
The Meal

Viktoria's heart was racing when she realised she could glimpse land in the distance. Finally! She had known for a few hours that she was getting close as she had seen land birds and a few boats in the water below. She could smell the sweet scent of the flora from the land well before she could see it.

Her shoulders, back and wings ached and her eyes were dry and sore. She could feel a tinge of burn on her tanned skin from the sun beating down on her and she was so thirsty her lips had cracked and dried. This had been an arduous journey across the ocean, and she knew she couldn't have kept going for much longer. There was a long way to go to reach her own kind, but at least she would be on land where there would be water and food and not the fear of landing in the ocean.

As she neared the shore, she could see human shelters stretch into the distance which meant lots of humans. She never flew over humans and human shelters in the daylight, not wishing to be seen or being shot with those nasty objects that had injured her thigh. In this case, she had no choice. She was weary to the point of collapse and there was nowhere else to go. She would have to fly over these shelters until she could find a quiet place to rest.

Reaching the shore and flying well above the shelters, below she saw many shelters of different shapes and sizes, shelters with wheels, trees and lots of humans. No one seemed to notice her above them, which was a relief. She flew on realising that these human shelters seemed to go on forever. She had not realised how far she would have to go to reach the other side of them.

Odours reached her from below and she could detect a multitude of different aromas, but the overpowering one was the smell of food cooking. She was salivating and her stomach was growling. It had been many days since she had eaten or enjoyed a drink of water. With reluctance, her body demanded she eat and drink before she could rest. Looking across the horizon and hoping to see where the human shelters ended and there may be farm animals to hunt, but she could see nothing. The shelters stretched as far as she could see.

Unsure what to do, she flew lower and lower until she was flying just above the roof of the shelters and could see narrow strips of land between each shelter. Many had humans walking in them but there were empty strips. Where could she find food? Where could she find water?

A strong smell of food cooking hit her and it was from the shelter ahead, with steam rising from a small object on the roof. Slowing down, she landed on the roof. For a few minutes, she stood quietly, listening for any humans that may have seen her, her wings outstretched and ready to flee. Sensing no one around, she relaxed her body but kept her wings ready. Her balance felt strange and she tottered as she tried to walk. The muscles in her legs had not been used for many days and needed to loosen up.

After a few minutes of hearing and seeing nothing to indicate humans had noticed her, she relaxed and withdrew her wings. She walked over to the steam coming out of the roof and put her face near it, smelling. The steam was hot and she pulled her face back, smelling food but where was it?

She walked over the roof to the edge and looked down. There was a narrow strip of land but nothing there, no food or water. Feeling frustrated and desperate, she walked around to the next edge and looked down. Another narrow strip but this one had an object sitting there. She cocked her head, looking at the strange object. What was it? It was large, about as large as a shelter with wheels, but there were only little, tiny wheels. The top of it was ajar slightly and she could smell food within.

The delicious aroma of spoiled meat and rotted vegetables reached her and saliva ran down her chin.

Looking around, she couldn't see any humans, so she jumped down and landed next to the object. It was as tall as she was and the colour of grass. Placing her hands on the top she hoisted herself up and over the edge of the object, landing in a massive pile of mostly soft, noisy material. She could smell food all around her.

She tore into the noisy material and located small bits of food, recognising cooked chicken, raw chicken, cooked beef and fruit and vegetables. Many other foods she did not recognise but ate them anyway. She ripped and shredded, seeking every morsel of food she could find. Unfortunately, it was not enough food to satisfy her and she was still starving.

When she was confident she had exhausted all food in the object, she jumped out. Standing still and listening for humans, she heard a drip … drip sound. It was coming from a small object against the wall. She knew drip meant water, so she walked over to the small object on the wall and watched droplets of water drip and hit the ground, causing a small puddle. Dipping her finger in the puddle, she brought it to her mouth. Yes. It was water.

Placing her mouth under the object where drips were coming out, she sucked up the drips as they arrived, but it was not enough. She needed more drips. Scanning the little object, she couldn't work out where the water was coming from as there was no waterhole or stream nearby. With a moan of frustration, she struck the wall with her hand, but nothing happened. She thumped the wall again and this time her hand glanced off the little object. Something moved and suddenly, something was gushing all over her feet. She jumped back alarmed, then realising it was water, put her face under and drank and drank. The water ran over her face and down her body and it was the best feeling in the world. She lay down and rolled in the growing puddle, soothing her sunburned skin.

With a bang sound, a door opened in the shelter next to the gushing water. She stopped rolling and looked up to see a male human standing there dressed in white. He stood and stared at Viktoria with his mouth open. She used his moment of stunned belief to jump to her feet, quickly extend her wings and ran a few steps before taking off into the air. She flew up the narrow strip and up and over the shelters.

She needed a quiet place to rest now, but at least she knew where to find food and water.

Chapter 55
The Rock

"**A**re you guys ok?" asked Jacks, grabbing Arthur by the shoulder. Arthur turned to look at her, shocked by what he had seen, or barely seen. It was so dark they weren't sure they saw what they thought they saw. Stewart dropped the gun to the ground. It was dark so she couldn't see their faces clearly.

"We're ok," Stewart answered.

Arthur shook his head, trying to clear his mind.

"Holy shit! Did you see those things?"

"Come on guys. I want us to set up for tonight and then we can talk. I know it's dark, but I want to move our camp here next to the yard. Let's get the campfire started here. Nothing is coming back to get these calves tonight, not on my watch," she said, firmly.

"What about the horses?" asked Stewart, heading back to the camp to begin the move.

"Let's bring them closer to here as well," she answered. She didn't want the horses to panic, break their tether and abandon them here. She could see Arthur was a bit distressed, so she gave him instructions to keep him moving.

"Arthur, go collect the swags and bags and bring them back here."

"Yes, miss," he answered quietly and headed toward the former camp site.

It was not long before they were set up again and felt secure. Each had their shotguns next to them and knew there would be no sleep tonight. They discussed what each of them had seen and agreed they were not imagining things. They had all seen the same thing, dark or not.

"Jacks, are we heading for home in the morning?" asked Stewart. She thought he looked remarkably calm, but she knew him well and could hear the subtle shift in his voice. In his fifteen years on the station, he had seen many predators, but he'd never seen anything like this, none of them had.

Jacks shook her head.

"I've been thinking about that. I don't want to leave the cattle here. I'd rather herd them over to the east or near the house for now."

"Yes, good thinking," agreed Stewart.

"I've also been thinking about where those creatures might live. You know ... where they've come from, and it makes sense that they would be at Corner Rock. They didn't just appear out of the blue. They must live near here. At Corner Rock there's shelter, shade, water and it is only about one kilometre from here."

The two men were listening intently, and she could see the slight nod of agreement with what she had suggested.

"I'm going there in the morning to have a look."

"WHAT?" both voices responded.

"No way. You can't go."

"I'll be ok. I'll stay on horseback and have my gun with me. I'm not going right into Corner Rock. Just look from a distance and check it out. I need to know what we're up against."

Stewart looked at Arthur and a communication passed between them unseen.

"Then we'll come too," said Stewart, firmly.

"Yes. We'll come too," agreed Arthur.

"No. I'll be fine. I want you to immunise and worm the cattle while I'm gone. No point wasting them being in this yard. When I get back, we'll herd them and go home."

She looked at the two of them for agreement. Stewart looked doubtful and worried. Arthur was still shell-shocked but coping better than she thought he would. The rest of the night was quiet and uneventful, except for the occasional call from the cow looking for her calf.

Jacks headed off at first light after a coffee and making a sandwich for later. Her mare, Nelly, was always reluctant to leave the other horses but the mare begrudgingly left the camp, one ear flicked to the side listening for the other horses.

The countryside was beautiful at this time of the morning with the sun just rising. The dirt looked super red and the world appeared new and fresh. It made last night's events seem surreal and she almost felt silly heading to Corner Rock to chase a nightmare she'd experienced. In the clear light of day, it did feel foolish as if they had been under the influence of a drug that had brought on hallucinations. However, there was a calf missing this morning. She wished she had brought one of the station dogs with her. The dog would have alerted her to the predators before they managed to get the calf and possibly, the dog may have scared the predators off. However, then they would not have become aware of the creatures and she was glad they knew about them.

What if the creatures they had seen were not at Corner Rock? Where else would they have come from? All other possibilities seemed too far away. They had to be at Corner Rock. She was positive these predators were the same creature as the one she read of in the news. A creature had killed an Australian and the authorities captured the creature. When did that happen? Was it last year or the year before? Was this the same creature? She seemed to remember that creature had escaped. Could one of these creatures be that one? No. Surely, Australia was too far away from where the creature had escaped from for it to be the same one.

She could see Corner Rock ahead of her. It had been named Corner Rock by her grandfather as the rock formation was at a 90-degree right angle like a corner. Growing up, Corner Rock had always been their own mini-sized Kings Canyon. A natural spring flowed at the foot of the rocks with grass and trees scattered around the little valley. Many of the cows came to Corner Rock to have their calves or to shelter from storms. The right angle of the rocks gave them shelter.

Jacks did feel anxious about getting too close to these creatures, but the curiosity was too strong, and she needed to know so she could protect the cattle. She pulled the shotgun out and prepared it should she need it in a hurry. She really hoped not. She was approximately two hundred metres from the rock on the far side, and the plan was not to ride into the valley but ride to the front so she could look straight into the valley from a distance. She hoped Nelly wouldn't spook when the mare saw the creatures.

Jacks saw them immediately on top of the rock, a line of fifteen to twenty stood sentry. A number were scattered at different levels of the rock on ledges, and many were down in the valley. She could see young juveniles playing in the water with mothers nearby. It looked like a holiday camp, a town, and she couldn't believe what she was looking at. Was this earth?

This was the most amazing sight she had ever seen. Where did they come from? When? When was the last time she had been to Corner Rock or her father? She must ask him. She found she was smiling in wonderment. She stayed that way for ten minutes or so, watching the various little clusters of creatures going about their everyday activities.

Nelly started pawing at the ground restlessly, which shook her out of her trance. Had they noticed her? The ones in the valley didn't act as though they knew she was there. No one seemed to be moving or looking her way, so she thought it timely to leave. She had seen what she came for. She didn't wish to upset the creatures or make her presence obvious. Her intentions were purely to observe and report so she turned Nelly and gave the rocks a wide berth on the way back. She didn't need to tell Nelly which way to go. Nelly knew where the other horses were and was keen to get back to them.

A noise behind her made her heart race, and she knew one of them was in the air behind her. The hair on the back of her neck stood on end and she turned her head and glanced up, seeing a male slowing down. She thought Nelly was too big for the creature to pick up, but she wasn't. If they could pick up a calf, they could pick up her slim body and carry her off. She felt the first stirring of fear and the adrenalin rush through her body. She quickly leaned forward and wrapped her arms around Nelly's neck. Now she was a difficult target to attempt to pick up. She urged Nelly on and they galloped the kilometre back to the campsite. She had no idea if they were following her or not. She just left it up to Nelly to find the best way back to camp.

There was no sign of any followers when she reached camp. She jumped off the panting Nelly and watched from the safety of the trees surrounding the camp, but the sky was clear.

Stewart and Arthur were very relieved to see her and full of questions. They were just completely shocked and incredulous that there were so many creatures at Corner Rock. An hour later, they had finished the work with the cattle and began to drive them back home. The trip would take several hours, particularly with the young calves. She was keen to discuss the strange situation with her father. Although excited to have such an amazing and rare creature on their land, it also posed a dilemma with the fact that these creatures killed calves. The cattle were the Foster's income and life's work. They could not afford to lose calves.

"Stewart. Arthur," she called out to the two men, trotting Nelly up to join them. They halted and waited for her.

"You can't tell anyone about the creatures. No one at all. They are our secret for now. Just us and my parents. That's it."

She looked into Arthur's eyes.

"Do you understand?"

"Yes, miss," he answered.

"I mean it. If people find out about them, the police might come here and kill them. We'll tell people about them soon, but first we need to talk to my father and maybe the scientists. Is that ok?" she asked.

"Yes, miss," said Arthur.

Stewart caught her eye and she could see he thought there wasn't much hope of Arthur keeping this quiet.

Chapter 56
The Agreement

Clint and Bill met up in Bill's office at the Wyoming facility. Bill's office was more elegantly decorated than Clint's office had been, and Bill was seated in his large, comfortable, leather chair watching as Clint paced the floor agitated. Clint was dressed in casual clothing with his arm in a sling though there were no longer bandages on his shoulder.

"Bill, it's been four months now. GOD, WHAT WASTED TIME! I could have found Viktoria. I could have visited the flock in Australia."

"You couldn't have done all that in four months. Calm down. This isn't going to help anything. Let's talk about this ... calmly," Bill responded, indicating Clint to take a seat.

Clint looked at the chair for a minute as if it were an electric chair and then sat reluctantly.

"It's ok. The Australian flock is safe for now. There's a local family who own a cattle ranch in Queensland. The flock have moved into a part of the ranch where there are big rock hills and the family are keeping an eye on them."

"I do have millions of questions about the Australian flock, but what about Viktoria? WHERE IS SHE?" he asked in desperation.

Bill understood how passionate Clint was about Viktoria. He stood up and pulled a tab on the pull-down screen located on the wall. A large map dropped down with red markings all over it.

"From sightings, we've mapped exactly where she hit shore and which direction she's heading."

He pointed to a thick red line with large circles for verified sightings. Clint jumped up and walked over to study the map closely.

"She's clever. She's been raiding dumpsters all across here."

He pointed to the area on the map from the coast and heading inland.

"She's worked out how to turn on a water faucet and has been leaving them on all over the city." Bill shook his head in amazement.

"When was the last sighting?" asked Clint, following the red marks with his finger.

"Not for a month or so," Bill answered.

"Perhaps she's found what she was looking for." Clint spoke in a hopeful tone, but Bill saw his face fall at the thought that something may have happened to her.

"Clint, I know you're bursting to go look for her, but she can wait. We don't even know where she is. If you went after her, it could be going down a rabbit hole, and you may be looking for the rest of your life. You know that's true." He paused to let the thought sink in.

"What you need to concentrate on right now is the Australian flock. They're at risk. The word is out that they're there and the anti-Viktoria people may try to harm them. This is an opportunity for you to study them, report on them, help the family, work with the Australian government and keep them safe. I hear there are dozens of them. I need you in Australia."

Bill waited for a response, but Clint shuffled and looked around the room for a few minutes.

"I know you're right. I know I need to go to Australia. I agree with you, but it kills me. What if someone shoots Viktoria while I'm in Australia." His voice broke slightly and Bill could sense the emotion.

"You won't be able to stop that. You know it." Bill placed his hand on Clint's good shoulder.

"Give me a year in Australia and then you can go chase Viktoria," Bill proposed.

"One whole year?"

Clint looked surprised although he knew he shouldn't. There was a lot of work to do in Australia. In reality, one year was not long enough but Bill was dangling a carrot in front of him. He nodded his head.

"One year. Ok. One year. Is everything ready?"

"Sure is. Mary spent months researching Australia, the location, climate, wildlife, laws, culture and so on. She's put it all in this dossier for you to read. I have a working visa ready, and all we have to do is book the flight."

Bill lifted a thick folder from his desk and held it out to Clint. He was pleased with this outcome as he had expected this conversation to be more difficult, but he knew the scientist would not be able to resist studying a whole flock.

Clint nodded and took the folder.

"I want to go as soon as possible. I'll want to camp out with them."

Bill nodded. "I thought you would. Oh ... and one more thing ... stay away from alcohol while you're there. The hospital told me you were in a bit of a mess four months ago."

Chapter 57
The Secret's Out

Jacks pulled into the parking space in front of the supermarket in town. She loved it when she could find a free spot out the front, nice and easy to pull the Toyota four-wheel drive into. She collected her handbag from the passenger seat, and jumped out of the car, heading towards the entrance to the supermarket.

Hearing running footsteps, she turned to see Becky and her friend racing to catch up to her. The girls were teenagers from a local Indigenous community not far from town. They stopped when they reached her, puffing from their run. Jacks smiled at them, waiting to see what they were after.

"What're you girls up to?" she asked.

Becky spoke. "Jacks, is it true? You know … that Arthur saved the cows and scared those devil animals off?"

Jacks stared at her and was momentarily speechless. Damn. She knew Arthur would not be able to keep the secret for long, but she hadn't expected it to get around this quickly. She blinked and smiled, recovering her composure.

"Sure is. He's a hero," she said, trying to keep a smile on her face.

"He's so brave. He said he'll take me out to see them sometime. You know … the devil animals." Becky had a big grin which slipped from her face when Jacks grabbed her arm.

"Listen, Becky. It's a secret about the …. creatures. If people find out then they might go out there and get hurt, or they might hurt the creatures."

"But people already know. My uncle said he and his mates are going out to have a look."

"NO! No one's allowed out there. Do you understand? Tell them not to go out there. It's dangerous. I mean it, Becky. No one's allowed out there. Don't tell anyone else about this. Do you understand me?"

Becky pulled her arm away, rubbing the place where Jacks had grabbed her and pouting.

"Yes, I got it. I'll tell them but I can't stop them."

"Also, they are not devil creatures."

The two girls walked away looking over their shoulder at her, disappointed.

Jacks stood on the pavement unsure what to do now. GODDAMN IT! Where were the American scientists? It had been weeks and weeks since they were notified of the creatures. This was too difficult for her family to contain alone. They needed help urgently. How were they going to stop people from going out to Corner Rock?

Her parents agreed with her not to tell any officials in Australia about the creatures yet. They felt the risk was too great that the creatures could be rounded up, or the media would get hold of it and there would be panic in the area.

After hours of research and phone calls, they had tracked Bill Powell down to a facility in Wyoming and spoken to him directly. He was very helpful and she could hear the excitement in his voice. His people had since contacted Jacks regularly to discuss certain aspects of the creatures, their needs and plans for the future. Bill Powell informed her he would send a scientist out as soon as possible and to wait for his arrival before doing anything.

Where the hell was the scientist? This latest news heralded a major problem, and it wouldn't be long until the media and authorities heard about the situation, or the public. She felt overwhelmed by the responsibility. Jacks jumped back in her Toyota, supermarket forgotten and backed out of the car space to go tell her father the bad news.

Chapter 58
The Homecoming

Viktoria had been travelling east for several weeks now, flying over countless human shelters that stretched into the horizon and so many people, she thought it would never end. Gradually, there had been less shelters and less humans until finally, she could see fields and the occasional small animal to hunt.

When she had been flying over the busy places full of human shelters, she had easily found food in the large objects next to the shelters. Sometimes there had been a top on the object but she worked out how to push the top off. On a few occasions, humans came out of the shelter and yelled at her, but she just flew away and found another object. Water was easy to find once she understood to bang the top, then the water just came out of nowhere.

She had slept or rested when she needed to, sometimes in quiet shelters, sometimes in a narrow strip of land behind the food object and even on the roof of a building once. Now, there were trees so she could perch on a big branch like she used to.

Her excitement was building as she headed east, the territory was not familiar, but in many ways it was. So many things had changed since she last flew this way over one hundred years earlier. There were so many shelters and humans, and it no longer resembled little villages. Now, there were shelters as far as she could see in some places. She could remember the smells, the taste of the air, the type of trees and the colour of the dirt. Not long now.

She could take her time now the busy shelter places were behind her and not tire herself out. The trip across the ocean had taken its toll on her and she felt weary and run-down. Part of her weariness was due to the injury on her thigh which was healing well though still painful, and that she had suffered long periods of time with nothing to eat.

Despite her weariness, nothing compared to the utter despair she had felt alone on the island. Despair at not being able to fly and of living alone and dying alone. No matter how weary, run-down or hungry she felt now, she was free, she could fly and she was happy.

One night, as she settled to perch in a tree for the night, she heard the roar of the big cats and knew she was getting closer. It had been over one hundred years since she had left her homeland, but she remembered the noise of the animals. The big cats killed many hunters over the years, even climbing trees, so she only stayed at the top of the tallest trees. Another predator was the big, long slithering one. How she hated those! The large one wrapped around and squeezed the life out of the hunter and the smaller one would bite, resulting in the death of the hunter. The slithering ones could also climb trees.

The day was hot and the sun beat down on her as she flew east. The countryside was now as she remembered and she had memories of certain trees and rocks she flew over. Nearly there. She saw the massive rocks ahead and knew she was home. Until this moment, it hadn't crossed her mind that there may not be any hunters there. When she had left the homeland, along with the alpha male and other mature hunters to find Utopia, there were pregnant females, youngsters, sick hunters and old ones that stayed behind. She sucked in her breath as she looked around for signs of life. What if they were no longer here? Where would she go? What would she do? Had the alpha male and her flock come back here?

Water glittered in the sun from the valley further down the hill, which was a good sign. Water meant life and food. She landed on a rock near the cliff face, holding her breath and looking around eagerly. She had stood on this very rock many years ago, before leaving with the flock. Aware she was making little whimpering noises, but unable to control it, she couldn't see anyone but was confident she could smell the hunters. Perhaps the smell had permeated into the rocks. She inhaled the smell and retracted her wings. If there was no one here any longer, she would stay here. Alone. Forever.

Suddenly, a face appeared from the cave in the cliff face above. A male strode out onto the rock ledge and stared down at her. He was the leader, but not the alpha male she knew. She looked back at him calmly and waited. He was assessing the situation to determine who she was.

A few minutes passed and more faces appeared, all around him. Hunters appeared out of everywhere, behind rocks, caves and shrubs. A large group assembled in various positions in the rocks staring at her intently. She looked around, recognising a few faces and was so excited she could barely contain herself. She didn't recognise the alpha male and realised the flock she had been with on the island had never returned to the homeland. She could not see any of the hunters from the flock who left to fly over the ocean. She wondered if they had found Utopia or had not made it.

The new alpha male flew down and landed not far away from Viktoria. An unknown hunter appearing and flying into an existing flock had never happened in her memory. The alpha male was unsure how to act and sized her up and down with a stern look on his face. He was particularly focused on the wound on her thigh. It was his duty to protect his flock and ensure there was no danger from this hunter he was not familiar with.

The minutes ticked by as the male continued staring at her and looking her up and down. She could see that he was much younger than the other alpha male she had known. Perhaps, this one was a youngster when her flock had left and had since grown to lead the flock. She twittered and placed an amiable look on her face, a friendly look. He stepped closer and she could detect his strong odour as he inhaled to detect hers. He moved close enough to bump his chest against her, a slight bump, but deliberate. He waited for her reaction as this was a sign of strength and dominance. She stepped back a few steps with her head down and eyes averted, to show respect and accept his leadership. This gesture seemed to satisfy him, the tension left his body and he exhaled. He turned to the rest of the flock and made a loud, calling sound. From all around, there was movement and twittering. She could hear the flock were excited that she was there and were welcoming her.

A female hunter landed to her left and she turned to look. The female looked very aged with brown, wrinkled skin especially on her face, neck and arms. There were strands of grey through her hair and her arms were thin. The old hunter had tears running down her face, streaking her cheeks. She twittered and put her arms out to Viktoria. Viktoria walked over and put her head down on the female's chest. The female patted her head and twittered quietly to her, shushing her. Viktoria stayed that way for a long time with the hunter who had given birth to her.

Chapter 59
The Long Socks

Jacks drove back to the station in record time, encountered Arthur as she headed into the house.

"Arthur," she called out to him.

He stopped and looked back, breaking out into a large smile at the sight of her.

"Hey, Jacks."

Arthur was so likeable with a smile that lit up a room. It was difficult to stay angry at him.

"Did you tell anyone about the creatures we saw at Corner Rock?" she asked.

"Just my girlfriend, Miss," he answered, not missing a beat.

"Well, she's told all the community, and they want to come out to Corner Rock to take a look."

Arthur looked suitably horrified, and a little embarrassed.

"I want you to sort this out. Go to the community and tell everyone they can't come out. Tell them the American authorities are on their way, and they don't want anyone near the rocks. Tell them my father and I will be very angry if they go against what we've said. Do you understand?"

She looked into his eyes so he could see how important this was. His eyes were wide.

"Yes ... Jacks ... Miss. I will fix it. I will."

He hurried away and climbed in the old Ford farm vehicle, speeding off down the driveway. She hoped he could stop what she knew was a disaster waiting to happen. Now that this information was public, it was only a matter of time before people came out to the rock.

After filling her parents in on the situation and brainstorming scenarios and solutions, she headed back to town to collect the groceries she had originally planned to purchase earlier.

It was a sense of déjà vu as she parked out the front of the supermarket, fortunate to secure a park right at the front again. Feeling pleased, she stepped out of the vehicle and turned to close her door. A Toyota Prado four-wheel drive caught her attention, and she stopped to watch as it turned into the side street in front of the shopping centre, driving on the wrong side of the road and pulled up at the café next door. Amused, she watched as a man climbed out and walked into the café. Jacks quietly watched him, stifling the laugh that was threatening to escape her lips, then made her way to the café, grocery shopping forgotten.

The man was standing at the counter having just ordered a coffee. He looked an average height with dark hair, slightly curly and unruly to his shoulders, black glasses and smooth skin on his hands which appeared to have only seen the inside of an office. It was easy to identify non-locals in town as they were the ones with pale skin, even though his skin had a natural light olive colouring. She watched him for a few seconds and then walked over to him, stopping a few metres away.

"So, you're the American scientist." It was a statement not a question.

The man turned and looked at her in surprise, and she saw he had warm, dark brown eyes with an attractive face and she estimated him to be in his late thirties or early forties. Momentarily speechless, he just stared at her.

"Umm. Yes. Dr Clint Marne." He recovered and offered his hand. She reached for his hand and they shook.

"Jacks Foster. I've been waiting for you."

"Jacks? Your name is Jacks?" he asked, looking puzzled.

"It is."

She stared at him as if daring him to make any comment about her name and not offering any further information. He thought better of further questions in that regard.

"How did you know I was American?" he asked, looking around at several other men in the café.

Jacks laughed, a humorous and natural sound.

"Oh, that was easy. You drove into town on the wrong side of the road, and no Aussie in their right mind would wear long white socks like that."

Clint's eyes immediately spun down to stare at his socks in surprise. He was wearing khaki shorts, khaki short-sleeved shirt with brown leather shoes and white socks reaching just below the knee. He looked ready for a safari in Africa, just as Mary had documented he wear. Clint then looked around the room at what other men were wearing and seeing no other long socks, his face reddened with embarrassment.

Seeing how uncomfortable the scientist had become, Jacks felt guilty. She shouldn't have teased him, but she couldn't help it. Most people were aware of her smartarse sense of humour, but he didn't know her.

The waitress passed him his coffee to go. He took the cup and turned to face Jacks.

"Come on. My parents own the station where the creatures are. I'll take you out to meet them. There's a lot to talk about."

"Jacks, I made you a coffee too," said the girl behind the counter, handing her a take-away cup.

"Thanks, Deb."

Clint followed her vehicle to the station and found it much easier to stay on the right side of the road when following someone else.

Chapter 60
The Meet and Greet

Steve, Evie, Jacks and Dr Clint Marne sat around the kitchen table at the farmhouse drinking coffee and talking. She had introduced the doctor to her parents and tried to hide her giggle as she watched both their eyes travel down the doctor to his feet. She also noted the brief pang of anxiety on his face when he realised, they were checking out his socks. Poor guy, she thought. He would have no idea what was wrong with his socks.

Clint brought in photographs of Viktoria and everyone was fascinated, asking many questions.

"Is there any chance Viktoria is here, travelled here after you saw her last?" asked Evie.

Clint shook his head. "No. She was headed in a different direction. I'm positive she was heading back to where she came from."

He looked around and the other three were staring at him, hanging on his every word. They did not appear upset or threatened by the look of Viktoria in the photos. In fact, they seemed enthralled, which was the perfect audience for him to talk about his passion.

"My theory is there was a flock somewhere in Africa which is where Viktoria came from. For whatever reason, perhaps drought, perhaps disease, predators or urban development, part of the flock left to find a new home, probably the strongest."

"Why do you say only part of the flock?" asked Jacks. "How could you know that?"

"With a community, whether it be humans, animals or this new species, there are men, women, children, babies, pregnant women, elderly and the sick. I don't believe all of them would be capable of flying thousands of miles across the ocean to have reached that island in South America and then flown all the way across to Australia."

He could see the others digest this and were nodding in agreement. It made sense.

"I don't know how old they are when they learn to fly, but I cannot see babies flying across an ocean. I think the strongest females and males left and the elderly, sick and young ones stayed behind in Africa."

"That seems very brutal, to leave the weak behind," said Jack's father, Steve.

"It does seem like that to us, but it is about survival of the species. Better to abandon the weak ones than to lose the entire flock to famine, thirst or disease."

"So, you're suggesting there's still a flock in Africa?" asked Evie.

"Yes, I think so. Well ... I hope so. I think that is where Viktoria is headed. That would be the only place she knows. She wouldn't be aware her own flock arrived in Australia. That is ... if this is the same flock. Maybe, there's another flock somewhere or even a number of them."

Clint stood up and started pacing the kitchen then realised what he was doing and sat again.

"Sorry. I get a bit carried away."

He grinned weakly, feeling aware they must think of him as such a nerd. The three Australians were comfortably dressed, tanned, attractive and looked like country people. He knew he looked out of place and uncomfortable, the pale-skinned, nerdy scientist with the strange accent and nerdy clothes. Half the words the Australians spoke he had never heard.

Jacks thought for a minute and then spoke. "My parents and I have been trying to work out how long the creatures ... umm ... flock have been here at Corner Rock. We ride out near there often, but I think I've only been in the valley once, which is the foot of the rocks, and that was when I was a child. My father and I rode our horses into the valley and never saw anything. I guess they could have been there but I'm sure we would have noticed if calves were regularly going missing."

"Viktoria was on that island for over one hundred years, so the flock would have left over one hundred years ago. It may have taken them many years to travel across the South Pacific Ocean, and they most likely stopped at islands on the way for a period of time to eat, drink and rest. When I study this flock, I may be able to work it out from the age of the oldest infants. I believe this species would not breed until they felt it safe to do so."

Clint opened his reports, prepared for him by Mary and scanned to find the section he required.

"My reports indicate that animal life in this area consists of stock animals and wildlife, including cattle, camels, snakes, wild dogs, dingoes, echidnas, emus, wallabies, wombats, kangaroos, rabbits and ... bilbies. What is bilbies?" He looked at the other three puzzled, as he hadn't had time to google that animal.

Jacks laughed. "A bilby is like a little wallaby type animal."

"Can you tell me if there are any other animals?"

The three family members were silent for a few minutes as their minds raced through the animals they were aware of.

Steve cleared his throat and answered. "We're right on the edge of where feral camels live. Occasionally, we see a herd of camels but not very often. There are snakes of all sorts including pythons. Native animals ... yes. Pests like rabbits and hares, yes and the occasional fox, tons of birds, hmmm ... "

"Would the flock eat all those animals?" interrupted Jacks.

"Small animals and young stock, they would. Snakes ... I doubt it. Wild dogs, I'm not sure. Kangaroos, wallabies, emu and rabbits are most likely, yes."

"Oh, the greenies and most Aussies won't like them touching kangaroos and wildlife," said Jacks.

Clint looked puzzled and his eyebrows shot up. "What are greenies?"

The three Australians laughed realising how Australian the word 'greenies' was.

"They are the conservation and environment advocates who don't like trees to be cut down or anything to harm the wildlife. Australians are very protective of our native animals and it wouldn't go down well for anything killing native wildlife," Jacks answered, concerned.

Clint nodded. "I see."

"More importantly, will they eat humans?" asked Evie, with a serious look on her face.

All eyes turned to the doctor for his response.

"No. They won't eat humans." He saw the skeptical look on their faces. "You would have heard that Viktoria did eat humans on the island."

Everyone was nodding, keenly watching his reaction.

"She had no choice. The person tasked with caring for her and providing regular food to the island, starved her for months on end and when he came across tourists, he left a human or two for her, for his own amusement, I assume. She hunted humans to survive though I believe, it would have been difficult for her."

The others didn't look convinced. They stole glances at each other to judge if the other believed this.

"Difficult for her? I would imagine it was difficult for the victim's family," Evie said, quietly.

Clint looked horrified at his slip with word choice. "Oh. Of course. Sorry. I didn't mean the way that sounded. What happened was an absolute tragedy and a terrible act by the man supposedly caring for Viktoria." His face reddened. "When there is other food, they would never touch a human."

He said it as convincingly as he could. "I can't say they would not injure a human if they felt their youngsters were at risk or the humans were there to harm them. I'm not sure but best to keep the public away from them."

"What are your plans now?" Steve asked.

"I need to buy supplies and then I will be camping out with them for who knows how long."

The other three looked at each other in surprise, all thinking the same thoughts.

"You ever camped in the Australian outback before?" asked Steve, peering at the pale-faced scientist.

"No," he answered, with a look that inferred he didn't expect it to be too difficult.

Steve and Jacks looked at each other for a few moments.

"Doc, the boys and I are riding over to the west side of the station tonight and that's near Corner Rock. We need to check we didn't leave any cattle over there. Why don't you come with us? You can check out the scenery and the rock, but more than that, we're camping the night so you can get a feel for Aussie outback camping. You might even learn a thing or two."

He thought for a few minutes and had to admit he felt quite overwhelmed by the thought of buying supplies for the complete unknown, a place he had never been and had no real understanding of. All he knew of the Queensland outback was what he could see in photos and what was in the report Mary had prepared and until Mary conducted the research, she had never heard of Australia. Accepting help from these experienced people was very appealing.

"Great. That would be appreciated. Thank you," he said, breaking out into a grin.

Steve looked down at Clint's clothing again, noting the safari style shirt, shorts, socks and shoes.

"Jacks," he said. "You'd better take the Doc into town and help him with supplies and some suitable kit."

Jacks laughed.

"Come on, Doc. By the way, you can ride a horse, can't you?"

Chapter 61
The Cattle Yard Camp

Jacks placed Clint on the quietest and oldest horse they owned. Old Ned had not been ridden for two years. The old bay gelding looked pleased to be pulled out of retirement and saddled up. The fact that the doctor had never ridden a horse was a worry, but Jacks felt confident that Old Ned would look after him and they would just ride at a slow pace.

Clint was dressed in his new tough jeans and shirt with his R.M. Williams boots and an Akubra hat. He still managed to look nerdy, Jacks thought, but at least he was dressed for the environment and didn't look so American anymore. She was sure that once he had toughened up and the clothes looked more worn, then he would look the part. As they left the house, Jacks signalled for him to halt while she kicked dirt on his new boots. He looked at her as if she had lost her mind.

"Now they're broken in," she said, simply.

Clint had his new swag fastened on the back of the saddle. He looked at the saddle again and wondered how the hell he was supposed to hold on. He imagined the saddle would look like the ones he'd seen in Western movies with the horn on the front. This saddle had a flat pommel at the front and Jacks explained it was an Australian stock saddle.

He had also purchased a tent, tarp, billy, camp oven, frypan, cooking utensils and solar powered lights among other items for camping on his own. He wasn't sure what some of the items were for, but Jacks assured him they would show him what to do and how to use these strange things.

Jacks, Stewart and Arthur nearly fell off their horses laughing when Clint first mounted Old Ned and held the reins up high with one hand like he had seen in the Westerns.

"Whoa, slow down, John Wayne," said Stewart.

"Better for staying on if you hold the reins like this."

Stewart showed him how to hold the reins, one in each hand, and to place his hands just in front of the pommel at the front of the saddle.

"If you need to, you can always grab hold of the pommel or the mane," he explained.

They headed west on horseback at a walk, and after a few stretches of trotting, they reached the camp site in just over two hours. The three Australians pointed out various features and native animals they saw along the way.

Stewart thought the doctor was walking like John Wayne with bowed legs after he dismounted Old Ned and knew he would feel muscle sore the next day in muscles he never knew he possessed. Jacks tethered the horses and they set up a campsite. This was the same camp where they had first encountered the creatures, a grove of trees with the yards in the middle on the west side of the station – Cattle Yard Camp. Jacks took Clint to the outside of the trees and pointed to Corner Rock in the distance to the west, barely visible on the horizon. She explained that this was the outside of the rock and the valley was on the far side. Clint could just see the terracotta colouring of rock formations on the horizon.

"Do you have binoculars with you today?" she asked.

"Yes, I do." He rummaged around in a backpack and pulled out a fancy looking pair of binoculars.

"The boys and I are riding out to scout around for any cattle. I want you to stay here. OK? I've let your horse go in the small yard, so he's fine. Just relax here and check out the rock. You may even see them flying or whatever they do."

She waited for his reply as the last thing they needed was him taking off for Corner Rock on his own so she had unsaddled his horse, knowing he would find it very difficult to saddle up on his own.

"Thanks," he responded. "I'll be here."

He smiled back at her, happy with this arrangement. In truth, the inside of his thighs and his rear end were feeling a bit tired and sore from the horse ride, and he was keen to observe the rock on his own.

He peered through the binoculars at the rock, amazed at what a beautiful, natural structure it was. Tall, orange in colour and almost eerie next to a background of flat land. It reminded him of parts of Arizona though not as dry. In fact, the report Mary put together indicated there was a high rain fall in this part of the world much of the time. The species may have chosen the location well, a place with plenty of rain and water, warm temperatures most of the year-round, animals for prey and vegetation. Whether there was enough food without cows might be concerning but he would investigate this in his research of them.

He moved the binoculars all over the rock, understanding that the activity was on the other side. He happily stayed in his position for hours checking out the rock and the surrounding territory. Every now and again, he thought he saw something in the air but then reasoned that he was a long way away and could be imagining it.

Camping out in Australia would be a challenge. He had travelled across many states of America, but he had slept mostly in his vehicle or the occasional motel. He was an expert at vehicle sleeping but this was a whole new ball game. He realised he didn't even know how to light a fire without tons of paper and a lighter. What did people do out here without McDonalds or diners? Well, he was up for the challenge.

The three horse riders returned late in the afternoon, not having found any cows but had found a few carcasses devoid of meat. That did not necessarily indicate the creatures had killed the cows as dingoes, foxes or crows will polish off a dead animal. Clint thought it more likely that the flock would take the animal with them to devour in their own space rather than feed on an animal out in the open.

Arthur took charge of showing the doctor how to light a campfire, using dry sticks and twigs from the area. He liked the fact that he was the expert and could take on the mentor role and instruct the doctor in everything about Australia and camping. Jacks thought it was a good experience for Arthur to take a bit of responsibility and share his knowledge. Arthur happily showed Clint how to wait for glowing embers and then place a large lump of beef, a few potatoes and an onion with water in a camp oven, bury it in the embers, placing embers on top as well, and wait a couple of hours for a camp stew. He explained about damper being a quick and easy bread, and how to make it as well as other things he could cook in the camp oven.

"You can do this with rabbits as well. Once you catch the rabbit, you skin it and cut its guts out. Have you ever skinned and gutted a rabbit?" Arthur asked, pleased he was so experienced in the art of gutting animals.

"No, I haven't done that, but I have dissected and operated on hundreds of animals from frogs to a gorilla, so it should be ok," Clint answered.

"Oh," said Arthur, deflated.

Clint was fascinated with the idea of sleeping in a swag and not a tent. Arthur explained that it was common in Australia for campers to sleep under the stars in just the swag, the canvas pulled up over the head if it rained. Clint had his concerns but prepared to trust the other three that they knew what they were talking about. Arthur also had plenty of instructions for Clint once he was on his own at Corner Rock.

"Now, make sure you set up camp on flat land not far from water, but don't sleep too close to the water because wild animals and snakes come to drink each day," he said, solemnly.

"You could sleep in your car but it would get hot. You can also put a swag on the roof rack of your car and sleep up there. But just remember, snakes can climb. We don't have crocodiles here so you are safe with that, but we do have leeches in the water and cane toads. Cane toads have poisonous stuff on their backs and if an animal eats a cane toad, they die."

Jacks could see the doctor turning a bit grey, trying to remember all the advice.

"I'll make sure I don't eat any cane toads," Clint answered and every-one laughed.

The evening passed with a good meal of beef and potatoes, salad from the station and a stubby of beer per person. Clint thought it didn't taste as good as bourbon but the more he tasted it, the more he liked it. Arthur showed Clint how to boil water on the campfire with the billy and how to make the fire safe for the night. There was a lot of chat and fun. Clint explained he planned once a week to head into town to phone his boss and stock up on supplies. They swapped phone numbers and he promised to contact them if he ran into problems.

Clint slept well and was surprised in the morning to find that sleeping in a swag had agreed with him. He woke to bright sunshine filtering through the trees as the sun rose on the horizon. The landscape was beautiful, a scene of red and green.

Jacks had brought along eggs and bread, so they cooked in a frypan over the fire – eggs on toast with coffee. Life was good.

Chapter 62
The Drone

"I have a surprise for you," Jacks said to Clint.

They had finished breakfast, packed up the camp and were about to saddle the horses. She pulled a box out of her pack and Clint was surprised to see a drone.

"This is the drone we bought for the property recently. We can send it out to check on the cattle as long as they're not too far away. It has a limited reach but has still been useful at times. I thought we might send it over to Corner Rock and we can see what's happening here on the tablet," she explained.

"Fantastic!"

Even though Clint had known they wouldn't be venturing as far as Corner Rock on this trip, he felt disappointed he had not seen any of the flock, so was excited at the thought of possibly seeing them with a drone. Seeing footage of Corner Rock would assist him identify the lay of the land and where he would camp as well as the possibility of seeing the flock.

It took fifteen minutes for the drone to reach Corner Rock and using a remote control, Jacks was able to steer the drone around to the left of the rock to the far side where the valley was. It was like reaching an oasis with water, bushes, green grass and the concave of the rock face.

She steered over to where she imagined the best place to camp would be. It was on the far side of the water to the rock, slightly up hill and offered a full view of the entire interior of the rock face. They discussed the camping position and Clint mentally marked where he would drive the Prado to. Jacks then guided the drone to turn toward the rock face and very slowly close the distance. The flock would hear the humming sound of the drone and Clint hoped they wouldn't be too alarmed.

For a while, all they could see on the tablet were the red rocks, then the camera panned across a few faces. Jacks backtracked and there were three faces staring at the drone, spellbound.

"Wow! Will you look at that!" Clint said. "It looks like three girls."

"How can you tell?" asked Jacks, frowning with concentration.

"They have a look like Viktoria, though not very feminine. I can't wait to see a male," replied Clint.

Jacks moved the drone over the rocks further until it showed a ledge on the rock face with what looked like a cave behind it. This was half-way up the rocks and the creature in the front was a male with several males behind him. His face was large and very masculine compared to Viktoria's face. He was watching the drone and keeping his flock behind him, away from danger.

Jacks could see Clint was mesmerised, eyes wide and mouth slightly ajar. She moved the drone away and over more of the rocks. More faces and bodies were visible and although he knew the flock was here, seeing them on the tablet blew his mind. Jacks thought he looked like an excited kid with his face lit up. His enthusiasm was contagious and she felt the excitement. Stewart and Arthur were watching the tablet over her shoulder and were expressing amazement at what they were seeing.

On the ride back to the house, everyone had questions for the doctor.

"What happens if you get hurt out here and no one knows?" asked Stewart.

"I'll have a phone which I'll charge each day with the solar charger, and I have a satellite phone. I have your phone numbers now so you may get a frantic call." He laughed.

"Yes, please do that if you're hurt," said Jacks in all seriousness.

"Maybe for the first few days you should text us that you are doing ok so we can relax," said Stewart.

"Sure thing," said Clint feeling warm at these strangers caring for him and his safety.

"What will you do if the creatures attack you?" asked Arthur.

"I doubt that will happen. I have studied Viktoria for a long time now and I know how they respond and although I've not seen them interact, I have a good idea what will work with them," Clint replied. He looked at Arthur. "I will be careful though."

"How long will you be out there for?" asked Jacks.

"I plan to go out to Corner Rock tomorrow and stay until next Friday. Then I'll head into town for supplies, a shower and a good sleep for the night. Back out here on Saturday. Hopefully that's what I'll do each week," Clint replied clutching at Old Ned's mane as the horse stumbled.

"I'll be back in town Sunday night until Friday night. Why don't we catch up for lunch on Friday? I'd love to hear how your first week went," said Jacks.

Clint brightened. The thought of lunch with Jacks was something to look forward to.

"Sure. That would be great. Meet you at the 'Long Socks Café," he teased.

They both laughed. Arthur and Stewart looked confused.

Chapter 63
The Sergeant

Steve knew a car was coming well before he saw or heard it as Rocky, the old cattle dog sat up, stared down the driveway, then jumped up barking. He cleaned his greasy hands on a rag where he had been working on servicing one of the farm tractors and made his way out of the shed to greet the visitor.

With such a long driveway, it took time for the car to reach the house and there was always plenty of time to guess who the visitor was and what they wanted. Usually, the position of the visitor was easily spotted by the plume of dust created by the vehicle.

Steve was surprised to see the local sergeant step out of his unmarked car.

"Afternoon, Steve." G'day, Rob. What's up?" Steve asked, wondering what would bring the senior policeman out for a home visit.

"I'm hearing talk around town of gorilla animals living on your station. Some of the locals are getting pretty worked up about it. There's talk of people coming to chase them out."

He peered at Steve's face to ascertain whether this sounded nuts or not. Rob had ignored the talk for a while thinking it was fantasy, but he needed to sort it out.

Steve sighed in resignation.

"You'd better come in the house." Steve motioned for him to follow, and Rob followed him on to the verandah.

Over coffee, Steve explained the story regarding the creatures and what the current status was with Clint's plans to camp out at Corner Rock. He could see the sergeant was not happy.

"I'm surprised the media hasn't got hold of this story yet. You might wake up one morning with half of Australia camped on your front lawn," Rob told Steve, shaking his head with concern.

"It's really important that we keep this quiet for now until the Americans work out what to do," Steve explained.

"Too late for that. I would say the cat is well and truly out of the bag now. You better talk to the Americans and look at a Plan B. I'm not sure what will happen now. You say there's an American scientist out there with them?" he asked.

"He goes out there today. He needs at least one week to assess the situation. Can we keep everyone at bay for one week?" Steve asked, starting to feel some real concern about what could happen.

"What happens in one week?" asked Rob.

"Well ... I don't know. The doc will see how many of them are out there, how they are doing and all that, then he will need to report on what the options are, can they stay there, what do they eat, what environmental impacts there may be and so on ... I hadn't thought about what the locals would say or do."

Steve was feeling more alarmed, imagining the entire town marching out to Corner Rock.

"Do you really think they could storm the place and what ... shoot these creatures?"

Rob sighed and shrugged his shoulders.

"I'm really not sure what they might do. There is always a lot of bravado when people get scared, and trust me, this is scaring the shit out of them."

"I don't want anyone coming out here on my land even if it's just to look. The damn place is too large for me to guard the boundaries. What am I supposed to do?" he asked.

Rob looked thoughtful for a few minutes.

"The public will have to know about this. They can't be kept in the dark. What about if I try to keep everything quiet and calm as best I can for the next week. Then, I want a meeting arranged with me, you and the scientist at the end of week. Depending on what he says, I think there needs to be a meeting organised with the locals. This needs to be explained to them. They will be worried whether they're safe, whether their children are safe, whether their animals are safe. We need to talk to them and answer their questions. Do you get what I'm saying?" Rob was firm and he maintained eye contact with Steve.

"Yes. I think that's the best way forward. I'll phone the Americans today and talk to them. We may not be able to contact the doc until he returns next weekend but don't worry, I'll be on to it," answered Steve.

"I'm not sure how I can prevent people from coming out here. All I can do is warn them that they will be charged with trespass. We'll have to take that one as it comes." He stood to leave. "Keep me updated with any change of circumstance."

"Will do," answered Steve. They shook hands and the sergeant left.

Chapter 64
The Corner Rock

The Prado slowly made its way around the left side of Corner Rock. The going was tough as there were no roads or tracks, just dry, red dirt, rocks and tufts of grass. The last thing Clint wanted was to bog or break down out here before he even started the research.

On his Viktoria chase across the United States, he had suffered his share of vehicle malfunctions including flat tyres, dead battery, broken windscreen, minor scrape with a tree and had been bogged in the mud more than once. For the first time in his life, he had been forced to learn the basics of vehicle maintenance and problem solving. However, vehicle problems in the outback was not something he wished to encounter. He couldn't exactly phone an emergency service to come out and change a tyre in the middle of nowhere.

He rounded the rock and made his way to the location he and Jacks had picked for him to camp. It would give him a perfect view straight into the concave of the rock where the ledges and cave openings were. He would be right near water and far enough from the flock that hopefully, he could observe them without interacting. His biggest fear was that they would leave this location out of fear of him.

He reached the camping location faster than anticipated, turned off the vehicle and sat watching the rock face. No sign of movement but it was likely they were hiding, having heard the vehicle approaching. He stepped out of the car and stretched. The morning sun was warm and the sky was a clear blue. Although he had a tent, he had decided that for tonight, he would sleep in his swag either on the roof of the vehicle or inside. Truth be told, Arthur had scared him with talk of snakes and creepy crawlers.

Clint headed to the back of the Prado and lifted out the firewood he had brought along, a chair and tarpaulin to make shelter from the hot sun. He made up the campfire though it was way too early to light it and set up camp how he wanted it. He had brought a drum of water but Jacks assured him the water here was fed from a natural spring and was good enough to drink.

Summing up his courage, he wandered down to the water carrying a bucket. It was around one hundred metres from his camp on a slight downward incline. There was still no movement or sign of life. His skin prickled as he imagined dozens of eyes watching him from the rock only a few hundred metres away. He bent down and washed his face and hands in the water. The water did look clear, clean and inviting, and he imagined immersing himself in it, but not today. He made his way back to the camp, carrying his bucket of water, and sat comfortably in a chair under the tarp and scanned the rock face with his binoculars. Close at hand, he had the camera, pen and notepad, recorder and gun in case of trouble.

Time ticked by slowly. He ate the sandwich he had bought in town and drank water but other than that, his eyes were glued to the rock face. Every now and again, he thought he saw movement, but it was gone in a flash and he was left wondering if he imagined it. Maybe the flock had already left. No, he didn't believe that. They were doing what any living being would do in this situation. They were hiding, watching, and waiting. Sooner or later, they would come out for water. Maybe they would wait until dark. He hoped they would accept his presence without too much drama.

Around five in the afternoon, he heard a sound, then another, and another. It was a strange noise, and he racked his brain for what the sound could be. The sound became louder and more frantic and bounced off the rocks, echoing around the valley. He suddenly realised it was an infant crying. The sound was similar to a human baby but louder and at a faster tempo. He pictured the mother frantically trying to quieten her infant. Would anything change now their hiding spot was found out?

An hour later he saw movement. Slowly, he lifted the binoculars to his eyes and could see a number of the flock wandering around halfway up the rock face. A few were standing still and watching him, on sentry duty, while others were milling around and playing with youngsters. He was elated. Never in his wildest dreams could he have imagined a whole flock like this living within his reach. Within minutes, there were tons of them around. He could see them down the bottom of the rocks, on various ledges and crevices, a few were flying and several were heading to the water. He had no doubt that any sudden movement from him would send them scurrying back to their hiding spots. He was happy not to move and to just watch them. Very slowly, he lifted the camera and filmed them. Wait until Bill saw this footage. He would pee his over-sized pants.

Clint watched as two females, both with infants and a male bent down at the watering hole. They did not use their hands to cup water like humans did. They drank by putting their mouths down into the water as he had seen Viktoria do at the facility.

Time passed quickly and suddenly, he could see the night approaching. Time to light his campfire and boil the billy for coffee. The billy took his mind off bourbon. For this first night, he had brought along a beef and salad roll. After that, he would begin cooking and thank goodness Arthur, Stewart and Jacks had shown him how to light the campfire and how to cook on the fire. He knew that he would have made a disaster of it otherwise.

It was too dark now to see the rock face although he could still see its silhouette against the night sky. He wondered if the flock had seen fire before. He hoped they were not afraid, but he also didn't want them to come and investigate in the dark. He had decided he would sleep on top of the Prado especially as darkness fell. His swag was up there already and although he was excited about the flock, he wanted to ensure plenty of sleep so he could rise early. He doused the fire with water as Arthur had shown him and climbed up to his lofty bed under the stars.

Chapter 65
The Encounter

Clint's eyes snapped open and he became aware of the early dawn light. It took him a few minutes to remember he was on top of the Prado, snuggled in a swag with the roof rack for company and in the middle of nowhere. He blinked a few times and sat up looking around. The sun was peeping over the horizon casting its ginger glaze over the landscape.

Feeling his hair stand on end and sensing something to his right, he turned to see a male of the species standing ten metres away from the Prado staring at him. Stunned, all he could do was stare back at him. Wow! What a magnificent specimen he was. So much larger and more powerful than Viktoria, very bronzed with his skin having a leathery look to it. His hair was long, similar to natural dreadlocks with grey hairs and streaks contrasted with the dark hair. Clint wondered how old he was. He was much older than Viktoria as he had never seen any grey hair on her and her skin was much more supple than the leathery skin of this male.

The leader did not appear afraid, and Clint thought his expressive face showed interest and curiosity. A little unsure what to do, Clint carefully climbed out of his swag and down via the back of the Prado. He moved very slowly and steadily, not wishing to alarm the leader or appear threatening in any way.

Once down, he stood next to the vehicle in front of the leader and watched him, waiting. From the ground, he realised how tall the leader was. He would easily be six foot six inches, or over two metres in Australian measurement.

The doctor became aware of other males and a few females gathered around behind the leader. They were curious about this human and what he was doing there. He hoped they were not aggressive or violent and although he had studied Viktoria intently for some time, he had no knowledge of their culture, their group behaviours or correct etiquette. He was ready to act subservient if the leader started acting aggressively.

The leader looked down toward the doctor's feet continually and Clint looked down to see what he was looking at, puzzled. All Clint could see was his bare legs, well ... pale white bare legs, actually. Maybe the leader had never seen a nerdy, white skinned scientist before. Having slept in boxer shorts and a T-shirt, Clint looked down at his legs again and wondered if the leader was confused about clothing. Slowly, so as not to alarm the leader, he pulled his t-shirt off over his head to reveal his bare chest. Clint looked down at his own chest and across at the leader and saw the leader cock his head slightly and stare at the human's white bare chest. Clint took a deep breath and stepped out of his boxer shorts, standing there in the middle of the outback, naked as the day he was born. He saw the leader look down and thought his expression was one of relief, as if realising that this strange human was similar to them.

After a few minutes, the leader gave his head a little nod, as if he was satisfied, and then extracted his wings and flew back to the rock. The other creatures followed suit except for one male who stayed behind, investigating the campfire, which was now cold and a mound of grey ash. The male smelled the ash, leaning in close enough that the ash went up his nose when he sniffed. He snorted and poked at it with his finger. Finally, he stretched out his wings and left.

Clint dressed and rekindled the campfire to boil the billy for coffee. He had brought along eggs and bread, so cooked eggs on toast as Jacks had shown him. His mind was on the encounter and how unbelievable it seemed. He had not expected this and so soon. He thought they would watch him from afar and disappear if he came close or made too much noise. He wished the encounter had been filmed as Bill would never believe him. Oh, wait a minute. He should be glad it wasn't filmed as he had stood butt naked. He laughed to himself as he ate his eggs on toast.

For the next few days, he stayed at his camp site, only venturing down to the waterhole on two occasions to collect water for washing himself and the cooking utensils. Both times, there were males and females around and they stopped and stared at him until he was gone. At least they did not run away and hide which he was relieved about. None of them visited him at his camp site again though he could see the leader often watching him from afar.

He collected much in-depth footage of the flock and wrote many notes, the material so essential to the research, and he witnessed re-markable things. It appeared the leader had several female partners, and many offspring belonged to him. The other males had one partner each and a small group of offspring. This method of breeding ensured that the future was reasonably clear of in-breeding.

Studying the approximate maturity of the flock, he tried to gauge the age of the youngsters. It was difficult to be accurate, but he saw what looked like teenagers flying around and play fighting, and it seemed the flock may have been here for a considerable amount of time.

The males were protective of the females and young ones. At the slightest noise, he watched the males push the females or young behind them. They hunted and brought back food for the ones who could not fly or were caring for young. He saw small hunting parties fly out regularly and return carrying food, but it was difficult to see what the food consisted of. They willingly shared their food with each other and there was no fighting or squabbling that he could see other than in fun. He also saw what appeared to be fruit brought back. The flock that he could see all appeared to be well-fed and healthy, with no over-weight ones but neither did he see any that were undernourished. This did seem to be the perfect place for them with plenty of food, water, a good climate, rock sanctuary and privacy. He hoped it would remain that way.

Chapter 66
The Rain

Jacks and Arthur rode out to Cattle Yard Camp, not far from Corner Rock. They wanted to check that the doctor was ok and that there were no other people hanging around to cause problems.

Her father had phoned her only a few hours after she left the farm to inform her of the sergeant's visit and concern. Jacks kept an apartment in town and spent her weekdays at university. She had just returned to her apartment when she received the worrying call from her father so decided to return home and help out with the situation. She could hear the concern in her father's voice and didn't want to leave her parents in a potentially violent situation. She was also worried about the doctor camped out where there could be trouble with not only the creatures, but other people.

Steve, Evie and Jacks discussed the possibilities of what could happen for hours and came up with a series of plans. Hopefully, they would not need to execute the plans and no one would try to sneak out there. Jacks and Steve planned to patrol as much of the boundary as they could with Evie and Stewart, staying at the farm to keep an eye on the house and surrounds. They decided not to tell Clint just yet as they didn't want the situation to affect the research. Instead, they would concentrate on keeping people away from the area. Jacks and Arthur hatched a plan to camp out at the Cattle Yard Camp and send the drone to the doctor's camp so they could see with their own eyes that everything was ok.

From town there was only one road north where the driveway to the farm branched off. It was the only way people could enter if they were looking for the flock. From the farm driveway, they would turn off into the bush to the north-west and Corner Rock was a few kilometres away across rocky and bumpy terrain. Steve was worried there may be tyre marks left from Clint's entry into the bush and wanted to check. They didn't want any easy markers for intruders to find. Steve would be camping out for the night in the north-west area.

The drone whizzed off across the afternoon sky which was still blue, but Jacks knew there was a storm coming in and they would likely be wet before bedtime. This would be the doctor's first rain experience in Queensland, Australia. It should be interesting as this part of the country often had severe storms with torrential rain.

With Arthur and Jacks staring at the small monitor of the tablet, they saw the doctor's camp site come into view. He was in the perfect position to camp, and they could see the tarp he had tied up and there he was, sitting in his chair under the shade. He had his hat on and appeared very comfortable. The drone hovered in front of him and he grinned and gave them the thumbs-up sign.

"Check out his campfire, miss," said Arthur, excitedly. "He's got the billy on just like I showed him." Arthur was grinning like a proud teacher.

"He looks like he needs a good shower," she replied.

They both giggled and turned the drone around to return. Once it had landed, she sent him a text message,

'Are you doing ok?'

His answer came back quickly.

'Yes. All great here'

'Storm coming in next couple of hours. Lots of rain'

'Thanks. Will get ready'

The storm hit at 7pm when it was still daylight and started with booming thunder and spectacular lightning. Great jagged electrical bolts lit up the purple sky and then the boom so intense that the ground felt like it was shaking.

Jacks was glad they were in the shelter of trees and not out in the open. The doctor had trees behind him higher up the hill so he should be safe. Jacks and Arthur had eaten early and were comfortable in their swags when the rain hit. She usually didn't pull the hood flap over but tonight she did. She was safe and dry and slept listening to the rain hitting the outside of the swag.

By morning, the rain was no longer teeming but was still constant. They would be wet this morning and there was nothing that could be done about it. She couldn't stay in the swag all day. They saddled up the dripping wet horses and headed back to the farm. Both wet through but pleased they knew that the doctor was ok.

Chapter 67
The Intruders

Steve packed his wet swag and saddled his black gelding, Jay, after the storm overnight. He'd experienced many storms while out camping and always felt a thrill at the spectacular ones. What would have made it perfect this morning was for the rain to stop.

He reached the farm driveway not far from the front gate with a 'No Trespassing' sign in his saddle bag and for the first time ever, he planned to lock the front gate and add the sign. Jay snorted and Steve quickly looked around trying to determine what was spooking the horse. Ahead and just inside the farm gate was an old Holden ute. It had crashed into a tree just twenty metres inside the gate, probably during the storm the night before when vision was poor.

Steve tied Jay to a nearby tree and wandered over to the vehicle. Through the side window, he could see two men inside asleep, their heads lolling against the back of the seats. Well ... he hoped they were just asleep. The thought they may be dead or injured was a frightening possibility.

"HEY!" he yelled and pulled at the passenger door handle. The door opened and the two men jumped to life with a huge fright.

"HOLY SHIT!" one of them panted between deep breaths as he feigned a heart attack.

"You damn scared us half to death."

Steve could smell alcohol inside the vehicle. He also recognised the two of them as local married men who spent too much time at the pub and were loud-mouthed, big talkers.

"What are you boys doing out here?" he asked.

The driver looked a bit stunned at first like he had forgotten where he was and looked around feigning ignorance.

"Umm ... well ... we thought we'd go roo shooting," the passenger said.

"Really? Well, you boys would know I don't allow anyone out here on this farm to shoot kangaroos," Steve answered, calmly.

"We had a few drinks ... you know ... and we forgot ... just wanted a couple for the dogs," the passenger said.

"Well, that's not going to happen now, is it?" said Steve, getting agitated with them. "You can head back to town now and don't let me find you out here again."

"Hey, come on. Don't be like that." The driver tried to make light of the situation and the passenger joined in.

"Yeah, we're not hurtin' nobody. We just wanna shoot a few roo's and be on our way."

"No. Get out of here NOW!" Steve waved his arm in the air to signal for them to leave.

The two faces stared back at him through the windscreen for a few minutes, then spoke together and started up the engine. Steve breathed a sigh of relief when the engine started. The damage where they hit the tree didn't look too bad, but you never knew. They backed the ute up and there was a tinkling sound as broken headlight and indicator lights fell to the ground. The bumper was hanging on by a few screws, but the vehicle was still drivable.

They turned and headed back to town but not without flipping Steve the finger out the window. Steve breathed out and calmed himself. He knew they were not there to shoot kangaroos. He knew what they wanted. He locked the gate and hung the No Trespassing sign. Hopefully, that would put a few visitors off trying to drive onto the property again.

Chapter 68
The Baby

The rain was coming down so heavily at one stage that Clint couldn't see more than one metre beyond the Prado. He was thankful that Jacks had pre-warned him that the rain was imminent. He should have been aware of it himself, having access to the news and weather, but he had been so engrossed in the flock that he lost track of everything around him, until the drone woke him from his trance. He laughed when he thought about what would have happened if Jacks had sent the drone when he was standing in front of the leader butt naked.

With warning of the impending rain, he had quickly cooked dinner on the campfire, brewed a coffee, packed up his camp site and was safely tucked in his swag inside the Prado. This climate meant it was still warm even when it rained so he soon found he was too hot sleeping in his swag and ended up on top of it with a window ajar to stop them it from fogging up.

The morning was still raining, and he couldn't see the rock face. It was too wet to light the campfire so he ate dried fruit and an apple, wishing he could make coffee. The rain was falling at an angle from the south so he wound down his window on the north side. Now he could enjoy the fresh air without getting wet.

After a while, he realised there was a strange sound every now and again. It was a wailing, groaning sound and it sent a shiver up his spine. It must be one of the flock but what was wrong? Was someone dying? Was an animal eating it? The unknown was killing him, so he dressed quickly, donned his Akubra hat, grabbed his binoculars and camera and opened the door, stepping into the rain. Within minutes, he was drenched through, but he didn't care about the rain, he had to know what was happening.

He made his way down to the waterhole which was the closest he felt he should be to the flock. The rain had sent rivers of water down the side of the hill and into the waterhole. The water looked fresh and inviting and from here, he could see the rock face. There were little streams like waterfalls making their way down the crevices. Such beauty. It took his breath away.

He heard the horrible groaning again. It was coming from one of the deep crevices that act as a cave. There was no way he was going up there, so he had to sit down and wait it out. At least the hat kept the rain out of his eyes and he wasn't cold at all. He had the camera tucked safely and dry in his pocket.

After some time had passed, he became aware of movement in the cave. A few of the flock were moving about and the groaning grew louder. He still couldn't quite work out what it was. What was going on up there?

Further to the right, there was more movement and he saw the leader and other males sitting on a ledge mostly out of the rain. He smiled as he remembered how Viktoria had hated water. Why were the males not near where the groaning was? Then it dawned on him, a female was in labour and that must be the noise he was hearing. The males had made themselves as scarce as possible, considering the weather. He deduced the female had retired to a safe, dry location, possibly with other females, to give birth. Oh, how he wished he was there to see this happening.

The groaning became more intense as the time passed and he could determine the sound of straining. It was difficult to listen to, and he thought the males on the rock felt the same. It seemed to be taking longer than he imagined it should.

Suddenly, there was a long period of groaning and straining and he waited for the sound of an infant crying, the sound that everything is fine and a new life has entered the world. Instead, there was a long mournful scream, a sound that tore at his heart and he knew the baby was dead.

The screaming continued and he could hear other females wailing and the sound of panting. Clint felt sick with worry and grief as the wails came to him.

The leader and a few males flew over to the cave and the leader headed inside. The wailing and panting continued. One female emitted a sound that could only be described as a screech. It was piercing and he wondered how the leader and females were coping with the intensity of the sound from so close.

The ear-splitting screeching continued and the leader appeared, stepping out of the cave with the dead infant in his arms. Clint watched through the binoculars and could see the small infant covered in blood as newborns are. The leader was cradling the baby as if it were alive and had his head down as if talking to it. A female was grabbing at him and screeching, and other females surrounded the screeching female. It appeared to Clint that the female was trying to take her baby back and the leader was removing it. She grabbed at his arms and he swung his body away to deflect her attempts.

In all the commotion, Clint had forgotten to film it so he quickly found his camera and filmed as the leader continued holding the baby and murmuring to it and the female screeched, begging for her baby back. The other females seemed to be trying to calm down the female, and he could hear murmurs as they shushed her and touched her gently. Clint could see a blood trail down the legs of the female.

The other males stood back quietly and respectfully. Suddenly, the leader walked to the edge of the rock face and flew off with the baby in his arms. The female tried to follow but the other females held on to her. The wailing was loud and upsetting as the females held on to the wailing female tightly.

Clint put down the binoculars and was stunned for a few minutes, with tears running down his face as well as rain. Realising the leader had flown off with the baby, he jumped to his feet and ran in the direction the leader had flown, to the west of Corner Rock. His Akubra flew off as he ran but he didn't stop. The ground was slippery and he had to concentrate to stay balanced as he ran. At one point he realised the rain had stopped. Good. All the better to see into the distance.

He ran away from the waterhole and up a hill. At the crest he could see the leader in the air a few hundred metres away. He was descending so Clint stood still and brought the camera up to his eyes. He used the zoom to close in and see what was happening. The leader had his back to Clint so he couldn't see if he still held the baby, but his wings were flapping and gliding as he descended to the ground.

Once on the ground, the leader leaned down and placed the baby down gently. Clint strained to see. That area of the paddock was very flat ground with tufts of grass but no trees and not many bushes. The leader stood there for a few minutes and then flew off. Clint panned up to see if the baby was in the leader's arms, but it didn't look like it was. He quickly panned the camera back to the ground and thought he could see a little bundle. The leader flew back to the rock face. Clint stood on the top of the hill, looking up at the rock face then back at the bundle in the paddock and thinking. Decision made, he pulled out his phone and called a number.

"Jacks, you got a cool room at the farm?" he asked.

Chapter 69
The Cool Room

"So, we have a dead prehistoric baby creature in our cool room," stated Evie calmly, addressing the doctor as if it was just an everyday occurrence and nothing out of the ordinary.

Clint gave a weak smile. "Sorry," he said.

Steve hadn't returned yet from his boundary ride, and Jacks and Arthur were fascinated with the baby. They were even more fascinated when they found out that there was a creature graveyard on their station. Clint had found the baby boy's body, but the land around was littered with skulls and bones which could only be from the dead of the flock. It was an interesting question, and one which Clint had often wondered about. What did they do with their dead bodies? On the island, Viktoria had left all the remains of her prey in the hut she sheltered in, so they had no issue being around the stench of deteriorating bodies, but not their own. They took their own kind out to a designated area and left them for the elements, mother nature or animals to scavenge.

Clint explained that he would organise the forensic scientists to gather the bones and skulls but as he had taken the baby as a newborn, he didn't want any deterioration. Arthur looked troubled.

"Do you think they will mind that you took their baby?" he asked.

Clint looked at Jacks for reference.

"The Indigenous people have a high respect for the dead. With animals, they believe the spirit of the animal will return to the land," she explained. Arthur nodded.

"Oh, I see. The species ... creatures ... left this baby in the paddock to be taken. We have taken it as we respect it and will treasure it. We will learn by studying it and then we can know how to look after the flock better," he answered, hoping his words would be acceptable. Arthur nodded.

Jacks explained to the doctor what had happened with the sergeant's visit and what Steve had encountered on his boundary ride with the two men in the ute. Steve had phoned Jacks not long ago. Clint sighed. He had been afraid of this.

"Did your father phone Bill, my boss?" he asked.

"Yes. Bill was very helpful and proposed that he would notify the Australian authorities. We haven't heard anything since," she answered.

"I'll phone him and find out what is going on." He headed out the door.

An hour later he returned. Jacks had brewed coffee which was most gratefully accepted. Clint had consumed less than 10% of his usual coffee quota in the last five days and felt he had catching up to do.

"He's coming out here, to Australia. He'll be leaving in a few hours' time. So glad he will be here to face the inquisition as well as me," he reported. "He told me to call a town meeting next Wednesday night. This meeting is for the locals but there may be press there as well. Hopefully, it will just be local press for now. There will be a few meetings with the Australian authorities before that. They are keen to get updated before the public know, of course. Oh, he's very excited about the baby."

"It sounds like everything is moving in the right direction. Good. Hopefully by scheduling this meeting, people will wait and listen rather than charging out here and causing trouble," Jacks stated.

Steve opened the door and entered the room, home from his boundary ride. He greeted everyone and kissed Evie on the cheek. Clint marvelled how clean and tidy Steve looked after camping out, compared to himself who was filthy, still wet and had thick stubble on his chin.

"Dad, just in time for a coffee." Jacks smiled at him.

"Oh Jacks. You are a life saviour."

He went to wash his hands before sitting at the table to catch up on the latest information. His eyes widened and eyebrows raised at the news of what his cool room was being used for. Clint pulled out his camera and showed them footage from his five days camping at Corner Rock.

"Well, I don't know what to say. I never would've believed it had I not seen it," said Steve, awed at the photographs.

"There is so many of them," said Arthur.

"Such cute little ones but the big ones are a bit scary," admitted Evie.

Clint pointed out the leader to them, and they were suitably impressed, giggling at the story of Clint butt naked in front of the leader and the flock.

"What about that one?" Jacks pointed to an adult to the extreme right of the camera on the rock.

"It's in so many scenes but always over there and looking at the others."

"I noted that as well." Clint opened his notebook. "Here it is. I've called her Mona. It's a female and she is not accepted by the flock. I don't know why. She's large for a female but not as large as the males, and very muscular. There are no young ones with her and no one in the flock goes near her. It's like she's been ostracised or banned or something," he answered, impressed at Jacks' attention to detail.

"That's sad," said Jacks.

Clint stood up. "Well, thank you again for your hospitality and the use of your cool room."

"I'm off to town to shower, shave, eat and sleep. Bill will be here tomorrow, so I'll book him a room too. I'll keep you updated with what's going on."

He looked around the room at this group of people who only one week ago were total strangers to him, but today, they felt like family. He looked at Jacks and felt a stirring somewhere inside that had been dormant for so long. She was hard to look away from.

Jacks looked up at him and smiled. "Don't forget that shower."

Chapter 70
The Authorities

After Bill arrived in Australia, everything started moving at a faster pace. Bill had been busy on the phone to Australian authorities informing them of the flock, the baby in the cool room, the paddock of bones and offering joint cooperation which at first, Clint was not happy about. He felt they had a certain oversight of the flock, a responsibility, having done all the work and research for two years on the species. Bill explained that this flock was not Viktoria, not in the United States and that they were guests of Australia, and lucky not to get their white asses kicked out of the country. In fact, they should hope the Australian authorities would allow them to be joint partners in the research and care of the flock. Clint knew what he was saying was correct but damn, it was hard to relinquish control of the situation.

The Australian authorities were wetting their pants in anticipation of seeing the baby and the paddock of bones as well as the live flock. They were on the first plane to Queensland to meet with Bill and Clint. The meeting was arranged for 10am the following morning and a conference room had been booked at the hotel with a media projector so Clint could present his video footage of the flock and talk about his research. He was both excited at the prospect of presenting to these distinguished scientists and dreading, fearing they may take over and he would have no say.

He was particularly surprised the next morning to see at least twenty people making their way into the conference room. There seemed to be a representative from every official Australian department in existence, and he could hear the hushed whispers and feel the excitement in the room.

The conference commenced with Bill introducing himself and asking each person in the room to introduce themselves and their department. Both Bill and Clint raised their eyebrows at the depth of people in the room. He was pleased they were taking it so seriously and with such excitement. Bill went on to describe Viktoria and the association and research that had been undertaken to date, plus the amount of time and money spent on tracking her and protecting her. Clint knew he was establishing they had a strong knowledge base and a history of care and commitment to the species.

The group of people were speechless and hanging on to every word Bill spoke. He explained who Clint was and invited him to the podium to report on his findings as well as show footage of Viktoria and the Australian flock. The floor would then be opened to questions.

Clint cleared his throat and stepped up to the podium. Public speaking was not his forte. He assimilated more as the nerdy scientist in the background, avoiding the public. For the next forty-five minutes, he spoke of Viktoria, her discovery on the island, how she had lived, her capture, the research and her escape. He explained how he had tracked her across the United States until she left to fly towards Africa where he suspected her original flock had originated. He then spoke of the Australian flock, his week studying and filming them and of finding the paddock of bones.

Next, he pressed a few buttons and an image of Viktoria appeared on screen. There was a collective gasp from the group, who had been silent up until that point. A series of footage of Viktoria played on the large screen; in the custom room they had built for her, eating a mango, eating meat, drinking from the waterhole, sleeping against the rocks in the room, exploring the room, Viktoria in the smaller study room where she was shown videos and given puzzles, there was also footage of her under anaesthetic having her wing repaired. The footage zoomed to a close-up of her body and her teeth. Clint followed up with a series of images from her time fleeing the United States. Several were photos he had taken, and many were photos from social media channels. His favourite was the shot he had captured early in the morning when

Viktoria was perched on a dead tree branch. He sighed when that photo appeared and smiled, remembering the wonder of it at the time.

Finally, he showed footage from the Australian flock, flying, hunting, drinking, eating, caring for their young, of the isolated female and the last day when the leader had taken the dead baby. He pressed a button on the remote control, and the screen froze with a still of the leader with dead baby in his arms, his head down twittering to it. He could see the group were mesmerised. He signalled for the lights to be turned on and opened the meeting up to questions.

There was a few minutes of dead silence as the group tried to absorb what they had just seen and shake themselves out of the coma of wonder. Suddenly, there were hands up everywhere and murmurs.

Question time went on for the next two hours.

"Doctor, is there any danger to the humans in the area?"

"What are they currently hunting and eating?"

"How many do you estimate to be in this flock?"

"Doctor, what about diseases? Are they carrying any or are they susceptible to our ailments?"

"Dr Marne, will they hunt dogs and domestic animals?"

"How long do you estimate they have been in Australia?"

"Where did this flock come from? How did they get here?"

"Why are there no elderly or infirm?"

"Doctor, what is the forecast for their population growth?"

"How will we feed them should there be not enough food for them in the future?"

"Who owns the land they are on and are they amenable to leaving the flock there?"

"Do you have any plans to take the flock or a specimen back to the US with you?"

"How scared are they of humans? How can we study them?"

"Has there been an environmental study undertaken?"

"Are they considered an animal like a gorilla for example, or are they closer to a human?"

"There will be a cost associated with their upkeep, keeping them fed when food is scarce, studying them, maintaining them. Has anyone thought about how the money for this cost can be raised?"

"How will the public react to this information?"

"How will we stop the public from going out there?"

"Doctor, are you married?"

A break was finally called, much to the doctor's relief. His mouth felt dry from talking non-stop for so many hours. Coffee, tea, finger food and sandwiches were brought into the conference room and Clint gratefully accepted a coffee from the tray. Never had he been so popular and a large circle of people vied for his attention. He thought of Jacks at that moment. She would laugh at this crowd of people wanting to talk to the white skinned Yank, her name for Americans. He wondered what Jacks was doing right at that moment. He looked across at Bill and ran his eyes down his over-the-top safari outfit with his long white socks and broke into giggles. Sneakily, he snapped a photo of Bill and sent it to Jacks.

The meeting reconvened and continued until five in the afternoon. Clint felt pumped. It had been a great day, a great meeting with many topics covered. He felt that rather than the Australian team pushing him out, they were counting on him to lead them and be the expert.

Decisions had been made and an order had been agreed to.

a.   The local morgue was to be used as the base for the autopsy of the dead baby and where the bones would be collated.

b.   Permission from the Foster family would be sought to enter their land and start collecting material from the 'paddock of bones' as it was now officially called. Ongoing support and transparency would be discussed with the Foster family.

c.   The local police sergeant was to be brought into the loop on decisions made.

d.   A meeting in the town arranged for the public, so they would be aware of the flock in their presence.

e.   A media conference was also arranged for the morning after the public meeting.

No decision had yet been made as to further research of the flock. Clint would be meeting with his Australian counterparts to discuss this.

Clint thought of Jacks as he climbed into bed. She had sent back laughing emojis in response to his sneaky photo of Bill. He slept well that night and dreamed that being in the spotlight was not as bad after all.

Chapter 71
The Coffee

Jacks was finding it increasingly difficult to consider returning to university with so much activity going on. Yesterday, the scientists arrived in white coats and a van and removed the dead baby to the morgue. She had felt distressed having a practically extinct dead baby of a human-type species just a few metres away and was pleased to see it removed.

Groups of people met with her family to discuss the welfare of the flock, its location, their commitment and the possibilities or problems that may occur. Her parents were very amicable and open to supporting the flock on their land, as she had expected, despite the difficulties that this may pose.

Arthur, Stewart and Jacks had ridden out to Cattle Yard Camp to check on the group collecting the bones. It was not that they were not trusted, but she just felt safer keeping an eye on the situation. She sent a drone over to check they were in the right place and they were. She hoped their presence would not upset the flock. Would they be upset if their graveyard was robbed of its dead?

She wondered about the doctor and what he was up to. She hadn't seen or heard from him in days and understood how incredibly busy he must be with all the scientists and people in town. She chided herself for feeling a little deflated that she had not heard from him. Why should he keep in touch with her? He didn't owe her anything. Still, she thought about him more than she cared to admit.

The entire town was abuzz with the news of what was going on, the scientists and the meeting scheduled for seven on Friday evening. Many friends and associates were calling her for information, but she told them to wait and find out at the meeting. She was itching to be more involved but knew that was foolish as she wasn't a scientist or had any qualifications that made her useful to these people.

Her phone rang and the screen told her it was 'Doc' calling.

"Jacks, how about meeting me at Long Socks Café?" a voice asked.

"Be there in 30 minutes." She laughed, suddenly feeling light and warm.

She had to blink and look around the cafe a second time before she saw him. He didn't look like the long socked American she had first seen here only two weeks ago. This man looked like an Aussie or almost an Aussie. He was wearing khaki-coloured casual chinos, black T-shirt, Akubra by his side, RM Williams boots and a slightly tanned face with stubble. He didn't look out of place and seemed totally at ease as if he had been here all his life.

She sat at his table, wondering how he managed to secure a table as the cafe was so crowded. With all the scientists and authorities in town, the whole place was full and buzzing. Car spots were now rare and highly sought after, supermarkets had queues for the check-out and restaurants and motels were booked out.

"I don't even know your first name," she said as she sat down.

"It's Clint," he answered.

"OK. I'll stick with Doc." She raised her eyebrow at him in jest and they both laughed.

"Well, speaking of first names. What's Jacks short for? Is it Jacqueline?" he asked.

She nodded.

"Jacqueline or Jacky sounds like a Barbie doll. I was always more the tom boy type."

A waitress hovering just at the back of Clint's chair, saw her opportunity to address the doctor, and stepped forward.

"Excuse me, Dr Marne,"

Clint turned, giving her his attention. The waitress fluttered her eyelashes and blushed.

"Would you like your usual coffee?"

Clint turned back to Jacks. "Yes, thank you, and Jacks will have a strong black?" He queried Jacks and she nodded. The waitress moved away slowly.

"So, tell me what's been going on."

Curiosity had been killing her. What was happening? She almost couldn't bear the suspense.

"It's been crazy. The Australian authorities have been great so far. The baby's being autopsied today, and the paddock of bones has been photographed, mapped and the bones are in the process of being removed, but you would know that."

He looked at her. It was a statement, not a question. She nodded.

"What will happen with the rest of the flock?"

He raised his shoulders. "I don't know yet. There are studies to be undertaken including an environmental study. That is the one I am most concerned about. Generally speaking, they are not native animals, so could be deemed not sustainable or environmentally friendly. For example, they may determine that leaving the flock in situ will cause a loss of too many native animals in the area and change the eco-system."

She nodded. She understood the ramifications, having studied the environment in her university studies.

"They're not really animals, are they?" Jacks asked.

"No. They are not animals but there is nothing like them, so they have to be slotted into a category for these purposes."

"What would they do in the case that they don't want the flock eating native animals?"

"Who knows? They may choose to relocate the flock somewhere, though I can't think of anywhere where they will not impact the environment, except perhaps Africa, if that is where they came from initially and I cannot see how they could transport a flock this size internationally."

It was a huge concern to them, forcibly moving the flock to a place not of their choice was devastating. They discussed the upcoming town meeting and possible outcomes, plus the media conference and what could happen once the larger public found out about the flock.

Their discussion was interrupted at one stage when the waitress returned with the coffee cups. She tried to attract the doctor's attention, but his focus was firmly riveted on Jacks. As Jacks looked around, she saw many of the customers looking at their table and whispering. The doctor was hot property she thought, giggling.

"Speak to your parents, and Stewart and Arthur and explain they are not to talk to the press under any circumstances. Lucky you have a padlock on that front gate, but that may not stop them for long. I wouldn't put it past them to cut the fence wire or send helicopters in to ferry journalists to your front door."

"But they could send choppers over Corner Rock to see the flock," she said, suddenly alarmed, not having thought of this earlier, and now picturing how this would terrify the flock.

"An emergency order is currently being approved that turns the entire area into restricted air space. That'll stop them."

He had been thinking of the media scrum that this announcement was going to produce, and how it would affect all involved. Suddenly, he remembered one Australian journalist who he knew and trusted. He reached out and grasped Jacks hand, leaning across conspiratorially. She didn't pull it away.

"I do know a journalist based in Melbourne, who I trust. Do you remember the articles on Kim? She was one of the backpackers. Viktoria killed her husband."

"Yes. I did read them. Sad story," she replied, looking down at his hand in hers.

"The guy who wrote those articles came to visit with Kim at the facility where Viktoria was being kept, in Wyoming. Nice guy. Great writer. I trust him. Maybe I should contact him and offer him exclusive interviews. You know ... ask him to write the story. At least the truth will be told."

The more he thought about the idea, the more he liked it.

"Sounds like a good plan. I wish there was some way I could be involved," she said.

"I'm sure you will be. The flock is located on your land and you'll know everything that's going on." He tried to look in her eyes to read her thoughts as her voice had changed. He knew he was still holding her hand, but she had not retrieved it.

"I'm ... finding it difficult to go back to uni. I don't want to miss anything that's going on with the flock ... and I can't leave my parents to face all this on their own." She looked down again, a bit embarrassed at her admission.

"How far through college are you?" he asked, giving her hand a squeeze of reassurance.

"Six months to go and I'll be qualified. I wanted this qualification to better run the station one day. The lecturers are sending me the classes I'm missing so I'm keeping up."

He held eye contact with her, and a special moment happened, or he thought it happened. It was a connection of spirits or souls, or was it just animal magnetism or his imagination?

"You'll have no problem catching up your classes. You are so incredibly intelligent, and I have total faith in you and your abilities."

He still held her eyes, and her hand. She knew he was trying to give her confidence, and she appreciated it.

"Thanks, Doc."

Chapter 72
The Scoop

Coop popped his phone back in his jeans pocket and stood for a moment staring into space, then turned to Kim.

"You are not going to believe this ..." he started.

He could barely believe it himself. Was he dreaming? Was this for real? Had that phone call just happened? Kim paused the sandwiches making in the kitchen and looked across at Coop in anticipation.

"They have found a whole herd of creatures like Viktoria."

He stared at her face and saw her eyes widen and mouth fall open. Her hands fell to her sides and she stood, stunned.

"Dozens of them, males, females and infants, and that is not the best part." He waited for her response.

"What?" she asked, breathlessly.

"They are in Australia, in Queensland!"

He dropped the bombshell and watched her hand fly up to her mouth automatically in shock and disbelief.

"No. Is this a joke?" she asked. Surely, this was not logical. Someone was pulling her leg, or maybe Coop's leg.

"I'm dead serious. That was the scientist from America ... you know, the one we met, Dr Clint Marne. He's in Queensland studying the group and wants me to do the exclusive stories on them."

Kim was picturing Dr Clint Marne, the nerdy, excitable scientist, who had asked her questions, and then freaked out when Viktoria escaped. She remembered him.

"But ... if this was true, your paper would already know about it."

She was trying to be logical. How could this be true when it had not been on the news, or the papers? It had not even been mentioned on social media.

"Apparently, there will be a media conference in two days' time where they will break the news to the world. Only a few people know about it."

He pulled his phone back out of his pocket and started shuffling through his address book, looking for a number.

"I need to speak to my editor." He wandered into a different room to make the call. This was an extraordinary situation that he did not plan to miss out on.

Kim walked into the lounge room, sandwiches forgotten, and sat down, staring at the photo of Jamie on the shelf near the television. Was this really happening? How did she feel about this? How did she feel about Coop covering this story again? Was Viktoria with this herd of creatures in Queensland? She needed to think through this.

James gave a little cry and she stood up and walked into his room. He was awake now and sitting up in his cot. He had grown out of his cot, but she still didn't want to move him into his own bed. He was only two years old so she felt she could still get away with him sleeping in a cot. She lifted the side of the cot down and he scampered out, his little feet running as soon as he hit the ground. Coop was off the phone and waiting in the lounge room when James scurried out, holding his arms up to be picked up.

"Coo, Coo," he called when he saw Coop.

Coop reached down and picked him up.

"How are you doing, big boy?"

He gave the boy a hug and James snuggled.

Kim looked at Coop expectedly, waiting to hear what was happening with the story.

"What does Roger think?" she asked.

"Are you kidding? Roger is peeing his pants about this. This will be the story of the year, like yours was two years ago. I'll be on the next flight up there."

He tickled James and the little boy giggled and squirmed in his arms.

"Let me know all the details once you know them. I'll be keen to hear about it."

He gently lifted James down to the floor where the boy zoomed off to find his toys, then he wrapped his arms around Kim in a hug. She buried her head into his chest, and he knew this news tormented her. She had closed that chapter of her life the day that Viktoria escaped the facility in Wyoming and flew off into the distance. In many ways, Kim had made her peace with Viktoria that day and returned to Australia thinking that was the end. Now, this news brought memories back, good and bad and stirred her emotions.

She pulled back gently as she always did when the embrace became too intense and looked up at him with a small smile.

"Be safe. We'll miss you."

Chapter 73
The Town Hall Meeting

The town hall was full to overflowing. It seemed every person in the entire town had turned up, as well as the rural families from out of town. There was a lot of noise from the crowd and speculation.

Coop stood at the back of the hall watching everything happening and feeling the mood of the audience. As a good writer, he felt it was important to look at all the various aspects of a story, and public opinion was going to play a major part.

He was pleased he had flown up immediately to get a head start on the situation and met with Dr Clint Marne and Bill Powell. He felt up to date on happenings and had already prepared a draft of the first article for the newspaper. The plan was to release the article tomorrow morning while the press conference was on. His paper would be a step ahead of the competition.

There were excited murmurs among the people in the hall, and Coop could see a variety of official people as well as the town folk. He fervently hoped this meeting would go well, as there was some negative feeling around.

Coop looked across at Dr Marne and marvelled at how different he looked compared to the scientist he had met in the US a few years earlier. The doctor looked so much older and wiser, not the youthful, excitable person he remembered.

Bill approached the podium and welcomed everyone. The plan was to work along a similar routine as they had with the authorities a few days ago but in this case, keep it simple and brief without all the complicated details. It was only fair that the people view the video footage so they could see what was residing not far from their town. He started the spiel. Immediately, he was interrupted by a middle-aged man in the front.

"Don't give us any shit here. Tell us truthfully, are we in danger?" the man yelled out.

Bill turned to look at him directly.

"No, there is no danger. The flock are many miles from town and keep to themselves. They do not hunt humans ..."

Again, he was interrupted.

"That's not true. That other demon they found, it ate people and killed an Aussie bloke," said the same guy.

Many others in the crowd were murmuring and agreeing. Bill put up his hand to silence the crowd.

"That was an extreme situation where she was starving to death ..."

"Well, that could happen here. There could be a drought or no food available, then they'll come and kill us all in our sleep," said another man.

A few people were yelling out different things.

"How will we keep our cows and sheep safe?"

"Get them out of Queensland! Send them to New South Wales."

Voices started overlapping each other and trying to shout the loudest. Clint tried holding his hand up and calling for quiet, but to no avail. Eventually, the police sergeant stood up and yelled for everyone to calm down. Perhaps it was the voice of authority, but people started to quieten down.

"Give these guys a chance to talk. Yelling and screaming isn't going to do any good. We need to hear all the facts about this and then ask some questions. EVERYONE GOT THAT?" he asked in a loud, firm voice.

There were a few murmurs but generally, the hecklers had been silenced, and the meeting was ready to proceed. The Australian equivalent of Clint stood up and made his way to the podium. He was a middle-aged guy with short grey hair named Dr Ian Baldrick. He pointed Clint out to the crowd to introduce him and talked on what had been learned to date about the new species, what they ate, how they lived, what we knew about them and then he showed the footage Clint had taken when he was camped out with the flock. Everyone was silent as they watched the footage in awe. The room had been darkened, and the screen was bright and clear. Everyone's focus was on the screen and the moving images on that screen.

There were a few awed whispers when they saw the first creature fly and some oohing and aahing when they saw the babies and infants. Dr Baldrick could sense the change in the crowd once they saw the footage. Suddenly, these creatures were not the demons they had envisaged. They were human-like beings with mothers and babies and children. The footage finished and he turned off the projector.

"As you can see, they are real flesh and blood. They are not monsters or demons. This is a wonderful opportunity for us here in Australia to study and learn from this primitive species so closely related to our own. We need to protect them, ensure they have food and are healthy, not drive them away or harm them."

He looked around and didn't meet any resistance or trolling, other than a few murmurs here and there.

"Tomorrow morning, we are holding a press conference where the rest of the world will find out about this flock. We imagine it could be chaos here in town after the media gets on to it. I ask you all to be hospitable and friendly but careful with the media. Help us to protect these special creatures."

"Can we go out and see them?" asked a woman.

"No. We want to keep them away from human contact as much as possible. It is important that they maintain their own natural abilities, skills, life and death without any obvious intervention from us. We understand you are all curious. So are we. We will regularly bring you information, photos and video footage so you can see what is going on. In time, we may ask you to help us and get involved with collecting food for them, or donations or a number of other things. We appreciate your interest and hope that you accept them and begin to be proud to have them living near you."

He smiled at the room. The crowd broke out in applause.

Clint shook his head and grinned. What a showman! If only he had those skills instead of being the nerd scientist. He looked across the room and on the other side, he saw Jacks clapping and watching Dr Baldrick. Her dark burgundy hair shining in the lights of the room now the lights were back on. She was laughing and turning back to say something to Steve and Evie. They were applauding as well and smiling.

Did he feel a pang of jealousy that Jacks was enjoying this great speech from Dr Baldrick? He had to admit he did feel a twinge and his eyes kept travelling back to look at Jacks. Why couldn't he be as dynamic and entertaining as Dr Baldrick and maybe Jacks would be as impressed with him as she appeared to be with Dr Baldrick?

Chapter 74
The Interview

A storm was unleashed the next day after the media conference at 10am. Coop's article hit the papers in Melbourne and was syndicated worldwide. There had been a few headlines and hints in the media the night before, but Coop was well ahead of the competition with his timely and detailed article along with photographs.

Within hours the town was inundated with journalists, photographers, sightseers, activists and weirdos. All hotels were full to capacity, restaurants and cafes were flat-out and the town was bedlam. Extra police were called in from neighbouring towns to help keep the peace. Coop was pleased he had secured a hotel room when he did and instructed Kim to fly up with James. He was going to be in town for at least one week and thought she may enjoy a change of scenery. She had been a major part of the earlier story of Viktoria and Coop felt she should be included and to see what was happening.

She arrived mid-afternoon on a very full flight with young James who behaved impeccably on the flight. Although she had not been to Karana before, she was surprised by the sheer number of people and vehicles around. The town was full of excitement but there was also a strange sensation she felt the moment she stepped out of the car. It was a guarded, tense energy as if everyone was waiting for something to happen. She could understand this feeling of suspense as the creatures were frightening.

Coop took her to the hotel room where she and James would share the queen-sized bed and he would be sleeping in the single bed. There was no hope of booking a separate room for them in the current situation. Their relationship was one of deep caring and respect for each other, a platonic friendship though Coop often thought of initiating a romantic gesture, but always chickened out, not wishing to jeopardise the close friendship they had. If he tried and she rejected him, he couldn't bear the thought of losing Kim and James from his life. She had only been a widow for two years and how could he compete with Jamie? Jamie had been a strong, athletic, handsome and adventurous man whereas Coop was just a middle-aged writer who lived for the story.

He had also let Dr Marne know Kim was arriving and suggested that Kim and James accompany him out to the station while Coop interviewed the Foster family. Dr Marne thought it was a good idea and was keen to see Kim again and apologise for his mistake at the facility when they last met. He also thought Jacks and the Fosters may be interested in meeting Kim and her son and hearing her story directly.

Coop watched her that night as she tiptoed into the queen bed trying not to wake James and his heart lurched admiring how beautiful she was. Her hair had been short and spiky blonde when he first met her and now, it was down past her shoulders and a rich honey blonde. He feigned sleep, watching her through nearly closed eyes, wishing he were braver and could tell her how he felt.

The Foster family were waiting for them the next day and the group sat out on the sweeping verandah which surrounded the homestead. The day was warm and humid after early morning rain. Clint introduced Coop, Kim and James to the family. James was a big hit with the ladies and Evie took him for a walk to see the chickens. His excited giggles were heard as Evie showed him how to throw grain to the hens.

Coop explained his role and who Kim was. After expressing their sympathy for her loss, they asked many questions and were pleased she still supported looking after the flock and ensuring their survival despite her tragedy. They were fascinated with her retelling of the episode at the facility, when Viktoria escaped after wanting to touch her baby, and Kim told her to go and signalled to her to fly away.

Clint told the group his personal story of shadowing Viktoria across the country after her escape from the facility. This was the first time he had ever vocalised the chase to anyone other than Bill at the time. He found it surreal when talking about it now and wondered what head space he had been in at the time, sleeping in his car, drinking too much bourbon, eating fast food and guessed it was depression. He explained to Kim how he had also told Viktoria to go and signalled her after he had been shot.

Coop frantically wrote notes as Clint spoke and took a ton of photos of the group talking on the verandah. He felt this was a very important part of the story that Kim, as one of the original survivors of Viktoria, was fully supportive of the flock and vocal in her support. Kim, who had lost so much, didn't blame the species for her loss. The man responsible, Juan, had been jailed for the rest of his life in South America the year earlier.

Clint explained that the Australian team wanted him to camp out at Corner Rock again and spend time researching and photographing. They did not want to send a new team out and risk upsetting the flock. The flock had already accepted Clint, so they wanted to remain with what was comfortable for them. Also, Clint had so much earlier knowledge and was in the best position to carry out the research although Dr Baldrick required he be kept up to date on a weekly basis. Clint's trip to Corner Rock was scheduled to start in a few days' time and there were still decisions to be made.

Coop asked a few more questions of Jacks and took a few photos. He wanted to write about her experience camping out with Arthur and Stewart on the night the creatures had taken the calf. He was also keen to meet with Arthur and Stewart and talk to them about the same incident. Fortunately, the two of them were found in the home yard so Coop was able to interview and photograph them.

By the end of the day, Coop had sufficient material to write many future articles for the paper. After that, he planned to keep in contact with the doctor so he could publish regular updates on the status of the Australian flock.

Chapter 75
The Report

Clint set up camp at the same site where he had earlier, feeling it had been a perfect location. Again, he was well stocked and more organised this week than he had been the previous time. He knew what to expect and felt quite at home with building a campfire and cooking his meals. It wasn't long before he had the camp as he wanted and could retrieve the binoculars out and see what was happening with the flock.

He didn't know if the flock had hidden when he first arrived but if they had, they were now moving around in full view. He felt they remembered him, his equipment and the camp site where he had set up and could see the leader standing at the front of the rocks looking at him intently. It had not been long since they had seen him last. This was a good sign that he would be able to regularly come and go without stressing the flock.

The leader unfurled his wings and flew down to the camp site where Clint was standing. A few other males followed as they had last time, and they landed in the same spot as two weeks earlier. The leader stared at Clint but this time, he was not looking down at his clothes and Clint was relieved he wouldn't have to strip off again. After a few minutes, the leader turned and walked over to the campfire watching the flames for a few minutes before putting his hand out towards it. Startled, he jerked his hand back as it touched the flame. Again, he stretched his hand out testing where the heat was tolerable and where it stung him. He was fascinated with the fire. Clint thought it likely the flock had witnessed fire before in their long history, but perhaps only from a distance. He imagined they would fly away at the slightest hint of a bush fire or grass fire.

The billy for coffee and a frying pan were sitting on the ground near the fire. The leader poked at them with his finger, touching them a few times. Once he was satisfied they were not going to hurt him or burn him, he picked them up and turned them upside down trying to work out what they were. The other males stood watching the leader.

It was so tempting to Clint to offer the leader something to eat or a gift like the early Americans had with the Indians. What held him back was the fear that the flock should not become accustomed to humans or look for treats from them. This could lead to problems in the future. It was best to offer nothing and let them look around. Limited curiosity was fine, but he didn't wish them to become too familiar with him. Hopefully, they would soon be on their way back to their own world.

Within a few minutes, the leader made a twittering sound and all the males flew off back to the rock. The leader looked at Clint again and then followed them. Clint breathed a sigh of relief that the leader had not taken the billy with him. What on earth would he do without his coffee? He laughed thinking it would have made a good excuse to call Jacks and ask her to do a mercy dash out to deliver a new billy.

The days were warm and Clint stayed under his tarp roof and drank bottles of water. He liked to watch the mothers and infants head down to the waterhole each morning. The youngsters splashed the water at each other but instinctively didn't like water just like their parents. A few larger youngsters were trying to fly, standing on medium sized rocks and flapping their wings. The braver ones jumped and managed to glide down to the ground gracefully.

Clint spent his time watching the flock and their behaviours, making notes and taking photographs. He also watched the lone female that he had nick-named Mona, and was confident she was estranged from the rest of the flock. No one went near her and she stayed away at the edge of the rocks. When males came back with food, they did not share any with her. She went out hunting on her own and Clint wished he understood the reason behind this.

One afternoon, Clint became aware of a noise and saw a male fly in twittering excitedly. A few males were suddenly alert and flew off with him in a northerly direction. An hour later, they returned and two of them were carrying a newborn camel. Mercifully, they had killed it first. These camels were feral and the farmers despised them as they ate crops and grass intended for the cattle. The camels had come across from the Northern Territory at some stage and bred in the wild. The males landed on the rock and tore apart the camel offering pieces to the females and the females fed the young ones. Clint had watched them do the same with mangoes they had found.

There were no obvious signs of sickness or disease, and he wondered if this was because they were segregated from humans. The Aboriginal population had been decimated not long after Sydney was settled from diseases including smallpox, introduced when settlers had arrived. It would be a disaster should something similar happen to this flock.

The autopsy on the baby from the paddock of bones had not yet identified a definitive cause of death, but the most likely scenario was the cord had wrapped around the baby's neck during labour, a tragedy also faced by humans throughout time.

The flock appeared well-fed and life ran smoothly for the species living at Corner Rock. Clint spent time on his report, using a laptop that he was able to charge each day using solar power. He hoped the Australian authorities would agree to the flock staying where they were. He could see some human intervention may be required regarding food. If the food source became low, then the flock would move on, so it was important that they had a continuous food supply. Water was not an issue as this waterhole was spring based. It was also important that the flock not hunt the cattle too much or venture into the towns or small hobby farms. He envisaged a meat delivery every few weeks to ensure they remained well fed. His report just needed a few tweaks and tomorrow, he would run it past Bill.

Chapter 76
The Leader

Jacks unsaddled Nelly and turned her loose in the cattle yard. Nelly snorted and walked around sniffing the ground and checking out who had been in the yard before her. Nelly had not been impressed to be leaving home on her own, without any other horses. Jacks had ridden out to Cattle Yard Camp this afternoon without really knowing why. The doctor had been out at the rock for five days now and Jacks had not heard anything. She assumed he must be ok or she would have heard. In some ways she felt a bit silly riding out to Cattle Yard Camp, but something drove her to come and see if he was ok.

She couldn't ride over to the rock and risk upsetting the flock and he probably couldn't leave camp yet, but she just had the urge to be close and send a drone or talk to him on the phone. She hoped he wouldn't feel like she was spying on him as she could have sent him a text message or phoned him, but here she was.

With a couple of hours of daylight left, she wanted to ensure that the camp was ready for night so she set the campfire and unpacked her swag. She didn't mind camping on her own and had done it ever since she was a teenager. Her father had taught her well and she was aware of the risks such as snakes. Another reason she liked to get the fire going was that snakes were less likely to show themselves when there was a fire.

She retrieved her binoculars from the backpack and looked across at Corner Rock. It looked so still and majestic rising up out of the flat land around it. She wondered what the doctor was doing right at that moment. She had the urge to phone him and find out. He answered eventually and she pictured him frantically trying to find his phone in the vehicle.

"Hey, Doc. It's Jacks."

"Jacks, how are you?"

He sounded pleased to hear her voice, she thought. "I'm great. I was just wondering how you're doing and when you plan to head back."

"Well, I'm packing up in the morning. It's been a great week, and I have tons of material."

She heard her mare trotting around snorting, always a bit jittery on her own.

"That's good news. I can't wait to hear all about it," she replied, picturing the two of them chatting over coffee.

Her mare was trotting around now quite agitated. Jacks looked up, listening. She wondered if a snake was nearby. Nelly was often a good warning system, especially when there were snakes around.

"Jacks, I can hear your horse. Where are you?" asked the doctor.

"Well ... guess what? I'm at Cattle Yard Camp. Nelly's a bit spooked for some reason." She started heading toward the yard to check on her.

"Jacks ... Jacks ... JACKS ..." The doctor was yelling into the phone.

Jacks was half aware of his voice but more concerned about what was wrong with Nelly. She never behaved this extreme when on their own before.

"Hang on ...," she said into the phone as she pressed the speaker button and placed the phone in the back pocket of her jeans.

"Can you hear me, Doc? I'm just going to see what's wrong with Nelly."

"JACKS. WAIT!" Clint yelled.

"I SAW SOME OF THEM FLY YOUR WAY!"

She stopped dead in her tracks. With a loud thump, a male landed in front of her, only ten metres away. With his wings extended to the side, he appeared to be ten times larger than he was. She held her breath in shock and could feel her heart thumping against her chest. His eyes were on her and she looked at his face, so human-like and yet so very different. She couldn't move and stood rock still while the leader stared at her.

He was looking down at her with his head slightly to the side. She could see his brown leathery skin, hair sprouting all over his body and greying long hair on his head. His wings reminded her of bat wings. She felt her legs turn to jelly and the hair on the back of her neck stand on end.

"Oh shit," was all she could say.

"Oh shit ... oh shit ... oh shit ..."

"Jacks. Are they there? Where are they?" Clint asked and she could hear concern in his voice. She wasn't sure she could speak or was brave enough to try.

"Oh shit. There's one in front of me. Oh shit," she answered, quietly.

"What's he doing?" he asked, urgently.

"He ... he's looking at me. Oh shit. He keeps looking down at my feet and back up. Oh shit."

"Keep calm. He's not going to hurt you. Listen to me," Clint spoke calmly.

"OK," she responded.

"This is the leader, I'm assuming. The leader has grey in his hair."

"Yep. That's him. Oh shit," she answered.

"It's ok. Just stand still. He's curious about you."

"OK."

"Is he still looking at you?" Clint asked.

"Yes."

"OK. Now, take your clothes off," he said, calmly.

"Say what?" Jacks must have heard wrong.

"Just slowly take your clothes off. He wants to know if you're female or male."

"Oh shit ... oh shit."

"It's OK. No one else is around. Just do it slowly. He's just curious. He won't hurt you."

Jacks looked around. There were a few other creatures in the background. One was standing up on the top of the yard fence looking at her mare. She hoped it wouldn't try to hurt Nelly. Surely, Nelly would be way too large for any of them to take on. She could hear Nelly snorting and cantering in circles to keep away from the creature on the fence. She wondered what would happen if she didn't take her clothes off. Would this stalemate continue into dark? That was a scary thought.

"It's ok. Just take your clothes off slowly," Clint repeated.

Slowly, she pulled her T-shirt up and over her head and softly dropped it at her feet. The leader continued watching her. She slowly kicked off her boots and pushed them away with her feet. The leader had a puzzled look on his face. She undid her jeans and pulled them down and off, thinking how lucky she was that she had not worn tight ones where she would need to lie on the ground and wriggle out of them. For a few minutes, she stood in a bra and pants. The leader was still looking at her with a puzzled look on his face. She sighed and unfastened her bra, letting it slip to the ground. Then with one slow but fluid movement, she pulled her pants down and stepped out of them.

She stood up and looked at the leader, feeling self-conscious even though he wasn't human like she was. He was studying her body and she could see a frown on his face. She worried what this might mean.

"Can you still hear me, Doc?" she asked.

A muffled voice came from her jeans on the ground beside her.

"Yes. What's happening?"

His voice sounded so far away and with background noise.

"I've taken off my clothes but something's not right. He's pulling funny faces like a frown and looking at me and looking around my camp and on the ground around me. I don't understand what's wrong. I'm scared," she admitted. "It's like he is looking for something. Does he think there's another person here?"

She could hear noises coming from the phone and then Clint answered.

"This will sound strange but trust me. OK?"

"OK."

"Look sad," he said.

"What?"

"Just trust me. I'll explain later. Look sad. Make an obvious sad face and make some whimpering noises. Trust me," he urged.

Jacks had no idea why she had to do this, but she trusted the doctor. Maybe the leader didn't like people being sad. She pulled her mouth down in an extremely sad fashion and pulled her forehead to frown, stuck out her bottom lip out a little and made a few whimpering, sobbing sounds.

The leader reacted immediately with eyes widened and stared at her face. He looked around quickly and then back to her face. He frowned and made his own sad face, then with a twittering noise, he turned away, twittering at the other creatures. All of them opened out their wings and with a few flaps, they rose and disappeared into the early evening sky.

Jacks stood there naked, staring up at the sky. What had just happened? She felt relieved, but also shocked and bewildered. Did she dream this just happened? She wasn't sure how much time had passed while she had just stood there in shock and naked, but an engine sound shook her out of her trance.

Quickly, she picked up her clothes and dressed, just in time to see the doctor's Prado pull into the camp. The doctor jumped out of his car and ran over to her, wrapping her up in his arms. She let him hold her tight and burrowed her face against his chest, crying.

"Are you OK?" he asked.

"I am now."

Chapter 77
The Swag

Clint and Jacks sat in front of the campfire and talked for hours. She had always been such a tough cookie, nothing bothered her and she liked to think she was a classic tomboy, but this incident had really affected her, chilled her to the bone and shaken her confidence. She sat close to Clint as though touching him would make her feel safe.

"I saw the leader and a few males fly off in the direction of Cattle Yard Camp, but I didn't know you were there at the time, of course," he was saying.

"Once I knew what was happening, I basically just unhooked the tarp and took off. I left a bit of a mess back at the camp."

She smiled and rested her head against his arm and he put his arm around her, giving her a squeeze. She was soft and warm, and he liked how she felt in his arms.

"Are you sure you are OK?" he asked.

"Yes. I am now. I just got a bit of a fright," she admitted, then sat up and looked back at him.

"I understand why I needed to take my clothes off, so the creature could see that I was female, like what happened with you. What I don't understand is why I had to put on the sad face. It really worked but I don't get it," she said, puzzled.

Clint grinned. He'd been trying to work out how to tell her and was silent for a moment wondering where to start.

"Well, he wanted to know if you were male or female and obviously, he worked it out."

He looked away slightly, blushing.

"The females don't have breasts unless they are lactating, and you ... ummm ..." He looked away.

"Doc, I do believe you are blushing," she said.

"Well ... you have breasts, so he assumed you had an infant. He wanted to know where the infant was."

"Oh," was all she could think of to say.

"Making the sad face made him think you had lost your infant, that you were in mourning."

She frowned and thought about it for a few minutes.

"So, he was making a sad face as well ... and that was saying he understood and felt sorry for me?" she asked.

"Yes, I think so," Clint answered.

"What a sweetie he is," she smiled, touched at his empathy.

She felt better about the incident with a better understanding. Jacks shivered as she thought of how frightening the experience had been and hoped she wouldn't be in that position again. Clint looked at her and smiled, seeing her start to relax.

"Lucky there was not a drone in the air recording you standing there stark naked," he teased.

"Well, I wasn't totally stark naked you know. I had my socks on." She laughed.

He laughed as well and before either of them knew what was happening, they had moved into each other and their lips touched. Slowly at first, they started kissing, and then more urgently. It felt so right, like it was meant to be, out in the middle of nowhere in the Australian outback. He pulled back slightly and ran his hands through her hair, pulling out the tie that held her ponytail. He'd been wanting to do that almost from the moment they met. She shook her head and her burgundy hair fell around her shoulders.

"Your swag or mine?"

"Mine's closer."

They made their way to her one-person swag.

Chapter 78
The Announcement

"YOU'RE WHAT?" demanded Bill, louder than he had intended but surprise had caught him off-guard. He gripped the phone tighter.

"I'm not coming back to the US. I'm staying here."

Clint sounded resolute and calm, annoyingly so, thought Bill.

"Have you completely lost your mind?" asked Bill.

"What are you going to do, become a jackeroo?"

Clint laughed. "Oh, I'm going to get married and have a family here."

"YOU'RE GETTING MARRIED? Are you talking about Jacks?" Bill asked.

"I am."

"Does she know yet?" he asked.

"No. She doesn't know yet."

"You have completely lost your mind. You are the world's most knowledgeable scientist on this species. You could be writing for journals, touring as a keynote speaker or doing further research in the laboratory. You could go down in the history books. Clint, are you listening to me?"

Clint laughed. Bill had never heard him laugh so much as he was on this call.

"Yes, I'm listening. I plan to continue to research the species, from here. I've presented a report with recommendations to a panel of Australian experts in Sydney, and they have accepted my proposal. I will be based here. We will be setting up surveillance cameras at Corner Rock so we can monitor the species 24/7. I'll spend a few days there each month at my camp and will also bring some meat or food for them once a month. I also plan to submit to the journals regularly."

Bill sighed and rocked his chair back and forward. He did not want to lose the doctor. He could not lose him.

"Clint, are you sure about this? This is a huge move. Would you consider still doing some work for us?"

"I'm sure. This is my future. I would very much like to continue my work with the facility and I hope the facility and the Australian authorities will continue to share knowledge and research."

"What about Viktoria?" Bill asked.

Clint breathed out. He knew Bill would bring up Viktoria.

"I haven't forgotten about Viktoria and if ever there is a genuine sighting of her, I will be there in a flash, but I can't spend my whole life chasing a ghost. I have a real chance of a life here with a beautiful girl and a wonderful opportunity to study a whole flock. How can I possibly turn this down?"

Bill sighed and leaned back in his chair.

"No. Of course you can't. I'm very jealous and I do wish you the absolute best."

Bill felt close to tears. He blinked them away, genuinely happy for the doctor.

"Thanks Bill. I hope you can make it to our wedding," said Clint, also feeling a bit emotional.

"I wouldn't miss it for the world, but you'd better ask her first."

Epilogue

The jeep halted with a jerk, sending a puff of red dust out. Clint looked across at Bill, sweating and panting in the heat. He took in Bill's outfit, his extreme, khaki safari shirt and shorts with the long white socks and lace-up boots, along with the safari hat and overweight body. He smiled to himself and thought what Jacks would say. Bill was determined to be here for this great event, even though he was not accustomed to heat as Clint now was. He felt a responsibility for Viktoria and had been such a support and champion for her over the years. He also wanted to spend time with Clint, having not seen him since Bill visited Australia a few years earlier.

Clint could barely contain himself in anticipation. Finally, after all these years, there had been a sighting of the species in a small village in South Sudan. A young village man heard his goat crying and had rushed out of his hut just in time to see two large humans with wings take the goat with their feet and fly off into the sky. Of course, it had taken a considerable amount of time for this news to find its way out of the village, out of Africa and to the United States where Bill finally heard the story.

When Clint had laid out a map on the table and drew a line from where Viktoria left the US coast in Florida, across the North Atlantic Ocean to Mauritania and across several states where there had been sightings of her, the small village in South Sudan was in a direct line. This was real and a genuine sighting. He believed the original flock Viktoria came from was not too far from this village. For two of them to steal a goat suggested close proximity. Clint used a series of satellite images of the region and pinpointed where he believed the flock were living.

This was also based on his knowledge of the habitat the flock preferred at Corner Rock in Australia.

The plan was for Bill and their guide to stay in the jeep and try to film as best they could. If the flock were in these rocks, they would be more likely to come out if it were just Clint visible rather than three people. The jeep was very close to the rocks so they could still see what was going on by zooming the camera. Meanwhile, Clint was fitted with a small Go-Pro attached to a button on his shirt so he could record.

The tracking equipment, which had served Clint so well tracking Viktoria across the United States years earlier, sat still and silent in the jeep. The tracking implant in Viktoria was no longer working so Clint hoped his estimates on their whereabouts was accurate.

Clint hadn't considered he may be wrong and the flock would not be here. He felt he knew them and what they needed and where they would go. This had to be the right place. It had water, plenty of animals for hunting and rocks for hiding and sheltering. There were a few villages scattered around, western civilisation had not yet made an impression here.

With determined effort and barely contained excitement, he left the car and headed toward the rocks. Clint had warned Bill about the naked strip-down, just in case it was necessary. He hoped it would not, particularly with a camera on him. The heat was intense and he could feel sweat trickling down his forehead. Clint wondered how cold Viktoria must have been at times in the US if this was her normal habitat.

As he drew closer, he looked up at the rocks but could not see any movement. If they were there, they would be hiding and watching him. There was such a sense of déjà vu. When within fifty metres, he stopped and turned to look back at the jeep. He could see two faces intently watching his every move, camera on.

Clint took his small binoculars out of his pocket and scanned the rocks. Nothing. He was an expert at being patient, but he was so excited Viktoria might be here that it was difficult to be patient. Minutes ticked by and nothing. Doubts started sneaking their way into his mind. Maybe he was wrong. Maybe they weren't here after all, or maybe the flock had been here and Viktoria had not made it. He knew she had made it across the ocean as there had been sightings of her, but he didn't know for sure she had not been shot or speared flying across the African nations. He couldn't bear the thought of her not being alive anymore.

Walking closer, he stopped and scanned the rocks with the binoculars, hoping the small camera on his shirt was working adequately. Still nothing. An hour passed. He walked closer again. He was only ten metres away now when he became aware of an odour and he knew - they were here. He had smelled this odour many times when near the flock in Australia and even when working with Viktoria back at the facility. His heart started racing. Perhaps he was too close.

A movement behind him and he spun around to see a huge male standing not far away looking at him, towering over him. The face did not look interested or curious like the leader in Australia. This one looked angry and had a scowl on his face. He was a magnificent looking young male, so different from the Australian leader. This one had jet black hair, very matted and in dreadlocks. His skin was tanned and glowing with the sheen of youth. He was incredibly strong and athletic, and Clint estimated that he would be much younger than Viktoria. That made sense considering he most likely had not been part of the original flock that ended up in Australia. Perhaps he was too young at the time.

The two stood there staring at each other. Stripping naked somehow did not seem the right thing to do in this case. This male was not happy that he was there at all. The doctor could feel a tension, almost like a controlled rage in this creature. How different this was to the leader in Australia.

For the first time he felt afraid for himself. This male had the strength to pick him up and throw him around like a ragdoll or crush him in his bare hands. He thought of Kim's husband, Jamie, and how he had been slashed across the throat with a talon. The doctor didn't carry any weapons to protect himself. That had been his choice, and he was prepared to take the risk of harm. It didn't mean he wasn't afraid though.

He could hear a low sound and realised it was very similar to a quiet growl, and it was coming from the male's throat. The hair on the back of his neck stood on end. The male extended his wings to make himself look more threatening and intimidating. Oh shit, was all Clint could think and it was an apt description. He had been too complacent, too confident in his own knowledge of these creatures, and he had been wrong.

Suddenly, another figure stepped in front of the male and bumped chests, making grunting noises. This figure was smaller and Clint stepped back, confused. The male lost his momentum and stepped back, staring at the smaller one, then slowly withdrew his wings. At the slightest provocation or threat, he had witnessed the creatures withdraw their wings for protection. Clint could now see it was a female. The grunting and pushing continued. Clint likened it to a wife telling off her husband. The male was scowling and grunting back at her in defiance, but the pushing was firm. Eventually, he backed off and relented. The female watched him for a few minutes and then turned around to face the human. It was Viktoria.

Clint's heart skipped a beat. Here she was. Safe, healthy and with a pregnant belly. He stared down at her rounded stomach in delight. He was aware of having the biggest grin on his face and he couldn't help but give a few little laughs. He would swear she was smiling too. There was no doubt she recognised him and appeared relaxed in his presence. He scanned her body and could see she was well fed and looked about half-way through her pregnancy. He was so pleased. She would finally be a mother.

He became aware of other members of the flock standing in the background watching the encounter. The male had moved back now but was watching as well. Viktoria moved a few steps closer to him and was holding her hand out toward him. He looked down at her hand, not sure what she wanted. The hand was empty and the palm was open. She was making low twittering noises and reaching her hand out. She stepped forward again. He held still watching her hand, trying to understand. He didn't feel threatened, so he held his ground, waiting. Her fingers touched his right shoulder, and suddenly, he understood. He undid the buttons of his shirt and slipped the shirt down to expose his shoulder. The last time she saw him he had been shot in the shoulder and was bleeding. She remembered and wanted to see the injury. She reached her hand out again and touched the scarring on his shoulder. Her touch was light and her face was calm. She twittered and withdrew her hand. He slowly lifted his shirt back over his shoulder, watching her. She reached down and touched her thigh and as he looked closely, he could see scarring where she had been shot too.

He found it fascinating what this little show meant. She was communicating with him that she remembered who he was and wanted to compare battle scars. Somehow, she knew he had not come to recapture her, perhaps because there was no rifle. She trusted him. Her face still displayed a slight smile, and he could feel tears welling in his eyes and threatening to spill over. He couldn't be happier to see Viktoria and how well she was and carrying a baby.

A small sound and movement caught his eye, and he looked down toward Viktoria's legs. A little face looked up at him, curious. A young male who appeared to be around two years old had his arms around Viktoria's legs and was looking up at the strange human. Clint had an 'Oh my God' moment when he realised Viktoria was already a mother. He gave a little cry of pleasure and Viktoria smiled as a proud mother would. He could now feel tears openly sliding down his cheeks. Nothing could make him happier now. This was the ultimate outcome for Viktoria.

He stood for many minutes just staring at Viktoria and her youngster. Maybe this male would one day be a leader. This flock looked strong and in good numbers. He looked around at the assembled and could see many older members, much older than the Australian flock, but also a good number of youngsters and infants. This flock were in their natural habitat and hopefully, would not need any human intervention.

"Goodbye Viktoria."

He said it softly to her and watched her face as her head moved slightly to the side, listening. He stepped back one step, then two. She watched him and twittered. Slowly, he backed away from the flock until he was a good distance, then turned and walked back to the jeep. Tears were still streaming down his face and he wiped at them with his sleeve.

He hoped Bill had managed to film most of that and that the Go-Pro had worked correctly. What an amazing encounter and one that he would cherish forever. They would arrange to mount a number of CCTV in the area to keep an eye on the flock, but he felt confident they were going to be fine.

He knew this would be the last time he would see Viktoria face-to-face. He was walking away from her now and back to Australia. He had a wedding to attend in one week's time in Melbourne. An invitation had arrived in the mail requesting the attendance of Dr Clint & Jacks Marne to attend the wedding of Miles Cooper to Kim Anderson.

He reached the jeep and grinned at Bill in triumph. Bill gave the thumbs up that all the cameras had worked. Mission accomplished. He climbed in and looked back at the rocks, imagining Viktoria watching him leave. He was going home, home to Australia, home to his wife, Jacks, and her pregnant belly.

About the author

L.J. Fox holds a Bachelor of Adult Education, Master of Business Administration (Internet Marketing), as well as qualifications in Information Technology. She has worked as a computer programmer, taught business computing at a TAFE College and managed the online presence for a number of corporates including the State Library of Victoria in the role of Web Manager. She has now retired to the mid-north coast of NSW where she grows Clivia plants and independently publishes novels in a number of genres.

'I am a story-teller from Australia and my primary writing goal is to entertain you, to keep you turning those pages not anticipating what will come next, not to mention - the story must involve something a little morbid or downright weird. If you found the stories easy to read, fast-paced, interesting, enjoyable and little bit quirky then my work is done.'

L.J. Fox

If you enjoyed this book, view other books or join the mailing list, visit https://ljfox.com.